MISFIT MILLENNIALS
...where Shimla Falls in love with Bihar

SAMITABH SARKAR

BLUEROSE PUBLISHERS
India | U.K.

Copyright © Samitabh Sarkar 2025

All rights reserved by author. No part of this publication may be reproduced, stored in a retrieval system or transmitted in any form or by any means, electronic, mechanical, photocopying, recording or otherwise, without the prior permission of the author. Although every precaution has been taken to verify the accuracy of the information contained herein, the publisher assumes no responsibility for any errors or omissions. No liability is assumed for damages that may result from the use of information contained within.

BlueRose Publishers takes no responsibility for any damages, losses, or liabilities that may arise from the use or misuse of the information, products, or services provided in this publication.

For permissions, requests or inquiries regarding this publication, please contact:

BLUEROSE PUBLISHERS
www.BlueRoseONE.com
info@bluerosepublishers.com
+91 8882 898 898
+4407342408967

ISBN: 978-93-7018-867-9

Cover Design: Shubham Verma
Typesetting: Sagar

First Edition: June 2025

Contents

Disclaimer	1
Acknowledgement	3
Prologue	5
1. Aakanksha – The Ridiculous daughter	7
2. Shahid – The Bihar ka Lalla	80
3. When dreams fall apart	131
4. Lust is to men – as – Flesh is to Lion	151
5. The Curse	168
6. Kismat Konnection	196
7. Love beyond Faith	218
8. Karma's a dog	240
Epilogue	257

Disclaimer

This book is a work of fiction. It is loosely inspired by certain real-life events.

Certain events, the characters, institutions, organizations, and public offices mentioned are entirely fictional and the products of the author's imagination. Few places, time of events, circumstances and incidents have been realigned to suit the appropriateness of the book. Any resemblance to actual persons, living or dead, or actual events is purely coincidental.

This work does not intend to offend or harm the sentiments of any individual or group. It neither promotes nor condones the use of cigarettes, alcohol, marijuana, or any form of substance abuse. The novel also does not advocate for or support live-in relationships or any other controversial lifestyle choices.

Please note that this book contains strong language and occasional adult themes. Reader discretion is advised.

The views and opinions expressed within this book are those of the fictional characters and do not represent the author's personal beliefs.

****

Acknowledgement

First and foremost, I bow my head in gratitude to God, whose divine grace and silent guidance blessed me with the idea, creativity, and strength to bring this book to life. Without His light, this journey would never have begun.

I am deeply grateful to my wife, **Madhulika Ranjan**, for constantly pushing me to finish this book and go ahead with publishing it. Her love, motivation, and belief in me made all the difference. Without her, this book would have remained just a dream.

I would also like to express my heartfelt appreciation to **BlueRose Publishers** for their meticulous editing—preserving the tone, flow, and emotional essence of the book while enhancing it with professional clarity. I am equally grateful for their thoughtful cover design and seamless support throughout the publishing process.

And last but not the least, to everyone who stood by me—whether in thought, in spirit, or in silent support—thank you for helping me turn an idea into a story, and a story into a book.

****

"Every fictional story and even the most fabricated tales, carries a whisper of truth within its pages."

Prologue

"In my end is my beginning"
- T. S. Eliot

14th January 2017 – Sultanpur, South-West Delhi.

It was a freezing winter night, the kind that pierces through your bones, and here we were, five millennials crammed into the cozy, yet chaotic four-storey apartment of Aakanksha and Shahid, the live-in couple whose birthdays we were toasting to. The arsenal for the night included two bottles of Old Monk, a couple of scotch, and a rogue bottle of vodka. By the time the clock struck 2:00 A.M., three bottles were already history, casualties of our midnight revelry.

Aakanksha, the birthday girl, shared her common birthday with Shahid. The birthday boy had earned himself the title, 'Chef of the Night', thanks to his killer fried chicken. The squad—Rijith, Arshit, and myself—completed the group of five.

Everyone, barring me, was deep into smoking up 'joint' and chugging rum as if tomorrow was a myth. With three bottles down, the consensus was clear: no one leaves until we are out of booze. Totally smashed, I watched as Arshit, high on the night's vibe, rallied for another round, his voice cutting through the haze, "Let's open another bottle, *saalo*!" His call went unanswered at first, but his persistence paid off. At that moment, I stood alone in my unwillingness, while everyone else was more than enthusiastic to obey Arshit.

Unwillingly, I gave in to the peer pressure, the brotherhood of the night winning over my sober senses.

Another bottle was freed from its cork. Joints were rolled, rum flowed like water. We smoked like a chimney and drank like a fish. As we cracked open the fourth bottle, the cold night air mingled with our laughter and the clink of glasses, celebrating the couple of the hour.

Midway through, Aakanksha's mood flipped like a switch, tears streaming down her cheeks, her sobs a sharp contrast to the evening's cheer. We rallied around her, followed by a chorus of soothing words, yet the more we consoled, the louder she cried.

Each of us prayed for her tears to cease, aware of the snooping ears of other residents of the apartment. The prospect of explaining why a young woman was sobbing at 02:00 AM, in the presence of four drunk guys was something we all wanted to avoid. Finally, her sobs quietened, and she whispered through her tears, "I'm sorry, guys. I just miss my mom a lot. Haven't seen her since that night in January 2013, when I fled from home for the second time. Since then, the relationship with my Colonel father had deteriorated completely. He cut me off completely and even told my relatives to ignore me or else..." Her voice trailed off, lost in the echoes of her broken family ties.

****

Aakanksha –
The Ridiculous daughter

*"There is a charm about the forbidden,
that makes it unspeakably desirable."*
- Mark Twain.

(14th January 1990 – Shimla, Himachal Pradesh)

Captain Jitendra Singh Rana, a third-generation army officer, had just received the biggest news of his life—he was a father now! But when he heard it was a girl, his smile flickered just a bit. Don't get me wrong, he was happy—super happy—but part of him had hoped for a boy. However, Captain felt more joy at the thought of having a son than a daughter because of his traditional Indian belief that sons carry on the family lineage.

Living in a bustling household with his wife Gayatri, his parents, and his two bachelorette sisters, everyone was over the moon about the baby girl. Still, Jitendra, being the only son after three sisters, had always imagined having a mini him first—a son to continue the family's legacy of military service. It wasn't that he completely rejected the idea of having a daughter, but he would have been happier if he had a son first, followed by a daughter, as it would have aligned better with his desires.

Just as Mr. Rana was about to leave for the hospital, to see his wife and their new little girl, a Subedar arrived, handing him an envelope straight from Army HQ. Ripping it open, Captain Jitendra Singh Rana's eyes widened—boom, he'd just been promoted to Major! From now on, it was 'Major Jitendra Singh Rana,' a title that rang with both pride and a touch of irony. Here he was, feeling a rush of joy with a side of regret. Turns out, his newborn daughter had brought him what you might call 'lady luck,' something he hadn't really banked on before. He'd been hanging on for this promotion for a whole year, feeling like it was dragging on forever, almost giving up hope. But hey, good things come to those who wait, right? And perhaps, good things come with new beginnings—or in his case, a new daughter.

As an army man, Major Jitendra Singh Rana had spent years perfecting the art of masking his emotions. In the army, you didn't flinch, you didn't hesitate—you just acted. But as he stood by the hospital bed, looking at the tiny bundle in his wife's arms, something stirred within him.

He had walked in with a mix of hesitation and duty, but the moment his eyes landed on her, he felt a strange sense of pride. She was stunning—not just in a delicate, newborn way, but in a way that made her look like she belonged to a soldier's family. Ivory-white skin, light brown eyes, and a solid 3.5 kg weight—she already looked tougher than most newborns. She looked like she had marched straight into the world, ready for battle.

"I'll name her Aakanksha," he said, his voice firm. "Aakanksha means aspiration. As the daughter of a third-generation Army Officer, she will fulfill her father's ambition, even in absence of a son." Gayatri, lying weakly on the hospital bed, glanced at her child. She had wanted to name her Apeksha—hope, not aspiration. But the words never left her lips. Rana had already spoken, and in their world, his word was final.

Major Rana, chest puffed with pride, went all out. He distributed sweets across the cantonment—neighbours, friends, relatives, even his battalion—no one was left out. He wanted the world to know that he had big dreams for his daughter. That she would be special. That she would make him proud.

But beneath all the laddoos and congratulatory pats on the back there was something else. A feeling he couldn't shake off. A feeling he never spoke about.

He still wanted a son.

No matter how many times he told people he was "more than happy" with Aakanksha, the truth was, a part of him still longed for a boy. Someone to carry forward the Rana legacy. But just when everyone thought it was all smiles and celebrations, there was an unexpected twist. And so, even as he celebrated, his mind was already made up. As soon as Gayatri recovered from stitches, they would try again.

And they did.

Two months after Aakanksha's birth, Gayatri was pregnant again. Just like that, she was thrown into a double battle—caring for her newborn daughter while bracing herself, mentally and physically, for another child.

(Who even thinks of having another baby when the first one is barely two months old? Seriously, what's the rush? Any sane person would wait at least a year or two before planning for the next. There has to be a limit to one's desires. This isn't just impatience–it's outright reckless. Some decisions need thought, timing, and a little bit of restraint. But clearly, for some, wanting more just never stops.)

December 10, 1990. A day that felt like it was written in the stars. Major Jitendra Singh Rana had never felt this kind of happiness before. His prayers had finally been answered—he had a son. His heir. His voice echoed through the house, louder than ever, as he celebrated what he believed was the moment he had been waiting for all along.

The family warmly welcomed the new addition, and despite being just 11 months old herself, Aakanksha found immense joy in the presence of her younger, delicate brother. Delighted, she gently explored the softness of his tiny hand. The newborn was named 'Adarsh Rana,' becoming Aakanksha's cherished brother.'

After her brother's arrival, something felt off for Aakanksha. She couldn't quite understand it, her tiny world had always revolved around Gayatri but she missed curling up in her mother's lap, feeling her warmth, her scent, the way Gaytari would stroke her hair while feeding her. Now, instead of her mother's embrace, she was handed a cold bottle of milk—something she neither liked nor wanted. It didn't feel the same —not even close. But no matter how much she sucked on that rubber nipple, it didn't bring her the comfort she craved. But with her brother now needing most of their mother's attention, Gayatri had no choice.

Gayatri saw the longing in her daughter's eyes, the silent confusion of a child too young to express her feelings. But what could she do? She barely had enough milk for one, and the newborn—fragile and helpless—had to come first. Aakanksha, still just a baby herself, found her tiny world shifting in ways she wasn't ready for, and for the first time, she felt what it meant to let go.

At first, Aakanksha didn't know what to make of this tiny intruder her mother had brought home. He was small, wrinkled and loud—really loud. He cried all the time, clung to her mother like a magnet, and worst of all, he stole all her food. Her mother was always holding him, feeding him, rocking him to sleep, while Aakanksha was left watching from a distance, confused and a little annoyed.

But over time something changed. She noticed how her mother's face lit up whenever she held him, how her mother smiled in a way Aakanksha hadn't seen in months. There was joy again. And that joy, even if it came from someone else, made Aakanksha feel warm inside. Maybe this tiny thing wasn't so bad after all. Maybe, just maybe, he was worth keeping around.

(Infants have an uncanny ability to sense their mother's emotions. They may not have the words to express it, but they just know. Every smile, every sigh, every flicker of joy or sadness—it all registers. And why wouldn't it? In the first few years of their life, their mother is their entire world. She's the one they see, hear, and feel the most. Every heartbeat, every touch, every moment spent in her arms builds an unspoken connection—one that doesn't need words to be understood.)

The siblings grew up side by side, sharing everything—toys, troubles, triumphs. Their father, Major Rana, had once longed for a son, but when it came to raising them, he played fair. Both Aakanksha and Adarsh were nurtured with equal care, held to the same gentle discipline, and encouraged to chase dreams that soared equally high. Playtime until 6:30 PM? Set in stone. Household chores? No exceptions. And of course, fitness was non-negotiable—military genes demanded it.

As time went on, Major Rana's sisters got married, life moved forward, and eventually, his parents, too, became memories, leaving behind a legacy of discipline and values.

Both Aakanksha and Adarsh attended Army School in Shimla, where Aakanksha, being a year ahead, had already made her mark. From the start, she was the more spirited, more driven one. Bright, energetic, and fiercely competitive, she was different from her brother in one big way—sports. While neither of them had much patience for household chores, Aakanksha was obsessed with basketball. Tall, strong, and unbelievably quick, she dominated the court. Even some of the boys struggled to keep up. She wasn't just another girl who played basketball—she was a player to watch.

As time passed, both siblings entered high school, and their differences became even more obvious. Adarsh wasn't cut out for the army life. Guns, drills, discipline—none of it excited him. What did? Music. He had a voice that could make people stop and listen, and he dreamed of becoming a singer. Aakanksha, being the older and more fearless one, pushed him to tell their father. "Just say it, Adarsh. What's the worst that could happen?" she'd urge. But Adarsh knew exactly what would happen. He could already picture his father's face—the disappointment, the outrage. So, he never dared to speak up.

That didn't stop him from singing, though. He performed at school events, learned to play the guitar, and thanks to his good looks and effortless charm, became quite the heartthrob. Even senior girls had crushes on him and often asked Aakanksha to introduce them to his brother. She always declined—not because she was jealous, but because, honestly, she couldn't understand it. "How the hell can anyone have a crush on this moron? The guy doesn't even have the guts to tell his own father what he wants in life!"

Aakanksha had fire in her eyes and confidence in her stride. She was the kind of person who didn't just dream—she made things happen. If she set her mind to something, there was no stopping her. Fearless, competitive, and fiercely independent, she pushed every boundary without hesitation. She wasn't just a top athlete; she was also a class topper. A rare combination. At school, they called her "Cowboy." Not because she dressed like one, but because she had the swagger, the grit, and the no-nonsense attitude that most girls didn't. Boys admired her, sure, but they also found her intimidating as hell. They'd rather admire her from a safe distance than actually approach her.

It was almost as if nature had played a trick on the siblings. Adarsh, with his good looks and charm, was adored by girls and envied by boys. Aakanksha? The exact opposite. The girls envied her and the boys admired her. Between the two, it felt like the universe had swapped roles.

Time moved on, and with it, Mr. Rana's relentless dedication paid off. His years of service and unwavering discipline finally got him the rank he had long worked for—Colonel Jitendra Singh Rana. Another feather in his already decorated cap. Meanwhile, his children were carving their own paths. Adarsh, despite his lack of enthusiasm, was preparing to join the National Defence Academy. It wasn't his dream, but in a family like theirs, personal dreams weren't always a priority. Aakanksha, on the other hand, was exactly where she wanted to be. She balanced her commerce degree at a college in Shimla with her true passion—basketball. And she wasn't just playing for fun; she was making a mark. Her skill, speed, and sheer determination landed her a spot in the state-level basketball tournaments. She was going places, and unlike her brother, she was loving every second of it.

Aakanksha's height and strength made her a natural fit for the Centre position in basketball—the tallest, strongest player on the team. Centre players are valued for their ability to protect their own goal while scoring with high efficiency. And she did all of it flawlessly in every tournament she played.

Her performance didn't go unnoticed. Coming from Himachal Pradesh, she could earn a chance to train for the National Level team in Delhi. Her coach, Mr. Manohar Karwal, a seasoned mentor in his 50s, saw something special in her. He believed she would ace the selection trials in September and go on to represent India. More than just a coach, he was like a father figure, always pushing her to train harder, knowing she had what it took to make it big.

Aakanksha was riding high on her basketball success, living by her own motto—"Train hard, party harder." Her adventurous streak often led to mischief, and she loved every bit of it.

One evening, in a classic act of rebellion, she swiped some scotch from her father's bar, carefully refilling the bottle with water to avoid suspicion. Post-practice, she and her partner-in-crime, Vishal—a commerce student juggling bank exam prep—headed to the city outskirts for their little celebration. Uncle Chips in one hand, scotch in the other. Vishal barely sipped, while Aakanksha, true to form, downed most of it.

Vishal, as always, had one job—get her home safe. Because if anything happened to her, Colonel Rana would personally destroy his existence. Their bond was rock solid. Technically, Aakanksha was the real troublemaker; Vishal just cleaned up the mess. But no matter what, he always had her back. And she knew it.

Aakanksha wasn't just a basketball star; she had a sharp business brain too. What started as sneaking a few drinks turned into something much bigger.

Using her cantonment privileges, she got scotch and rum at discounted rates and sold them to her classmates at a neat profit. It was a win-win—she had enough money to fund her parties with Vishal without touching her pocket money. But money wasn't the only motivation. Staying under the radar was just as important. With a Colonel for a father, even a tiny slip-up could mean all hell breaking loose.

She played it smart. No suspicious transactions, no unnecessary spending. And most importantly—no direct involvement. She had people within the cantonment handling the transactions, using her "Colonel's daughter" card to get things done. No one questioned her. New recruits, eager to stay in the good books of the Rana family, were always ready to help. And Aakanksha? She knew exactly how to make the system work for her.

Despite her sharp instincts and street smartness, Aakanksha knew where to draw the line. She never pushed too far, never dragged the wrong people into her business. Life inside the cantonment was all about balance—one wrong move, and everything could come crashing down.

Only two people knew the full extent of her hustle—Adarsh and Vishal. They weren't just her aides; they were her inner circle, her safe zone. And as long as they had her back, life felt like a perfectly scripted fairy tale. Every move was calculated, every risk managed. Somehow, everything just kept falling into place.

By the end of August 2008, Shimla was gearing up for its tourist season. In a month, the city would be buzzing with visitors, drawn to the perfect weather, snow-capped peaks, apple-laden orchards, and that crisp mountain breeze that felt like heaven. But while Shimla was recovering from two months of relentless rain and landslides, Colonel Rana's house was dealing with a storm of its own.

The cause? Lieutenant General Uddhav Singh. Colonel Rana's senior, boss, and old friend—and the reason behind a brewing conflict between Aakanksha and her father.

Enter Anshuman Singh, the Lieutenant General's golden boy. Fair, tall, ridiculously smart. The kind of guy every girl noticed. At 23, he had already checked all the right boxes—IIT Kharagpur graduate, a fancy engineering degree, and a jaw-dropping ₹45 lakh per year package at a multinational in Mumbai. Before starting his job, he had a two-month break to relax in Shimla with his family. And to celebrate his son's success, Uddhav Singh threw a lavish party, inviting everyone including the Rana family.

At the party, Anshuman saw Aakanksha for the first time—and he was hooked. Tall, confident, and effortlessly gorgeous, she was different from the girls he usually met. He walked up to her, striking up a conversation about IIT life, careers, the future, and even the weather. But Aakanksha wasn't impressed. Aakanksha quickly picked up on his subtle attempts to steer the conversation toward more sensual terrain, which she effortlessly dodged every time. "Looks great, talks nonsense," she thought. "Such a waste of intelligence. How can someone so smart lack basic decency? Total Intelligent Idiot."

Meanwhile, Anshuman couldn't get her out of his head. Even after the party ended, her face, her voice, her attitude—it all stayed with him. He tossed and turned all night, unable to shake off the effect she had on him. By morning, he had made up his mind.

At breakfast, he casually—or rather, desperately—brought up the idea of marrying Aakanksha before moving to Mumbai. His father, a seasoned Army man, instantly sensed what was happening. The sudden urgency. The restlessness. The testosterone-fuelled determination. Anshuman had spent years buried in books, chasing IIT dreams. Now, for the first time, he wanted something else. And it was written all over his face.

His father tried to reason with him. "Marriage isn't a decision you make overnight, Anshuman," he said. "Colonel Rana, his family, and most importantly, Aakanksha herself, need to agree." But Anshuman wouldn't budge. "Just give it a try, Papa," he insisted.

The Lieutenant General sighed. It made sense. His son was young, successful, and naturally drawn to a woman like Aakanksha. Why shouldn't he go after what he wanted?

"Alright," he finally said. "I'll talk to Colonel Rana today."

The Lieutenant General wasn't sure how Colonel Rana would react. After all, Aakanksha was just 18. Still, he brought up the idea of his son, Anshuman, marrying Aakanksha.

To his surprise, the Colonel didn't just agree—he was thrilled. In his mind, this was more than a marriage; it was an alliance. A chance to tie his family to the prestigious Lieutenant General's lineage. The perks? Unmatched status, career boosts for Adarsh, and an elevation of the Rana family name.

Aakanksha, his wife, or anyone else, none of them were consulted. The Colonel didn't see the need. This was happening. And in his world, decisions weren't up for debate. The wedding would take place within a month.

The Colonel returned home and informed Gayatri of his decision. She sat there, stunned. Marrying off Aakanksha? Just like that?

She didn't argue—she never did. But inside, she knew. Aakanksha wasn't going to take this quietly. A storm was coming, and the mere thought of an argument between father and daughter terrified her. That evening, Aakanksha walked in, tired from practice, unaware of what was waiting. The Colonel didn't waste time. He looked straight at her and dropped the bomb.

Aakanksha froze for a second before the words hit her. Then, her voice exploded. "Are you serious? You think you can just hand me over like some object? I'm not a damn puppet!"

The Colonel's face darkened. "Watch your tone, Aakanksha," he warned, his voice firm.

But Aakanksha wasn't backing down. "Watch my tone? YOU are the one making insane decisions about MY life, and I'M supposed to watch my words? Have you lost your mind?" Her voice shook the walls. "How could you even think of doing this to me?"

No one—absolutely no one—had ever spoken to Colonel Rana like that. Not in his entire life. In the army, such defiance would have been crushed in seconds. Respect wasn't optional—it was the rule. But this wasn't a soldier standing before him. This was his daughter.

Gayatri stood frozen, dreading his reaction. Aakanksha had crossed a line, but the Colonel didn't explode. Raising his hand wouldn't fix this. More than that, he had given his word to Lt. General Uddhav Singh. A scene now would jeopardize everything. Instead, he took a deep breath. "Go, have dinner. We'll talk in the morning. I won't force you into anything, so relax." He reached out, gently stroking her head.

Aakanksha wasn't expecting that. Her anger softened, and without thinking, she hugged him—so tight he almost lost his balance. And just like that, they burst out laughing and all that remained was a father and his daughter.

Aakanksha tossed and turned all night, cursing herself for ever stepping foot into Lt. General's house. Why the hell did she even go to the party? The more she replayed the evening in her thoughts, the angrier she got. Anshuman. That arrogant, overconfident idiot. She spent hours mentally hurling insults at him—some so creative that even a street thug would be impressed. But anger wasn't enough. She had to face the real battle in the morning—her father. She wasn't going to beg. She was going to make him understand. There was no way she was marrying Anshuman. Not in this lifetime.

Morning came and breakfast was tense. Afterward, father and daughter sat down for a conversation that neither was ready for—but both knew was inevitable. In the next room, Gayatri and Adarsh whispered silent prayers. All they wanted was a peaceful ending. But with Aakanksha and the Colonel on opposite sides, peace was a long shot.

Before the Colonel could say a word, Aakanksha spoke first. "Papa, I have a goal. I want to play basketball for India. There's a chance for players from our state to train at the academy in Delhi, and in two weeks, they'll be selecting the best for the National Team."

The Colonel raised an eyebrow. "You never mentioned basketball before."

"You never asked," she shot back. "You were so focused on Adarsh's career, you never once thought to ask about mine."

The words hit him like a punch to the chest. For a second, he felt his heartbeat falter. But he quickly regained his composure. "And after Delhi?" he asked, his voice calm but curious. "Then what?"

Aakanksha grinned—she had managed to get this far. Now came the real pitch. "After getting selected, we'll train in Delhi for two years at the academy. Then, the best from there make it to the National Team."

The Colonel leaned forward, intrigued. "And if you don't get selected for Nationals?"

"I will be," she said, confident as ever.

He wasn't convinced. "Competing at the state level is one thing, but Nationals? That's a different game. What if you don't make it?"

Aakanksha shrugged, completely unfazed. "Then I'll marry whoever you want."

The Colonel raised a brow. "That boy might not wait forever."

"He's not the last man on earth."

The Colonel hadn't expected that response. His patience thinned. "As of now, if there's someone, whom I can lay my hands on and who is also the best on earth for you, it is Anshuman."

A tense silence filled the room. Then, he pushed further. "And what if you don't even make it to the academy training in Delhi?"

Aakanksha barely flinched. "That's not happening. Coach Sir says I'm the best in the state. The only way I don't get selected is if I do something insane."

The Colonel wasn't letting go. "Just answer me. What if you don't?"

Aakanksha sighed dramatically. "Papa, you're getting old. Memory issues already? I told you—if I don't make it, I'll marry whoever you want."

"So, if not selected for Nationals, you're saying yes to marrying him?" the Colonel pressed again.

Aakanksha hesitated for a moment before muttering, "Yes."

The Colonel wrapped up the conversation with his daughter, advising her to focus on her selection trials coming up in two weeks, promising to discuss everything after the results were out.

Later, at Lt. General Uddhav Singh's residence, the atmosphere was light. The Lt. General, unaware of the storm brewing, greeted him with playful teasing. "So, Colonel, when's the big day? You seem more eager than the groom himself!" he chuckled, unaware of the weight of the news about to drop.

The Colonel's face drained of colour. It felt as if the blood had stopped flowing in his veins. Taking a deep breath, he finally spoke—"Aakanksha refused."

Lt. General Singh, instead of reacting with shock, simply smirked. "Honestly, I was more surprised when you agreed without consulting your daughter."

The Lt. General leaned forward, his tone softer. "Please don't take this the wrong way. I'm speaking as your friend, not your superior."

He gestured toward the glass of water the maid had just placed in front of the Colonel. "Drink up," he said before continuing. "There's nothing to feel ashamed or guilty about. Our children aren't like us—they're millennials. Audacious, independent, and sharp. Honestly, I would've been shocked if Aakanksha had agreed without a fight. You can't plan her future without involving her." He smirked, leaning back. "Think about it. Our kids grew up from radios to Nokia 6600s to having the internet at their fingertips. They don't need us to tell them what's best for them. And let's be honest—marriage is the last thing on their minds."

The Colonel, still tense, finally spoke. "With all due respect, Sir, if I had asked the same of my son, he would never have refused. He would've married whoever I chose."

In response the Lieutenant General quipped mockingly, "Then I must say, your daughter possesses a stronger spine than your son."

The Colonel sighed, shaking his head. Maybe, deep down, he had sensed this all along. Maybe that's why, on the day she was born, he hadn't felt the same joy as he would have for a son. Perhaps he had always known—raising her wouldn't be easy.

The Lt. General leaned back, arms crossed. "You're thinking like an officer, not a father." He spoke calmly but firmly. "We can't treat our kids like cadets. In the army, obedience is non-negotiable. But at home? It's different. They're not here to take orders. They need guidance, not commands."

The Colonel wasn't convinced. "We've given them everything—food, education, a privileged life. We've fulfilled every need, even their unreasonable demands. Therefore, treating them with the same expectations as cadets was not unreasonable."

The Lt. General sighed, looking at the Colonel with a mix of regret and wisdom. "We had sex for pleasure, and our children are the product of it," he said, his voice firm yet reflective. He reminded him that kids don't just appear on their own; they are born from the intimacy shared by their parents. Their existence isn't about orders and discipline—it's about bonds, love, and responsibility. They aren't recruits to be shaped and controlled; they are lives to be nurtured.

The Lt. General paused for a moment before continuing, his voice measured. "Some people have kids to secure their old age. Others see them as future breadwinners—sometimes even forcing them into begging. And then there are those who give birth to uphold their family's lineage and heritage."

The words, upholding the family's lineage and heritage, pierced the Colonel's heart like a thorn, stirring emotions and prompting introspection.

The Lieutenant General cut the conversation short, his tone firm and dismissive. "Enough of this discussion," he said, shifting focus. Turning to the Colonel, he asked about Aakanksha's decision.

The Colonel didn't hesitate. Frustration clear in his voice, he spoke about his daughter's refusal to marry. Her reason? She wanted to play basketball and represent India's national women's team. To him, it sounded absurd. Basketball? In India? For women? Basketball wasn't cricket; it had no real future in India, especially for women. He saw her decision as nothing more than a foolish dream—proof of her lack of common sense.

"Never underestimate anyone, Colonel," the Lieutenant General said, backing Aakanksha's decision. "People thought the same about Indian women's tennis—until Sania Mirza entered the court."

The Colonel smirked, "I think her looks had more to do with it than her talent," he said, his tone laced with sarcasm, trying to undermine the General's point.

"Beauty fades, skill doesn't. She's still India's No. 1 woman tennis player," the Lieutenant General snapped. "Don't throw baseless arguments just to prove a point, Colonel. And by that logic, isn't your daughter beautiful too? Therefore, if I were to believe your words then Aakanksha can become a star too."

The Lt. General continued, "And just in case you've forgotten, my eldest son is a successful businessman and also the President of the Sports Promotion Board in Himachal Pradesh. If she is a good player, then I can recommend your daughter's name. She'll get into the Delhi Academy for training—no hassle."

Colonel shook his head, as if emerging from a reverie, when the Lieutenant General mentioned his son, Ashutosh, who had recently become the President of the Sports Promotion Board in Himachal Pradesh. The Colonel nodded in recollection, acknowledging that it had only been few months since Ashutosh had assumed the role.

The Colonel paused, a sly glint appearing in his eyes. He leaned in and made an unusual request. He wanted the Lt. General to recommend his daughter for the position—but with a twist. No matter how well she performed, she shouldn't be selected.

The Lt. General frowned, "Why?"

With a smirk, the Colonel revealed his plan. His daughter had made a promise—if she failed to get selected, she would marry a suitor of his choice.

The Lt. General's expression hardened. "I can't do that," he said firmly. "I believe in fairness. I won't manipulate the system for personal gain. It's not just about her—every deserving candidate deserves a fair chance."

The Colonel leaned in closer and whispered, "Sir, who's going to know? Just us."

The Lt. General looked him in the eye. "God will know," he said. "And everybody is answerable to him, sooner or later."

The Colonel shook his head, "You think I don't want the best for my daughter? Of course, I do. She's bold, smart, and fearless—I won't deny that. But we have seen more of life than she has. Do you really think there's a better groom or a better family for her than yours?" He continued, his frustration evident. "Yes, she's a millennial, tech-savvy, glued to gadgets. But that doesn't mean she understands the weight of every decision she makes. I'll always want a stable, secure future for her. I'm her father, not her enemy."

The Lt. General leaned back in his chair, exhaling deeply. His silence spoke volumes. He was stuck in a dilemma, lost in thought. Sensing the hesitation, the Colonel stepped in. "You don't have to talk to your son. I'll handle that," he assured. "All I need is your consent."

The Lt. General sighed, finally letting go. "It's your call," he said. "She's your daughter. But remember, every decision comes with consequences."

The Colonel remained unfazed. "Once the marriage is fixed, everything will fall into place," he assured the Lt. General, confident he could convince Ashutosh.

But being a man of strategy, he decided to speak to Anshuman first. Testing the waters, he eased into the conversation before finally asking the question that mattered most, "Son, do you really want to marry my daughter?"

Anshuman didn't hesitate. "I love her," he said with conviction. "I'll keep her happy and give her a secure life."

The Colonel, listening intently, nodded. "I know. That's why I need a favour." He paused before asking the real question, "Convince your elder brother to disqualify her at the trials."

Anshuman frowned, confused at first. But as the Colonel laid out his reasoning, the pieces started falling into place. If she got into the Academy, her basketball career would take off. That meant years of waiting, uncertainty—maybe even losing her forever. He took a deep breath. It felt wrong, but wasn't love about sacrifices too? In the end, if this was the only way to marry her, he had no choice. He agreed.

As the Colonel and Anshuman made their way to Ashutosh's office, the Colonel felt a quiet sense of victory. He had successfully won Anshuman over. The boy was so smitten with Aakanksha that the Colonel chuckled to himself—if he had asked for Anshuman's kidney, the poor guy might have handed it over without a second thought.

The moment they stepped into Ashutosh's office, the luxury hit them. Floor-to-ceiling glass walls, lush green plants in every corner, a sleek Italian sofa, and a massive L-shaped desk. On it sat a desktop flashing a logo of a half-eaten apple. Ashutosh, dressed in crisp formals, leaned back in an imported British armchair—a throne of sorts. As soon as he saw the Colonel, he stood up, his expression polite but curious. "Good afternoon, Uncle," he said, his voice smooth. "To what do I owe the pleasure of this visit?"

The Colonel greeted Ashutosh with a casual smile. "Good afternoon, Ashutosh. Just curious—why does your desktop have a half-eaten apple on it?"

Ashutosh chuckled politely. "Uncle, that's the logo of Apple Inc., an international brand from the USA."

The Colonel nodded, pretending to process the information. "Ah, I see. I recently bought a desktop for my kids too. It's HP—another American brand. At first, I thought it was *Hindustan Petroleum* and thought they had started making computers. Then my kids explained—it's Hewlett-

Packard." He burst into laughter, making sure others joined in. Whether he genuinely believed HP stood for Hindustan Petroleum or was just playing along to boost Ashutosh's ego—it was hard to tell.

Ashutosh also smiled and remarked, "It's alright, Uncle. The world's going digital. Sooner or later, we will all catch up."

The Colonel, after exchanging a few pleasantries, wasted no time in getting to the heart of the matter. He revealed a significant task he had in mind for Ashutosh, expressing confidence in Ashutosh's capability to handle it. Ashutosh, eager to assist, readily agreed, demonstrating his willingness to help. Then, the Colonel shifted the conversation to a topic of personal significance - the desire for Ashutosh's brother to marry his daughter.

Ashutosh, already in the loop, burst into laughter, his happiness unmistakable. The Colonel, however, wanted more than just a reaction—he needed assurance. "Do you truly support your brother's decision?" he asked, watching Ashutosh closely.

Without a second thought, Ashutosh nodded, "Of course, Uncle. I'm genuinely happy for him."

The Colonel leaned in slightly, his tone calm but firm. "My daughter wants to be a basketball player. She's adamant about training at the academy in Delhi. The selection trials are in two weeks. If she makes it, she'll be away for two years. So, if you want your brother's wedding to happen this season, then..." He let his words hang, letting Ashutosh connect the dots.

"Then, what?" Ashutosh asked, his curiosity piqued.

The Colonel shrugged. "You know best."

For a moment, Ashutosh's expression faltered. He had expected a different conversation. Still, he kept his composure. As the President of the Sports Promotion Board, he believed in nurturing talent, not blocking it. "We're supposed to support players, not hold them back," he said, his tone calm but carrying a hint of displeasure—the kind the Colonel didn't miss.

The Colonel sighed, looking at Ashutosh. "I'm not against her talent," he said. "I just want what's best for her future."

Ashutosh frowned, "And that's by pushing her into a life where she becomes just another housewife?"

The Colonel shook his head, "Not at all. I respect her independence. But instead of basketball, I see a more stable future for her in academics. Perhaps B.Ed., maybe a Ph.D. She could become a teacher or a professor, and have a secure career." He paused before questioning Ashutosh about the viability of a career in women's basketball, to which Ashutosh found himself without a ready answer.

Ashutosh paused, caught off guard by the question. But he quickly regained his composure. "If every parent thought like you, Uncle, sports in India—except for cricket—would never stand a chance," he said, his tone measured but firm. He then added, "If she makes it to the nationals, she won't just play. She'll have real career opportunities—good jobs in government organizations through the Sports Quota. It's not as unstable as you think."

"What kind of job? A peon? A 'Group-D' attendant? A railway ticket clerk? Or maybe a constable?" The Colonel paused, letting his words sink in before continuing. "I'm not looking down on these jobs—they have their own value. But Aakanksha is my daughter. Colonel Jitendra Singh Rana's daughter. Do you really think these roles are better than becoming a lecturer or professor?"

As Ashutosh started to explain further, the Colonel cut him off. "See? Even if you're not fully convinced about a career in women's basketball," he said, raising an eyebrow. "That's why you brought up government jobs as a backup in the first place."

Ashutosh had no comeback. The Colonel's argument had backed him into a corner. He lowered his head slightly, acknowledging the logic in his words. "I don't agree with you, Uncle," he admitted, "but I can't completely dismiss your perspective either."

Anshuman seized the moment to justify their stance. "Ours isn't an orthodox family," he said. "We guide our own toward the right careers, encouraging them to explore their strengths." But then, with a firm shake of his head, he added, "Basketball? In India? Let's be honest—it's not a real career option."

The room grew tense as all eyes turned to Ashutosh. The Colonel waited, his expression unreadable. After a long silence, Ashutosh finally exhaled and spoke, his voice laced with hesitation. "I can't do this," he admitted. "If this gets out, it could ruin my reputation forever."

`The tension between Ashutosh and the Colonel thickened, the air heavy with unsaid words. The Colonel's voice, firm and unwavering, cut through the silence "Don't try to fool me, Ashutosh," he warned. "This isn't just about a favour. It's about my daughter's future." His gaze hardened as he added, "A father's curse is no small thing. Think carefully before you make a decision you'll regret."

Ashutosh swallowed, his distress evident. He opened his mouth to speak, but the weight of the situation held him back. His conscience battled against the Colonel's demand—one felt unjust, the other unavoidable. Seeing his hesitation, the Colonel softened, just a little. "Don't let guilt break you," he said. "Instead, find a way. No matter how difficult, there's always a solution."

After a long pause, Ashutosh exhaled and nodded. "Fine. I'll help," he said, his voice steady but reluctant.

The Colonel leaned forward, eyes sharp, "How?"

Ashutosh glanced around, as if ensuring no one else could hear. "There's a way," he said. "The official handling the selection trials is under the Sports Promotion Board—my board. He plays a key role in recommendations." He paused, choosing his words carefully. "I'll make sure he doesn't push your daughter's name forward. No official endorsement, no selection."

The Colonel listened in silence, absorbing every word. The plan was quiet, subtle, and most importantly, effective.

"And what if he doesn't listen to you?" the Colonel asked, his tone sharp with curiosity.

"His job, his increment, his promotion—all of it depends on me," Ashutosh said confidently.

The Colonel exhaled, relieved. A rare smile crossed his face as he pulled Ashutosh into a warm embrace. Anshuman, equally pleased, extended his hand, and the two exchanged a firm handshake. It was done.

As the Colonel turned to leave, he suddenly stopped at the door and looked back. "One last thing," he said. 'What's his name?"

Ashutosh responded, "Coach and referee for both the men's and women's basketball teams. Mr. Manohar Karwal."

On the day of the trial, Aakanksha stepped onto the court with fire in her eyes, ready to give it her all. But from the very start, things felt off. Every time she made a move, the whistle blew. Foul. Again. And again. Either she was actually making mistakes, or Mr. Karwal, the referee, thought she was.

She protested, her voice firm, insisting the calls were unfair. But Karwal barely flinched. "One more word, and you're out," he warned. With every questionable foul, her team lost possession, and before she knew it, the match was over. Defeat.

After the game, Aakanksha waited outside the campus, her frustration simmering under the afternoon sun. Three long hours passed before Karwal finally stepped out of the meeting room where the selection committee had gathered. She straightened up, her heart pounding. She needed an answer.

Mr. Karwal was surprised to see Aakanksha still waiting outside. "You're still here? Why haven't you gone home?" he asked.

Aakanksha, her patience wearing thin, got straight to the point. "What did the selection committee decide?"

Karwal hesitated, shifting uncomfortably. "I don't know," he admitted. "They just asked for my feedback. The final call isn't mine to make." He sighed, sensing her restlessness. "You'll find out tomorrow evening when they announce the results."

Aakanksha's voice wavered as she whispered, "Do you think I have a chance?" Her eyes glistened, caught between desperation and hope, searching for even the smallest reassurance.

Mr. Karwal sighed. "Look, I don't decide who gets selected. That's up to the committee," he said, his tone firm but calm. "You're a great player—your passes are sharp, your dodging is quick. But those fouls... they might work against you."

Aakanksha's frustration boiled over. "I didn't foul!" she shot back. "You got the calls wrong." Her voice was laced with anger, but beneath it was desperation. "I played fair." Karwal remained unfazed. "Argue all you want, but during the match, I had no choice but to warn you about expulsion," he said, his words carrying an air of finality. That was it. The last straw. Tears welled up in Aakanksha's eyes, and before she could stop herself, they spilled over.

Karwal, caught off guard, softened. He reached out, his voice gentler now. "Hey, don't cry. It's not entirely your fault." He had seen plenty of players over the years, but few had Aakanksha's fire. "You played with heart, with passion. But sometimes, when you're too driven, you don't see your own mistakes." He paused, letting the words sink in. "Still, you were better than most. Maybe the committee will see past the fouls. Your speed, your agility... that might just be enough."

Aakanksha wiped her tears and took a deep breath. "Do you really think they'll ignore the fouls and select me?" she asked, her voice quieter now.

Karwal offered a reassuring smile. "Anything's possible. But in the end, it's up to the Selection Committee. And why stress so much? If not this year, you can always try again next year."

"Sir, *next year may never come*", she said, her voice heavy with anguish. Without another word, she turned and walked away, not even looking back to wish Mr. Karwal goodbye.

Guilt gnawed at Mr. Karwal. He tried convincing himself—*I was just following orders. It wasn't my fault.* But no matter how much he reasoned, the weight of his actions refused to lift. What unsettled him even more were Aakanksha's parting words: *Next year may never come.* What did she mean? *There's always a next year,* he told himself, trying to shake off the unease. He reassured himself—he would make things right next year. In doing so, he sought solace in the belief that he could appease his troubled conscience.

The next day, when the results were announced, Aakanksha felt her world crumble. It wasn't just a loss—it was over. The kind that makes your stomach drop, your mind goes numb.

But it wasn't just about not making the team. The real fear? Facing her father. Telling him she had failed. And worse—the marriage that now loomed over her like a death sentence.

That evening, she sought an escape. She took Vishal to the outskirts of town, whisky in hand—bought with her own pocket money. She drank, hoping to blur out reality, but the hopelessness clung to her like a shadow. For a brief, reckless moment, she even wondered if an *early exit* from life would be easier. Vishal tried to lift her spirits with motivational quotes. She shut him down, as words meant nothing right now.

And then, as if the universe itself decided to intervene, the skies burst open. Within seconds, it threatened to turn into a downpour. Before they could get drenched, they ran, slipping through the muddy paths, taking shelter in an abandoned thatched hut. Aakanksha stumbled slightly—whisky playing its part—but she kept herself steady. The faint smell of alcohol lingered around her, she otherwise appeared outwardly composed and sober. Outside, the storm raged. Inside, so did she.

As they waited for the rain to pass, Aakanksha suddenly wrapped her arms around Vishal, holding him tightly. Caught off guard, he instinctively tried to pull away, but she refused to let go. Her body trembled, and within seconds, silent sobs turned into uncontrollable tears.

Vishal hesitated but then gave in, wrapping his arms around her, letting her cry. They stayed that way—her pain pouring out, his silence offering comfort—until her sobs quieted, and she finally pulled back, wiping her face. Then, out of nowhere, she whispered, "Will you marry me? Let's just run away from here."

Vishal blinked before breaking into a soft chuckle. "Aakanksha, you're my best friend. That's how I've always seen you," he said. "Even if I did say yes, I don't have a stable job, no money to take care of us." Vishal smirked and continued, "And I'm definitely not giving up my freedom to marry someone as dominating as you."

Aakanksha laughed and playfully nudged Vishal's chest. "Oh please! As if I'd marry you," she teased. "You're just 18. Boys aren't even allowed to marry before 21. I'm a grown-up, and you're still a silly kid."

Vishal smirked and let out a playful *"O-hoho..."* before swaying his head side to side like a Bharatanatyam dancer. "Girls, I tell you!" he teased. "Just a minute ago, someone was saying, *'Will you marry me? Let's run away from here.'* And now, look at the attitude!"

Aakanksha burst into laughter. "I never said that! You must be hallucinating."

"Oh, fantastic!" Vishal rolled his eyes dramatically. "So, I'm the idiot here, huh?"

"Obviously, you are! You'll always be my *idiot* friend," Aakanksha grinned. "You've been there for all my *chutiyapa*, sometimes even leading the charge. If you weren't such an *idiot* yourself, would you have joined me in all my *chutiyapas*?"

Before Vishal could respond, she pulled him into a warm hug and planted a quick kiss on his cheeks. They held onto each other, neither wanting to let go, as if the world outside had ceased to exist. In that moment, both wanted time to stop, the world to end—right there, right then—wrapped in each other's warmth.

Vishal stood frozen, unsure whether to feel flattered, embarrassed, or just plain confused. But one thing was certain—the kiss left a delightful tickle on his body, the warmth of that moment, that tiny spark, would stay with him for years to come.

The rain had stopped, and after much coaxing, she finally agreed to leave. By the time she reached home, it was 9:20 PM. Every step felt heavy, her body drained—not just from exhaustion, but from the storm brewing inside her. The tension in the house was palpable. Missed calls. Worried faces.

With a deep breath, she pushed open the gate, stepping inside like a soldier walking into a lost battle. She made her way to her father's bedroom, pausing at the door. Even in his drunken state, she hesitated before peering inside, feeling a mix of respect, fear and guilt. But no matter how much she wanted to, she just couldn't bring herself to go closer to him.

Aakanksha took a deep breath and steadied herself before pushing the door open. "May I come in?" she asked, her voice carefully measured. Balancing her steps and her words was tricky—because when you're drunk, even if your feet cooperate, your tongue might betray you.

The Colonel looked up and his expression darkened. "Are you drunk?"

"Yes, I am."

His eyes widened in rage. "Are you out of your mind?"

"No."

"Then why the hell did you drink?"

"Trying to forget the pain."

"What pain?"

She exhaled, staring at the floor. "I wasn't selected for the training academy in Delhi. The results came out today. My name isn't even on the reserve list."

The Colonel's anger cooled, just a little. "Oh... that's why?"

"Yes," she muttered, trying to act as normal as possible.

"Did anyone see you like this?"

"No."

His voice hardened again. "And how exactly do you *know* that? Do you even care about my reputation?"

"I've already told you; nobody has seen me. And it's not like this is my first time being drunk. I've been drunk plenty of times before, I just never mentioned it until now. Has anyone ever complained about me before? No. That means nobody has seen me." She spoke in one continuous breath.

The Colonel's eyes narrowed in surprise. "*You've* been drinking before?"

"For fun," she admitted, shrugging. "But this time, it was for the pain."

The Colonel sighed, rubbing his temples. His patience was wearing thin. "Enough. Go eat dinner and sleep. I don't want to talk about this anymore."

"I'm not hungry," she muttered. "I'm full."

"I don't care," he snapped. "Go to your room. We'll talk in the morning."

Aakanksha turned and left, her steps slightly unsteady.

The Colonel watched her go, a strange satisfaction settling in his chest. She wasn't going to Delhi. That meant one thing—nothing could stop the wedding now.

The next morning, Aakanksha woke up with a splitting headache. She couldn't remember what happened the night before, hoping it was all just a bad dream and that she hadn't caused any trouble. She clung to that hope as she rubbed her temples, wincing at the pain. Just then, Gayatri, walked in. Her face said it all—puffy eyes, dark circles, the unmistakable signs of a sleepless night filled with tears. She forced a weak smile. "How are you feeling? It's already 10. You should get up."

Aakanksha, still groggy, squinted at her. "Why have you been crying? Did Dad say something?"

Gayatri shook her head, "No, he hasn't said a word. He's not even angry at you."

"What did I do?"

"Are you mocking me?" Gayatri asked, irritated.

Aakanksha pleaded with her mother, insisting that she truly couldn't recall anything. She desperately asked what she had done. Gayatri recounted how Aakanksha had consumed so much alcohol that it seemed even the slightest movement would have made rum spill from her mouth.

"It was whisky, not rum"

Gayatri yelled at Aakanksha, insisting that it didn't matter whether it was rum or whisky and asked her to listen instead of arguing about the distinction. Aakanksha apologized and urged her mother to continue. Gayatri recounted how Aakanksha had entered her father's room, confronting him about her drinking while declaring she didn't qualify for a tournament. She also mentioned that Aakanksha had casually admitted to drinking before – just for fun.

Aakanksha was shocked to hear this and exclaimed, "What? No way. I didn't say that."

"Yes, you did."

"And... Did I mention who I was drinking with?" Aakanksha asked hesitantly.

"No." Confirmed Gayatri

"Thank God." Aakanksha mumbled to herself.

Gayatri asked who had been with Aakanksha while she was drinking. Trying to lighten the moment, Aakanksha said she had been in great company—just her and her solitude.

Curious about her father's reaction, she asked if he was angry. To her surprise, Gayatri shook her head, admitting that he hadn't shown any signs of anger and seemed completely fine. Perplexed, Aakanksha questioned why her mother was crying and had swollen eyes if her father wasn't upset.

"Shut up! My 18-year-old daughter is out drinking and coming home late at night, and you're asking why I'm crying?" Gayatri snapped, her voice shaking with anger and distress. Before Aakanksha could respond, she continued, "Get up. Your father's been waiting since morning to talk to you. Freshen up, eat something, and come to the lobby." After issuing the instructions, Gayatri left the room.

Reluctantly, Aakanksha dragged herself out of bed, her head throbbing from the aftermath of the previous night. Each step toward the bathroom felt heavier than the last. Standing before the mirror, she picked up her toothbrush, smeared toothpaste on it, and began brushing. As the foam filled her mouth, her tired eyes met her reflection in the mirror, she mumbled, barely audible even to herself, *"Oh God,* please kill me."

Aakanksha, dreading the inevitable conversation with her father, stretched her morning routine as much as possible. What usually took minutes dragged on for hours. By the time she finally stepped out of the bathroom, it was already lunchtime. Dragging her feet, she made her way to the dining table, where the rest of the family was already seated. Gayatri, as always, ensured everyone was served before taking her own plate.

The Colonel, without looking up, asked about her hangover. She sighed, giving a straightforward answer—*not good*.

Meanwhile, Adarsh, wore a subtle smile as he lowered his head, waiting for his turn to be served.

"Why do you drink so much when you can't digest it?" screamed Gayatri from the kitchen.

"Calm down, Gayatri," the Colonel said, his tone unusually gentle. Then, shifting his attention to Aakanksha, he continued, "She had a rough day yesterday. She turned to alcohol to cope. Let it go." His reaction stunned everyone. Aakanksha, Gayatri, even Adarsh—none of them had expected this level of understanding from him.

Looking at his daughter, the Colonel added, "Life doesn't always go as planned. Sometimes, things happen for a reason. You may not see it now, but there's always a bigger purpose behind it all."

Aakanksha nodded, absorbing his words. For the first time in a long time, she felt a sense of calm.

The Colonel leaned back, his voice thoughtful. He spoke about the role of guardians in shaping their children's lives, suggesting that sometimes, divine intervention is the only way because young minds often struggle to make the right choices. No matter the conflicts or differences, parents always have their children's best interests at heart. Aakanksha nodded, offering a quiet acknowledgment. After a brief pause, the Colonel asked Aakanksha if she still remembered a promise she had made. Aakanksha hesitated for a moment and said, "Yes, Papa."

The Colonel studied her carefully. "Are you ready to keep it?"

Aakanksha let out a small, ironic smile. "In the house of Colonel Jitendra Singh Rana, promises aren't just words. They're meant to be kept," she said, her voice laced with sarcasm, indicating her intention to keep her word.

The Colonel's chest swelled with pride. He had no doubt that Aakanksha would keep her word. His belief in her was unwavering. Though he felt a surge of emotion, he restrained himself from leaping out of his seat and dancing with exuberance, refraining from such a display.

The Colonel reminded her of the old saying, *"When life gives you lemons, make lemonade."* Selection or not, her life wouldn't lack comfort. She would still have luxury, security, and happiness within their family. With time running short, he had already made up his mind—after lunch, he would visit Lt. General's house to start the wedding preparations. But before taking the next step, he looked at Aakanksha, seeking her approval. *Was she ready?*

After a brief pause, Aakanksha voiced her wish to meet Anshuman before the wedding.

The Colonel's eyes narrowed with suspicion. "Why? You've already committed to marrying him."

She sighed, keeping her tone calm. "I'm not backing out, Papa. I just want to talk to him before we get married. He's going to be my life partner. Isn't it normal to meet him properly at least once?"

The Colonel reminded her that they had spoken at the party hosted by Anshuman's family. But Aakanksha shook her head. "That was just small talk—like any random conversation with a stranger on the street. It wasn't *us*, talking as two people about to share a life."

"He's not just some ordinary guy on the street. He's an IITian," the Colonel said, his voice dangerously close to shouting.

Before the tension could escalate further, Gayatri stepped in. She urged him to let Aakanksha meet Anshuman at least once. After all, she had never refused the marriage—she simply wanted a chance to have a conversation, perhaps a date, with her future husband. With a light laugh, half teasing, half persuasive, Gayatri tried to ease the situation. "Come on, don't take away this little moment from her," she said, hoping to sway the Colonel.

As the Colonel questioned Aakanksha about her intentions behind wanting a date with her future husband, Gayatri stood behind him, silently watching her daughter. With a quick blink, she sent an unspoken message—one that went unnoticed by the Colonel.

Aakanksha voiced her request, stating that she wanted to go on a date with Anshuman. Not just any date—something meaningful, something memorable. It would be both the first and last time she ever dated someone.

The Colonel didn't give an immediate yes, but he didn't refuse either. He assured her that he would convey her request to the Lt. General. If they agreed, she could go. But he made one thing clear—it was entirely their decision. He wouldn't insist.

The Lt. General's face lit up with delight as he embraced the Colonel, his joy evident. Anshuman, equally thrilled, couldn't hide his excitement. In response, the Colonel congratulated him, offering his heartfelt blessings for the future. After some discussion, they settled on a plan—the engagement would take place by the end of September, and the wedding would follow in mid-October.

Before leaving, the Colonel casually mentioned Aakanksha's wish to go on a date with Anshuman. The Lt. General burst into laughter at the unexpected request but readily agreed, giving Anshuman permission to take her out.

Back home, the Colonel shared the finalized dates for the engagement and wedding with the family. He also informed Aakanksha about her upcoming date and instructed her to coordinate with Anshuman for the time and place. Everyone seemed content with how things were unfolding—everyone except Aakanksha.

Resigned to the situation, Aakanksha decided to go with the flow and let destiny take its course. That evening, she called Anshuman and suggested meeting at a café on Sunday afternoon. Anshuman, however, preferred a quieter place—somewhere away from the usual café buzz, where they could talk in peace. But Aakanksha was firm on her choice. After a brief back-and-forth, they reached a compromise. They would meet at the café as planned, but if it was too crowded, they'd find another place after lunch. Aakanksha agreed.

Albert Einstein once said, *"Time flies when you're with someone you like, but a moment on a hot stove feels like forever. That's relativity."* For Aakanksha and Anshuman, this couldn't have been more accurate. Sunday arrived too soon for Aakanksha—she wasn't eager to meet Anshuman. But for him, the wait felt endless.

Sunday arrived, and Anshuman was up by 6 a.m., excitement making it impossible to sleep any longer. Meanwhile, Aakanksha, far less enthusiastic, dragged herself out of bed at 10 a.m. By 12:30 p.m., she figured it was time to get ready. Five minutes later, she was done—white top, navy blue jeans, nothing fancy. Even with her wedding barely a month away, her tomboyish style remained unchanged. No makeup, no jewellery. But mothers will be mothers. After some gentle persuasion from Gayatri, she reluctantly put on a small pair of earrings—*just* to keep her mom happy.

Anshuman pulled up outside the Colonel's house in his brother's car, ready to pick up Aakanksha for his much-awaited date. They headed to a popular restaurant on Mall Road, only to find it packed—hardly surprising for a Sunday afternoon. Luckily, Anshuman had planned ahead. A reserved corner table meant they didn't have to wait but the buzzing crowd still made it difficult for him to fully soak in the moment. He had even brought a rose for Aakanksha, tucked carefully inside his jacket. But with so many eyes around, he hesitated. Giving it to her in front of everyone felt too awkward. He decided to wait for the right moment.

As they finished their meal, Anshuman suggested moving to a quieter place where they could actually hear each other. The restaurant, packed with Sunday crowds, wasn't exactly ideal for a meaningful conversation. Aakanksha hesitated but eventually agreed. The noise was getting to her too. She suggested a secluded hilltop on the city outskirts, a spot she had frequented with Vishal, though she omitted any mention of Vishal and their drinking escapades. Instead, when Anshuman asked how she knew about it, she casually lied, saying she had been there once during a school picnic.

When they arrived, a wave of nostalgia hit Aakanksha. Her chest tightened, her eyes stung, but she blinked away the tears before Anshuman could notice. This place wasn't just beautiful; it held something deeper for her. For a moment, she let herself soak in its peace, knowing this might be the last time she'd ever be here.

Anshuman, too, found himself exhilarated by the prospect of reaching such a peaceful, hidden spot, especially in the middle of Shimla's chaotic tourist season. It was nothing like the crowded streets and cafes he was used to.

Some men, at times, fail to grasp the seriousness of a situation, letting their imagination run wild. The rush of testosterone blurs their judgment, making them see only what they want—sexual desire, temptation, a chance that never really existed. In those moments, they lose control, mistaking illusions for opportunities.

At that moment, Anshuman's mind started racing. Why had Aakanksha chosen such a secluded spot? The only explanation that seemed logical to him was that she wanted to get physically close. He overlooked a simple fact—most women wouldn't even consider engaging in sex on a first meeting, unless they were doing it for money.

Anshuman stood in silent admiration behind Aakanksha, his eyes drawn to the graceful contours of her figure as she lost herself in the beauty of the landscape before her. Wanting to start a conversation and connect with her, he decided to speak first, his gaze lingering on her curves.

"Nice view," Anshuman remarked, his gaze focusing on her butt.

Aakanksha, completely absorbed in the beauty of the snow-capped mountains and the lush greenery around them, assumed Anshuman was admiring the scenery. She smiled softly and said, "Yes, I know."

Immersed in the mesmerizing beauty around them, Anshuman couldn't help but remark, "Isn't this the perfect setting for romance?" Aakanksha, captivated by the scenery and perhaps unaware of Anshuman's burgeoning intentions, simply replied, "Yes, it truly is," unintentionally signaling a desire to steer the conversation elsewhere.

Aakanksha's unintended response only fuelled Anshuman's assumption that she was open to intimacy, making him believe he had the green light to take things further. Still standing behind her, he moved swiftly, wrapping his arms tightly around her. Though his hands didn't touch her bare skin, she could feel the firm grip through her white top—his right hand pressing against her abdomen, while his left clasped over her right breast.

Aakanksha froze, her mind going completely blank. The sudden turn of events left her paralyzed, unable to react. She knew this was wrong—every part of her screamed for it to stop. Yet, she remained motionless, trapped in a haze of shock and confusion. Her heart begged her to resist, but her mind, unprepared for something like this, simply refused to respond.

Anshuman mistook Aakanksha's lack of resistance as tacit approval, a silent nod that fed his confidence. Standing behind her, he couldn't read her expression, but even if he had, his desire had already clouded his judgment. Emboldened by her momentary stillness, he pressed on. He began by squeezing her right breast with his left hand while his right hand lifted the hem of her white top, fingers skimming her stomach, tracing the curve of her navel. He sought more, attempting to slip past the snug waistband of her blue jeans through a small gap between the fabric and her belly. Unable to do so, he resorted to partially unzipping her jeans, inadvertently scratching her belly with his nails in the process. The sudden scrape jolted Aakanksha back to reality. With a sharp intake of breath, she pushed his hand away from the zipper. She closed it and tried to create distance between them. With deliberate force, she removed his left hand from her breast and pushed him away with her buttocks in an attempt to free herself from his grasp.

Anshuman lunged forward, trying to grab Aakanksha in a forceful embrace, but she fought back, pushing against him with all she had. Yet, his strength overpowered hers. He tightened his grip, persisted in his attempt to hug her. She twisted, strained, but exhaustion crept in, her body betraying her. Tears brimmed in her eyes, spilling as she cried out—her voice cutting through the stillness of the mountains, carrying a raw, unsettling desperation that could shake even the hardest of hearts.

Anshuman froze, panic gripping him. He hadn't expected this reaction, and fear crept in as he realized the gravity of the situation. Instinctively, he stepped back, his confidence crumbling. Words tumbled out in hurried apologies, desperate attempts to calm Aakanksha down. But as her cries grew louder, anxiety took over. In a moment of desperation, he reached out, trying to cover her mouth—less out of concern, more out of fear of the consequences.

With frantic apologies, he begged her to stop crying, swearing he wouldn't touch her again. Yet, his hand remained over her mouth, desperate to muffle any sound that could escape.

Aakanksha gave a small nod, and Anshuman hesitantly let go. The sobs quieted, but she remained hunched over, her hands shielding her face as silent tears kept falling. Anshuman, attempted to justify himself, muttered apologies, insisting he had misunderstood—that he thought she wanted the same. But she didn't respond, her face still buried in her hands, her body trembling with quiet sobs.

Anshuman thought about pulling her hands away to comfort her but hesitated, fearing how she might react. Instead, keeping a safe distance, he softly suggested they head downhill to a small stream where she could wash her face and calm down.

Aakanksha got up and walked straight to the stream, lowering herself beside it. Instead of just splashing water on her face, she plunged her entire face into the cool flow. Anshuman stood behind, watching in silence, determined not to make another mistake. She let the water wash over her, its soothing touch grounding her. With her face still submerged, she took small sips of water, as if hoping the stream could wash away more than just her tears.

After a moment, she lifted her face from the water, taking a deep breath to steady herself. Without looking at him, she stood up and turned away.

"Let's go home," she said, her voice firm, already starting to walk.

Anshuman pleaded, "Can we stay till sunset? "

Aakanksha didn't stop. Her voice sharpened as she replied, "Just drop me home."

Anshuman, desperate to make amends, assured her he would do as she asked. He pleaded for just five more minutes, promising not to cross any lines again. Aakanksha's eyes burned with anger. Her voice was sharp, unwavering. "Don't even think about touching me," she snapped, her face flushed as she jabbed a warning finger in his direction.

Anshuman reassured her once more. "I won't touch you, I promise. Just give me five minutes," he pleaded.

Aakanksha's temper flared. "And why should I wait for five minutes?" She shot back, her voice sharp with defiance.

But then, he calmly reminded her—*In a month, we're getting married.* The words hit harder than she expected. For a moment, she had nothing to say. Because, like it or not, he wasn't wrong.

Anshuman and Aakanksha sat on the ground, a small distance between them, watching the birds. He questioned her frustration—wasn't this inevitable? In just a month, they would be married. What difference did it make if intimacy began now or later? With a quiet smile, he tried to reason with her, his voice soft but certain. Once they were husband and wife, he said, nothing would be off-limits—he could touch her anytime, anywhere, undress her, see her naked, and make love to her as he pleased.

Aakanksha's frustration spilled out as she questioned him, "Is that all this marriage means to you? Just an excuse for sex?" Anshuman reassured her, marriage wasn't just about that, denying such a simplistic motive, yet acknowledging that sexual intimacy is an integral aspect of married life that cannot be disregarded.

Aakanksha looked straight at him and asked, "What if I'm not ready? What if I want to wait after marriage—to take my time before intimacy?"

Anshuman nodded, his tone reassuring. "Then you take all the time you need. I'd never force you into anything you're not comfortable with." But after a pause, he added, "Still, physical intimacy is part of marriage. It's not about rushing into it, but it's a bond that comes with the commitment—whether it happens in a week or a month, it's something we'll eventually share."

Aakanksha lowered her gaze, her voice quiet but firm. She couldn't deny that Anshuman had a point. Sensing her acknowledgment, Anshuman smiled. "Thanks for understanding," he said, then hesitated before adding, "Shall we sit for a while? Talk a little more?"

She didn't object. They climbed to the top of the hill and settled on a rock, watching as the fog slowly wrapped itself around the distant mountains. Breaking the silence,

Anshuman said, "Colonel Sir mentioned you wanted to talk to me. So, go ahead—ask me anything."

"Why do you want to marry me?" Aakanksha asked.

Anshuman looked at her, thought for a moment, and said, "Because you're beautiful, smart, intelligent... and honestly, very sexy. A rare combination."

She raised an eyebrow. "You're an IITian, and I'm just a first-year commerce student. So, intelligence can't be the reason."

"Okay then, remove intelligent if you want. But beautiful, smart, and sexy remains," Anshuman said with a smirk.

A brief silence followed. Aakanksha didn't respond, but she didn't seem uncomfortable either. Sensing that she had relaxed a little, that she was now open to conversation, Anshuman leaned in slightly and asked, "Can I ask you something?"

"Yes, of course, you can. After all, you're my would-be husband," Aakanksha said with a hint of sarcasm.

Anshuman hesitated for a moment, then asked, "Are you a virgin?"

Aakanksha blinked, stunned by the bluntness of the question. She hadn't expected something so personal—especially from someone with such high qualifications. She just stared at him, trying to process the audacity. Then, her voice turned sharp. "And how exactly does that matter?"

Anshuman didn't hesitate. "It matters a lot," he said. "If you're a virgin, we go ahead with the wedding. If not, I'll have to call it off... and tell your Colonel father and both of our families the truth."

Aakanksha's blood boiled as she looked at him—another man chained to orthodox beliefs. She wanted to lash out, to call him out for his hypocrisy, maybe even lie about her virginity, just to shut him up. But she didn't. Instead, she kept her voice steady. "Why does a woman's virginity matter so much? Why is it always about her past and never the man's? Why the double standards?"

"Virginity matters because it reflects a girl's upbringing and character," Anshuman said, his tone unwavering. "It shows the values her parents instilled in her. It separates a decent girl from the ones who... well, don't have those values. So, let's not divert the topic. Just answer the question, dear."

"Let me be very clear—I'm not dodging your question." Aakanksha's voice was sharp, her patience wearing thin. "And yes, I'm a virgin. And no, I'm not a whore."

Anshuman tried to ease her distress, masking his curiosity behind a knowing smile. "I already knew," he said, his voice calm, teasing. "Otherwise, you wouldn't have reacted with tears when I touched you." He let out a soft chuckle before his tone shifted, laced with quiet desire. "Now that we agree intimacy is inevitable after marriage, tell me—what kind of sex do you prefer?"

Aakanksha frowned. "What do you mean by 'kind of sex'?"

Anshuman leaned in slightly, his gaze unwavering. "I mean... do you prefer something wild? Spanking, dominance, a little rough play? Or just simple, classic lovemaking?"

Aakanksha let out an exasperated sigh, a mix of frustration and disbelief flashing across her face, "So, you want a virgin wife, but you also want to discuss her sexual preferences? Do you even hear yourself?" She shot him a sharp look, arms crossed. "Are you genuinely this stupid, or are you just playing dumb? Honestly, how did you even get into an IIT?" she muttered, half in disbelief, half in mockery.

Anshuman, taken aback by Aakanksha's sharp response, tried to keep his cool. *"Relax,"* he said, attempting to explain himself. With measured words, he suggested, "I'm not saying we'd jump into bed right away. I just meant—people these days are exposed to things— Movies, internet.... porn, maybe? It was about understanding fantasies, exploring what one wanted in a partner." Yet, her hesitation intrigued him. There was a resistance in her, a guardedness he couldn't quite place. He probed further, genuinely curious. "Why does the topic make you so uneasy?"

Aakanksha shot back, her voice laced with irritation. "I've never watched porn," she snapped, exasperated by Anshuman's relentless fixation on sex. "Why is sex the only thing you want to talk about? Can't we discuss literally anything else? Careers? Hobbies? Life? Or is that too boring for you?"

Anshuman leaned back, unfazed. "Most couples about to get married talk about sex," he said, his tone casual. "But I guess you're the exception."

As the sun dipped below the horizon, Aakanksha saw her chance to put an end to the conversation. "We should head home". Anshuman, realizing he had pushed too far, nodded without protest. They drove back in silence, Aakanksha lost in thought, her mind circling the evening's events. Just as they neared her house, Aakanksha finally broke the silence, "Are you a virgin?"

The car rolled to a stop in front of her house. Anshuman with a hint of pride, said, "Yes, I am."

Aakanksha stepped out, her words slicing through the air, "Of course, you are. And if our wedding wasn't happening, you'd probably stay that way forever." She didn't wait for a response. With a sharp thud, she slammed the car door and walked off, not bothering with a goodbye.

At home, her mother asked "How was the date?" Aakanksha forced a smile and replied, "Good."

Anshuman clenched the steering wheel, his jaw tightening as Aakanksha's words echoed in his mind. His fingers drummed impatiently against the dashboard as he watched her walk away without a second glance. He thought, his pride bruised, "You can show your attitude all you want, bitch. But on our wedding night, I'll tie you to the bed rails and gag you to silence your screams. Then, I'll make you mine completely and you'd give in—body and soul." Without another word, he revved the engine and sped off, with frustration, wounded ego, and a nagging sense of unfinished business.

With just two days to the engagement, Colonel and his son, Adarsh, were completely caught up in the preparations—not just for the engagement but also for the grand wedding a month later. Everything was meticulously planned—guests invited, hotel booked, menu finalized, decorations set, and seating arranged. Anshuman's diamond ring was bought, Aakanksha's outfit was ready, and the Colonel had only one thing in mind—a spectacular, unforgettable celebration.

At 11:05 PM, just as Colonel was about to call it a night, his phone buzzed. He glanced at the screen—Lt. General. At this hour? A strange feeling settled in his chest. He hesitated for a second before picking up, his mind already racing, "Good evening, Sir," he greeted, keeping his voice steady.

There was a pause. Then, a hesitant voice came through. "Colonel, I... there's something you need to know."

The unease deepened. The tension in the Lt. General's voice was unmistakable. The Colonel sat up straight. "What is it, Sir?" he asked, bracing himself for whatever was coming next.

The Lt. General broke the silence, asking if the Colonel had caught the day's news. The Colonel, caught up in prepping for the big event, admitted he hadn't. That's when the Lt. General dropped the bomb—M/s. Lehman Brothers, one of the world's biggest banks, had collapsed and filed for bankruptcy, signaling the onset of a global economic recession.

Perplexed, the Colonel questioned the relevance of this news to their situation. The Lt. General explained that Anshuman had secured a lucrative job offer from a multinational corporation through campus recruitment, promising an annual salary of Rs. 45 lakhs. The Colonel, growing impatient, nodded. He already knew about Anshuman's offer.

The Lt. General revealed, "The multinational corporation that had chosen Anshuman for employment was M/s. Lehman Brothers. They just sent him a letter—an apology, nothing else."

The Colonel froze. His grip on the phone tightened as the colour drained from his face. For a moment, he couldn't process what he had just heard. His throat went dry. "So... Anshuman's job..." he finally managed, his voice barely above a whisper.

The Lt. General nodded grimly. The company had gone bankrupt, shutting down offices worldwide. Anshuman's dream offer no longer existed.

The Lt. General's voice softened. "I understand," he said. "If you want to call off the wedding, you have my support. There's no shame in reconsidering, especially when it's about your daughter's future."

He reassured the Colonel—there was no pressure. He should think it through, talk to his wife, family, and Aakanksha herself. After a brief pause, he added, "Let me know by tomorrow evening." With that, he wished the Colonel good night and ended the call.

The Colonel spent the night pacing in his room, his mind a battlefield of thoughts. His hands were clasped tightly behind his back, his face tense. Sleep was out of the question. Gayatri kept asking what was wrong, but he stayed silent, unwilling to share the storm inside him. Instead, he gently told her to rest. As dawn broke and the soft light seeped through the curtains, he made up his mind. No matter what, the wedding would happen. Taking a deep breath, he resolved to talk to Gayatri and Aakanksha—to reassure them, to move forward.

After breakfast, the Colonel finally spoke. He told them about the economic crisis in the U.S. and how it had brought down Lehman Brothers. Then came the hard part— Anshuman's job was gone. The company had sent him a regret letter, citing bankruptcy. But he left out one detail— the Lt. General's offer to call off the wedding, if Aakanksha desired.

Gayatri was stunned. The news hit her like a bolt from the blue. Aakanksha, on the other hand, looked sad on the outside. But inside? A tiny wave of relief washed over her. This had to mean the wedding would be called off. Right?

Gayatri, still reeling from the news, finally asked, "What about the wedding?"

The Colonel, unfazed, simply replied, "It will happen as planned."

Just as Gayatri was about to speak, Aakanksha cut in, her voice laced with concern. She questioned the logic of marrying someone who had just lost his job. If financial security was a reason for this marriage, what was left now; that it was gone?

Aakanksha voiced her frustration, uneasy about stepping into a future filled with uncertainty when she had been promised stability. The Colonel, however, remained firm. He reminded them that Anshuman was an IITian—highly qualified, intelligent, and capable. A lost job didn't define him. With his skills, he would find another opportunity soon.

Aakanksha didn't buy it. Frustration flared in her voice as she dismissed Anshuman's IIT degree like it meant nothing. "I'd rather die right now," she shouted, "than spend my life with a man who has no job and no money."

Aakanksha's frustration spilled over as she confronted her father, her voice charged with emotion. She wasn't just worried about marriage—she was thinking about survival.

"What happens if he stays unemployed?" she demanded. "How will I ever afford basics like sanitary pads or medicines when I fall sick?" Her voice trembled as she painted a stark picture—depending on her father-in-law for money or, worse, begging for help. The thought made her sick. To her, this wasn't marriage. It felt like a deal—one where her well-being was just a footnote.

The Colonel's expression hardened. "Enough, Aakanksha," he said firmly. "You won't have to beg for anything." His voice carried authority, but there was reassurance too. This was temporary, he insisted. Soon, she would have the life he had always promised. He reassured that she didn't need to ask anyone for help—he would take care of her expenses while Anshuman looked for a new job. And it wasn't just about essentials like sanitary pads. "You'll have money for clothes, jewelry, makeup—whatever you want," he added, as if that would ease her worries.

Aakanksha shook her head. "No, Papa. If I'm marrying Anshuman, my expenses should be his responsibility."

The Colonel sighed but stood firm. "Yes, it is. But as your father, it's also my duty to make sure you're okay."

She tried to protest, but he cut her off. "I'll support you until Anshuman finds a job. After that, I'll step back." His voice carried certainty. "And trust me, he will find one soon."

Aakanksha felt uneasy about her father's extravagant spending on the wedding. The gifts, the arrangements, and now, his plans to support her financially even after marriage—it was too much. She hesitated. "Papa, you don't have to do all this," she said softly. "I don't want to be a burden."

The Colonel smiled, his eyes full of warmth. "Burden? You and Adarsh are the reason I work so hard. What's the point of earning if not for your happiness?" Before she could say anything, he pulled her into a tight hug. "You'll always be my little girl," he whispered.

Aakanksha stood firm. She didn't want financial support and was determined to manage on her own. The Colonel looked at her with pride. He admired her independence but wanted to ensure she had everything she needed.

She smiled, appreciating his concern but still hesitant. "I don't want to add to your expenses."

Sensing her discomfort, the Colonel offered a different approach. "Then think of it as a gift," he said. Curious, Aakanksha asked what he meant.

He leaned back and did some quick math. "Let's assume Anshuman takes a year to settle, though I'm sure he'll land a job in two-three months. If I were to help you with ₹10,000 per month for a year, that would be ₹1.2 lakh. Consider it a gift from your father."

Despite Aakanksha's protests, the Colonel walked to the small iron vault in the corner of his bedroom. He unlocked it and pulled out a bundle of cash—money he had withdrawn earlier for wedding expenses and other necessities.

Without hesitation, he counted out ₹1.2 lakh and handed it to her. "This isn't financial support," he said gently. "It's a father's love." He reassured her, emphasizing that her happiness mattered the most. She didn't need to worry—he would take care of everything. Then, giving her a choice, he added, "Keep it as cash or go with your brother to open a bank account. Your call."

Despite Aakanksha's tearful protests, the Colonel remained firm yet gentle. With a soft kiss on her forehead, he silenced any further arguments. Then, without hesitation, he walked over to the landline and dialled the Lt. General, "The wedding would proceed as planned.".

Aakanksha hesitated at first, unsure whether to accept the money. But after much thought—and a little push from Gayatri—she decided to keep it, just in case. Until Anshuman found a job, it would serve as a safety net. Gayatri suggested a simple solution—if she didn't need it later, she could return it to the Colonel. Aakanksha agreed. She had no plans to use it anytime soon, nor did she feel the need to open a bank account. Instead, she tucked the cash into a suitcase, keeping it safe until the day she could hand it back.

On the day of their engagement, Aakanksha looked breathtaking in a peach-coloured lehenga, her wrists adorned with red bangles, and her hands covered in intricate mehndi designs. A diamond-studded gold necklace rested elegantly on her neck, while a garland of jasmine flowers wove through her long braid, adding to her ethereal charm.

She looked nothing short of a dream, leaving everyone around her in awe.

Anshuman, completely mesmerized, couldn't take his eyes off her. All he wanted was to hold her hand throughout the evening. But, of course, that wasn't happening.

The engagement was nothing short of a grand affair, drawing in a crowd of well-known and esteemed guests. Aakanksha, however, had chosen to keep it intimate, skipping invitations to her friends—including her closest confidant, Vishal. In fact, she hadn't even told him she was getting engaged. Vishal remained completely unaware that she was getting married. In contrast, Anshuman had wanted all his friends there—childhood buddies, schoolmates, college gang—everyone. But security concerns, thanks to the VIPs in attendance, made that impossible.

Despite the missing familiar faces, the occasion was enchanting. The guests couldn't stop admiring the glowing couple, and the event felt nothing less than magical.

The day after the engagement, some of Anshuman's friends weren't happy. "No invite? Seriously?" they complained.

Feeling a little guilty—but mostly excited—he made them a promise. "Chill, guys. I'll make it up to you with the best bachelor party ever."

Five days later, he delivered. The party was grand, no VIP restrictions this time. Everyone was invited, from childhood pals and classmates to Orkut friends and college mates. An open invitation was extended to his entire friend circle, encouraging them to bring along anyone they wished. The menu was as grand as the party itself—Blender's Pride whisky, Contessa rum, chicken lollipops, paneer tikka, tandoori chicken, mutton curry, and naan. For the perfect bar snacks, there were roasted peanuts, salted cashews, and masala *papad*.

Anshuman had expected a crowd of 200-250 at his bachelor party, and he wasn't disappointed. It felt like half of Shimla had turned up for the celebration. Friends, cousins, schoolmates, Orkut connections, and even distant relations—friends' cousins, nephews, and random plus-ones—all found their way to the party. Some came for the vibe, most for the free whisky and rum. A few even brought gifts, out of courtesy. Either way, the night was shaping up exactly how Anshuman had imagined—loud, chaotic, and absolutely unforgettable.

As the party kicked off, the air was filled with laughter, clinking glasses, and endless praise for Anshuman's top-tier hospitality. Drinks flowed, and soon enough, the dance floor was alive—some swaying tipsily, others pulling off moves they'd regret in the morning. A few self-proclaimed rockstars hijacked the DJ booth, turning the night into an impromptu concert. Meanwhile, a group of curious friends gathered around Anshuman, eager to hear the full story of how he had won over the love of his life.

With a proud grin, Anshuman grabbed the mic, all set to narrate his love story—complete with his so-called 'master moves' that won her over. But with a few drinks down, his filter was long gone. Somewhere between confidence and tipsiness, he started spilling more than he probably should have.

Anshuman cleared his throat, "The girl of my dreams? She's just 18. I'm 23. Stunning beyond words, but guess what?

She had no interest in marrying me—or anyone, for that matter." He continued, swirling the rum in his glass. "All she cared about was basketball. That was her world, her only dream. Can you believe it? Silly, right?" He paused, took a slow sip, and let the words hang in the air.

One of his friends, brimming with curiosity, asked "So? What happened next?"

"She had one dream—get into the National Academy in Delhi and to play for India. She even made a deal with her father—if she didn't make it, she'd marry me."

Anshuman took a slow sip, a sly smile on his lips. "Then came the big day. The results were out. She wasn't selected." He paused, letting the suspense build. "What she didn't know? I made sure she failed. A little nudge to the right people, threatening the referee... and just like that, her dream was over. With no academy to go to, she had no choice but to marry me."

The crowd erupted with cheers, whistles, and shouts of "All's fair in love and war!"

Anshuman chuckled, making fun of Aakanksha, "Funny, isn't it? She still thinks she lacked the skills to earn a spot in the Delhi academy." His laughter echoed through the room, quickly joined by the crowd.

Amidst the cheers, someone called out, "So, what's our *bhabhi-ji's* name?"

With a triumphant smile, Anshuman announced proudly, "Aakanksha Rana. But in just twenty days, she'll be Aakanksha Singh." raising his glass of rum high above his head and in a jubilant gesture, he exclaimed, "Cheers!"

As the crowd erupted in unison, raising their glasses and shouting "Cheers!", one person remained still. Unlike the others, he didn't join the celebration. Amidst the laughter and clinking glasses, he sat there, expression tense, fists clenched. He had come along with his cousin, a classmate of Anshuman's. But the moment he heard her name, something inside him snapped. A burning urge to confront Anshuman surged through him. But he knew, a fight here wouldn't end well—it could cost him everything, maybe even his life. Without a word, he pushed back his chair, stood up, and walked out. No food, no whisky. Just a quiet, deliberate exit. He was Vishal.

Vishal reached home, but sleep felt impossible. The clock read 11:45 PM. Restless, he grabbed his phone and dialed Aakanksha's number. The call barely rang once before he cut it, leaving her confused. Within seconds, her phone lit up again—she was calling back. He hesitated, then, with a deep breath, answered.

Aakanksha asked if he had called. Vishal hesitated for a moment before brushing it off, "Oh... that? No, it wasn't on purpose," he said. "I was trying to call someone else and accidentally dialed you."

"Oooh!... What a pity," Aakanksha teased. "For a second, I thought you called to say 'I love you'." Her laughter echoed through the room, so loud that her brother, sleeping in the next room, scolded "Slowly!", assuming she was on the phone with her fiancé. Meanwhile, on the other end, Vishal couldn't stop himself from smiling—his face warming up as he blushed.

"Ah, if only I had the guts to say those words... your reply would have been pure music to my ears," Vishal flirted back.

"Come on, just say it," Aakanksha teased.

Vishal chuckled, "No way. If you actually said yes, I'd be in serious trouble," he chuckled playfully.

"Huh! As if I'd ever say yes," Aakanksha scoffed with arrogance "Never. You're underage and not even eligible for legal marriage."

After a good laugh, they ended the call.

But twenty minutes later, Vishal dialled her again, waiting patiently. As soon as she picked up, he said, "Hello... can I ask you something?"

"Don't even think about asking if I'm a virgin?" Aakanksha teased.

Vishal chuckled. "Relax, that's not something I need to know."

Vishal casually congratulated Aakanksha on her upcoming marriage. She paused, surprised. "I was about to tell you," she said, trying to explain. Curious, she asked how he found out, but Vishal simply shrugged, refusing to answer. Instead, he changed the subject. "Heard the new movie's getting great reviews" he said, "Free tomorrow? Thinking of watching it with you."

Aakanksha smiled and nodded without a second thought.

"Great," he flirted "Let's call it one last date—with your *underage, not eligible for marriage* cum ex-boyfriend."

Aakanksha chuckled and corrected him gently. "You were never officially my boyfriend".

Vishal smirked. "Well, I'm a boy, and your friend. That makes me a *boyfriend* by default, doesn't it?"

Aakanksha chuckled at Vishal's enthusiasm and asked which movie he had in mind.

"*Rock On*," he said. "Heard it's really good."

He urged her to join him for either the morning or afternoon show, promising she'd be back home by evening—whenever she preferred. After a moment of thought, Aakanksha agreed and asked him to find tickets around noon. Vishal quickly checked and informed her that there was an 11:30 AM show at PVR, which he would book. Just as he was about to confirm, she added, "But I'm paying for my own ticket."

"Sure, buddy. Feel free to pay for my ticket too. No problem at all," Vishal said, his voice dripping with sarcasm.

Aakanksha chuckled. "I always knew you were a rascal, but I didn't realize you were such a big one."

They both burst into laughter.

The next morning, Aakanksha and Vishal met at PVR as planned. After enjoying the movie, they headed to a nearby restaurant for lunch. Since it was a weekday, finding a table was easy, and they could talk without distractions.

As they ate, Vishal struggled to bring up what he had witnessed at the party. The words sat on the tip of his tongue, but he couldn't say them. He genuinely believed Aakanksha was better off marrying Anshuman—he was rich, well-settled, and offered a secure future, unlike basketball, which was a gamble. She would have a comfortable life with him.

But a nagging fear held him back. If she ever found out what Anshuman had done, her reaction could shake everything—and everyone—around them.

When we truly care about someone, it's not just about their happiness in the moment—we think about their future too. We want to protect them, ensure they're secure, even if it means holding back the truth. Vishal found himself stuck in this exact dilemma. As a friend, he wanted to tell Aakanksha everything. But a part of him hesitated. Speaking up could risk the life of comfort and luxury that awaited her. And was that a risk worth taking?

During lunch, Vishal, lost in thought, barely engaging in the conversation. Noticing his silence, Aakanksha tried to break the tension. "The movie was fun, wasn't it?" Vishal nodded in agreement, but his lack of enthusiasm didn't go unnoticed. Sensing something was off, Aakanksha gently poked him. "You've gone all quiet. What's on your mind?"

Trying to deflect, he said, "Nothing... just thinking about the characters in the film," hoping she wouldn't push further.

"Yeah, absolutely! Joseph Mascarenhas, *alias* Joe, really struck a chord with me too. That last scene, where he quits his job to follow his dreams, was truly inspiring," Aakanksha said. She seemed to idolize Joe, almost as if she wished to be like him. Vishal, still lost in his thoughts, nodded absentmindedly, agreeing without fully processing what she had just said.

As the afternoon faded, Vishal stayed silent, unable to say what was on his mind. By evening, they parted ways with a promise to stay in touch even after her wedding and headed home. Night fell, and the sky lit up with countless stars. At Aakanksha's house, the Colonel and his family finished dinner and got ready for bed, the air calm yet heavy with her unspoken thoughts.

Lying in bed, Aakanksha replayed the afternoon in her mind. Something felt off about Vishal. He had never been this quiet before, and she hadn't even noticed how distant he seemed at the time. The thought nagged at her. She couldn't shake the feeling that something was wrong. Finally, unable to ignore it any longer, she grabbed her phone and dialled his number. After a few rings, he picked up. "Hello, Vishal," she said warmly.

"Yes, Aakanksha?" he replied.

She hesitated for a moment, then smiled. "I just wanted to say thank you... for spending the day with me."

"Oh, dear, the pleasure was all mine," Vishal replied warmly.

Aakanksha smiled and finally spoke up, her curiosity getting the better of her. She pointed out how unusually quiet Vishal had been today—so unlike him. It felt as if something was on his mind, something he wasn't saying.

Vishal, caught off guard, quickly masked his emotions. With a calm voice, he reassured her, blaming his silence on not feeling well. But deep down, hiding the thoughts he wasn't ready to share.

Acknowledging Vishal's explanation, Aakanksha admitted she had been too lost in her own thoughts to notice much. On paper, marrying into a wealthy, well-known family with a charming fiancé seemed perfect. But deep down, she wasn't sure she wanted it.

Vishal frowned, confused. "Wait... you *don't* want to marry him?"

She sighed, her voice laced with frustration. "I don't."

Vishal was taken aback. Trying to make sense of it, he asked, "But why?"

Aakanksha hesitated. "I don't know," she admitted. "My mind says this marriage is the right choice, but my heart... it's just not convinced." The conflict between logic and emotions was tearing her apart.

In an unexpected turn, Vishal felt a storm brewing inside him. Keeping quiet about what he had witnessed at the party felt like a betrayal— Aakanksha was his closest friend. His mind told him to keep quiet, but his heart refused. After a moment of struggle, he finally spoke. "Aakanksha, you were right. There's something I wanted to tell you today but couldn't."

Aakanksha got up from her bed and glanced out through the closed glass window. The night was eerily silent except for the distant barking of stray dogs. A cold breeze swept through the darkness, adding to the unsettling stillness. Wrapping herself in a warm blanket and pulling on a jacket, she slipped out through the back door. Her face hidden, she jumped over the boundary wall. With her phone's torch lighting the path, she made her way through the deserted road.

A patrol officer stopped her, but the moment he learned she was the Colonel's daughter, he let her pass without question. He even offered to accompany her, but she politely declined. The streetlights flickered weakly, struggling against the thick fog, barely lighting up the way. Yet, she didn't stop and pushed forward until she reached a house. The clock had just hit 1:30 AM when she knocked on the door, startling the sleepy homeowner inside.

"Why did you do this to me?" Aakanksha inquired.

Mr. Karwal looked at her, confused. "What have I done?" he asked.

"You know exactly what?" She shot back. "I trusted you like a father, and you betrayed me. Shame on you, Mr. Manohar Karwal." Her voice trembled with disappointment and anger.

Mr. Karwal didn't try to stop her, even though her voice could wake his family or neighbours. He knew he was guilty—she had every right to be angry. All he could manage was a quiet, "I'm sorry."

Aakanksha's voice was sharp with frustration as she confronted Mr. Karwal. But he stood there, silent, letting her words hit him like blows. She refused to accept his apology. "You ruined my career! You risked my entire future!" she cried, her voice trembling with anger.

Desperate for answers, she demanded, "Give me one reason. Just one valid reason for what you did!"

But the silence between them only grew heavier. Mr. Karwal looked away, unable to speak, unable to justify his betrayal. But Aakanksha wasn't done. She stepped closer, eyes burning. "Say something! Anything!" she pressed, refusing to let him escape without an answer.

"I have a family to feed, Aakanksha," Mr. Karwal said, his voice heavy. "My job is all we have. I'm just a small man—I can't afford to go against your father or your father-in-law."

Aakanksha took a moment, letting his words sink in. Then, with a sigh, she said, "Yes, indeed a valid reason."

As Aakanksha was about to leave, Mr. Karwal stopped her, his voice laced with regret. "I'm sorry for what I did," he said. "I can try to make things right."

She frowned, "How?" she asked, curiosity and confusion mixing in her voice.

Mr. Karwal hesitated before finally speaking. He told Aakanksha about a selection trial happening in Delhi in six days for players from the Delhi region. Through a friend, he could arrange for her to participate in the trials.

"Really?" she asked, barely believing what she was hearing.

"Yes. But after that, it's all on you. If you perform well, you'll secure your place in the training academy. No favours, no influence—just your game" he added. "If you're ready to take the chance, I'll make the arrangements."

Back home, sleep refused to come. Aakanksha lay awake, her mind racing with anger and desperation. She thought about confronting her father but knew he would dismiss Mr. Karwal's offer without a second thought. Worse, if he found out about Karwal's involvement, the consequences could be severe for him. As the clock hit 4 A.M., the icy Shimla winter seeped through the walls, but her mind was already made up. She needed help. Without hesitating, she picked up her phone and dialled Vishal.

Aakanksha asked Vishal to meet her at PVR at 11 AM. Half-asleep and groggy, Vishal blinked in confusion. "Wait... what? Why?" he mumbled, unsure if he was awake or dreaming.

"I'll explain everything when we meet," she said firmly. Before he could ask more, she added, "Goodnight, Vishal," and hung up.

By morning, Vishal was still unsure if their late-night conversation had actually happened or if it was just a dream. To be sure, he called Aakanksha to confirm their meeting at PVR. She simply said, "Be there."

When they met, Aakanksha wasted no time. Her plan was set—she was running away from Shimla to Delhi. She would stay at a friend's PG in Laxmi Nagar, far from her father's reach. She handed him ₹1.2 lakh in cash and told him to deposit it into his own savings account. Vishal stared at her, confused.

"If I put it in my account and then withdraw it, my father will know exactly where I am," she explained.

That wasn't all. To avoid being tracked, she had another request. She asked Vishal to buy a new SIM card under his name. Once he did, she took Vishal's SBI ATM-cum-Debit Card, handed him the cash to deposit in his account, and destroyed her own SIM card on the spot, replacing it with the new one under Vishal's name.

Aakanksha casually asked Vishal how much balance he had in his bank account. "About ₹1,400," he replied.

Without missing a beat, she instructed him to deduct that amount from the ₹1.2 lakh and deposit the rest. "From now on, I'll handle your bank account and your new SIM," she added, "No way my father is tracking me."

She then playfully suggested he open a separate account for himself, making it clear—his current one was now hers. With a mischievous laugh, she laid out her plan, fully intending to stay under the radar while using Vishal's resources to do it.

Aakanksha looked calm, almost carefree—no one would guess she was planning to run away. She radiated happiness, as if she were living out her own dream. In her mind, it felt like a movie, and she was the lead. She saw herself as Joe from *Rock On*, chasing her passion with the same fearless energy.

"Are you crazy?" Vishal asked, baffled by Aakanksha's sudden excitement.

"Maybe," she grinned, "But sometimes, extreme situations call for extreme actions."

Vishal hesitated. "Why don't you just talk to your dad? Or even Anshuman? Maybe there's a way to fix this."

Aakanksha scoffed. "My father won't listen. And Anshuman? That bastard isn't even an option."

Vishal tried to reason with her. "At least give it a shot—"

She cut him off, frustration boiling over. "Are you helping me or not? Because if you're not, I'll find another way."

Vishal gave up on convincing her and instead asked about her plan.

"I'm taking the last bus to Delhi tonight at 11:30," Aakanksha said. She explained that she'd wait until after dinner, when everyone was in their rooms, then quietly pack, slip out unnoticed, and leave.

"You've given me a lot of money. What if I run away with it instead of depositing it?" Vishal teased.

Aakanksha smiled, "I trust you with my life. This? This is just money."

Vishal smiled at Aakanksha and expressed his desire to meet her at the bus stop that night to say goodbye. She hugged him tightly and nodded. "Definitely, you can," she said.

As night fell, Aakanksha executed her plan with precision. After dinner, she quietly packed her belongings and slipped out through the back door. Moving swiftly, she scaled the boundary wall and disappeared into the night. At the bus stop, Vishal stood waiting, his presence a comforting sight in the dim glow of the streetlights.

Vishal handed Aakanksha the deposit receipt. She glanced at it and saw the full amount—₹1,20,000—had been deposited. Frowning, she looked up. "Wait... why didn't you deduct the ₹1,400 you already had in your account?" she asked.

Vishal shrugged and grinned. "Think of it as a loan. I'll collect it back—with interest—when we meet again."

Aakanksha, overwhelmed, pulled him into a tight hug. Vishal tried to stay composed, but his eyes welled up. Noticing his tears, she cupped his face and smiled. "Why are you crying, silly?"

Vishal quickly wiped his tears and put on a brave face. "I'm not crying, okay? Just... some dust in my eyes," he said, trying to sound casual.

Aakanksha teased, "Please don't start quoting some emotional movie dialogue now."

Curious, Vishal raised an eyebrow. "Which one?"

Smiling, she pulled his cheeks. "*Tussi ja rahe ho... tussi na jao!*" she said dramatically. That was it. They both burst into laughter, and for a moment, the weight of the situation faded. Vishal, still wiping his tears, laughed along, letting himself enjoy the moment.

Just before Aakanksha left for Delhi, Vishal handed her a packet of homemade snacks. "Eat properly," he said. "An athlete can't survive on emotions alone."

She smiled, touched by the gesture. Their farewell was brief but heartfelt. With one last glance at him, she stepped onto the bus, leaving behind the warmth of their shared moments as she set off for Delhi.

By 11 AM, Gayatri grew restless—Aakanksha still hadn't come out of her room. A nagging worry crept into her mind as she pushed open the door. What she found made her heart stop. A neatly folded letter lay on the desk, addressed to the Colonel. Gayatri's hands trembled as she picked it up, her breath catching in her throat. A sinking feeling settled in her chest.

She cried out loud. Within moments, the Colonel and Adarsh rushed in. The Colonel's sharp eyes scanned the room, searching for Aakanksha. But she was gone. Gayatri, still in shock, held the letter with trembling hands. It read:

Papa,

You destroyed what mattered most to me. So, I'm destroying what matters most to you.

You crushed my dream. I crushed your reputation.

Hope to never see you again.

Your Ridiculous Daughter

Aakanksha

****

Shahid – The Bihar ka Lalla

"Of all the lies you told me, 'I LOVE YOU' was my favourite."
                                    -Anonymous

(14th January 1988 – Siwan, Bihar)

Mohammed Farukh Eqbal, 62, was the respected chief of the gram panchayat in Habibnagar, Hussainganj block, Siwan district, Bihar. People didn't just listen to him—they followed him. His honesty, integrity, and commitment to the village's welfare made him a figure of admiration. Yet, despite the influence, he stayed grounded, always putting his people first. A father of three daughters and four sons, he had shared a deep bond with his wife, who lived long enough to see all their children happily married. Two daughters settled in Lucknow, and one moved to Dubai. Even after her passing, Farukh remained devoted to his responsibilities.

His household was a bustling joint family—four sons, daughters-in-law, grandchildren—a total of 21 members. And today, the family had one more reason to celebrate. His eldest son welcomed a baby boy, his fifth child—two boys, three girls.

The parents of the youngest member of the family wanted to name him, 'Fahid,' which means 'one who does good deeds in someone's absence.' But his grandfather had a better idea— 'Shahid,' a Persian name meaning 'beloved.' The family didn't need much convincing. The name was finalized in minutes.

Shahid wasn't just the youngest; he was also the most stunning. With sharp features, deep eyes, and fair skin, he often left people confused—they mistook him for a girl. He had inherited his mother's extraordinary beauty, something hard to put into words. But as he grew older, the narrative changed. The 'pretty boy' phase faded, and in its place emerged one of the most handsome men in the village. A beard and moustache later, 'pretty' became 'dashing.'

Bihar, in 1988, rich in minerals like coal, iron ore, copper, and uranium, was once among India's wealthiest states. But its potential remained locked away, thanks to decades of political instability. From 1961 to 1990, not a single Chief Minister managed to complete a full five-year term. The result? Poor governance, social unrest, endless bureaucratic red tape, rising unemployment, malnutrition, failing healthcare, and unchecked illegal mining.

A year after Shahid was born, Bihar seemed to be changing. The chaos of political instability finally appeared to settle as Lallan Prasad Yadav took office as Chief Minister with a strong mandate. It was a big moment—no CM had completed a full term since 1961.

During this time, fear ruled Bihar. If you weren't aligned with Lallan Prasad Yadav and his family, life felt uncertain. People avoided stepping out after dark, afraid of kidnappings, extortion, or worse. Opposition leaders and political analysts had a name for it—*Jungle Raj*. Law and order felt like a joke, and chaos became the new normal.

Jungle-raj refers to a criminalized nexus of politicians, government officials, businessmen and other entities. This criminalized nexus is responsible for illegal activities being committed in a sustained fashion, sometimes openly, and mostly with the use of violent intimidation.

Under their rule, Bihar's progress took a backseat, with the kidnapping industry being the only one to thrive. While the rest of India moved forward, Bihar fell nearly 30 years behind. A survey revealed that between 1992 and 2004, Bihar recorded a staggering total of 32,085 reported kidnapping cases. During their regime in Bihar, virtually every type of crime imaginable was rampant. Murder, dacoity, rape, burglary, bank robbery, and riots were commonplace occurrences, woven into the fabric of daily life for criminals.

In Bihar, ransoms were commonly referred to as "Rangdari." Under the guise of this "Rangdari tax," individuals were obligated to pay a portion of their earnings to local goons whenever they started a new business, purchased property, or acquired a vehicle. Refusal to comply with this tax often resulted in severe consequences, with death being the prescribed punishment by the extortionists.

Allegations ran deep – Lallan leveraged muscle power to retain control, with muscle men like Salahuddin, among others, gaining prominence and making their way into politics. And soon, blurring the lines between crime and governance.

Salahuddin wasn't just another muscleman in Lallan Prasad Yadav's network—he was *the* most trusted one. Whispers in political circles suggested that Lallan relied on him more than his own brothers-in-law, Bablu Yadav and Bittu Yadav. And over time, those whispers turned out to be true.

As Lallan's grip on power weakened, he began sidelining his own family. Or maybe, it was the other way around. When his influence started fading, Bablu and Bittu Yadav slowly distanced themselves. Either way, it marked the beginning of Lallan's political downfall.

Mohammad Salahuddin was born in 1963 in Pratappur, a village in Bihar's Siwan district. On paper, he was an academic—a Master's degree, a PhD in political science. But in reality, his path was far from what you'd expect from a highly educated man. Instead of using his degrees to build a respectable career, Salahuddin, like many others, chose the faster route to power and wealth—by any means necessary.

Rumors floated around that in the mid-1980s, Salahuddin took a trip to Dubai, supposedly to meet a Sheikh. The official reason? Seeking funds to build schools and colleges dedicated to Sir Syed Ahmad Khan's teachings. Whether his intentions were purely academic or there was more to the trip—that remained a mystery.

Sir Syed Ahmad Khan (born October 17, 1817, in Delhi) was a prominent Islamic reformer, philosopher, and educator in 19th-century British India. He founded the Muhammadan Anglo-Oriental College, which later became Aligarh Muslim University (AMU).

Salahuddin's true motives slowly came to light. He started pulling in jobless, uneducated men from his village, even roping in a few from nearby areas. While no one could say for sure if he was building a criminal gang using the funds meant for *Sir Syed Ahmad Khan's* legacy, the source of the money remained a mystery to all.

Salahuddin procured weapons and ammunition to fuel his local gang's reign of terror in the Siwan District. Around this time, he crossed paths with Lallan Prasad Yadav, a meeting that changed everything. Sensing an opportunity, he aligned with Lallan, using politics to strengthen his grip. By the early '90s, Salahuddin had climbed the ranks, becoming a key youth leader in Lallan's party. He won the state elections in 1990 and 1995, then took an even bigger leap—securing a Lok Sabha seat in 1996. With Lallan's stronghold over Bihar's government, Salahuddin's power didn't just rise—it skyrocketed.

During this time, Salahuddin, the gangster-turned-politician from Siwan, was at the peak of his power. With multiple murder allegations against him, his connection with Lallan gave him such a strong shield that even the police thought twice before taking any action. But as Lallan's hold on power started slipping, the tables turned. The authorities finally gathered the courage to go after Salahuddin, leading to his conviction in a kidnapping case.

His men were experts at the game—kidnapping candidates before they could even file nominations, eliminating them if needed, or scaring voters right before polling day to make sure they voted the 'right' way.

If their usual tricks didn't work, they had a backup plan—booth capturing, or as the locals called it, *booth management.* In Bihar's political battleground, *bahubalis* eyeing MLA seats often relied on this method to swing elections their way. They hired gangs skilled in taking over polling booths and paid private militias to scare voters into submission. The message was clear—vote as instructed, or face the consequences.

These power-hungry leaders, backed by armed goons, made their rounds from village to village before elections. Their message was simple—if they lost, the villagers would pay the price. But if they won? They promised safety from kidnappings, murders, and land grabs.

Salahuddin didn't just rule the streets—he ran his own version of the law. Right in his courtyard, he set up a makeshift court, controlling Siwan like a parallel government. He held *khap panchayats* based on Sharia law, settling family feuds, land disputes, even deciding how much doctors could charge. He meddled in marriages, dictated local affairs, and made sure everyone knew who was in charge. The District Magistrate of Siwan had only one way to describe him—a habitual criminal.

You're probably wondering— why this deep dive into Salahuddin's world when I started with Shahid's birth? Well, here's the twist— Salahuddin isn't just some distant figure in this story. He's Shahid's maternal uncle. Yes, you read that right. Shahid's mother and Salahuddin are siblings.

Mohammed Farukh Eqbal deeply respected Salahuddin's father, a government school teacher. Though aware of Salahuddin's notoriety, he had no qualms about accepting Sadiyah as his daughter-in-law, assured of her father's respectable profession. Back then, Salahuddin was just a notorious village brat, not yet linked to Lallan Prasad Yadav.

Sadiyah and Salahuddin had strikingly similar facial features, so it was no surprise that Shahid ended up looking like both of them. This uncanny resemblance, combined with

Salahuddin's fondness for him, made Shahid the most pampered kid in the village. Known as the *'bhanja,'* he wasn't just loved—he was treated with a mix of respect and fear, almost like royalty in the community.

Everyone knew about Shahid's special bond with Salahuddin, and no one dared to challenge him. This unearned power made him arrogant—he acted like he owned the place, expecting everyone to obey without question. Even as a kid, he would walk into a confectionery shop, pick up sweets, toffees, and Uncle Chips, and leave without paying. The shopkeepers never protested, knowing too well that complaining to his parents could mean inviting Salahuddin's wrath.

At home, he was just as demanding. He demanded things from siblings, cousins, even his parents, and they happily obliged, amused by his tantrums. If his parents ever refused him a toy or a treat, he had an easy solution—Salahuddin. One word to his maternal uncle, and his wish was granted, no matter what.

As a young child, Shahid's antics amused everyone. But as he grew older, his habits didn't change. By the time he was seven, no one in the family—or outside—had ever scolded him for his behaviour. His mother tried now and then, but every time she did, others would stop her, "He's just a kid. He'll learn as he grows," they'd say.

Then came the day that changed everything. Shahid ordered the maid to cook chicken for lunch. Busy juggling a hundred household chores, she didn't have time and handed him a boiled egg instead. That was enough to set him off. Furious, he screamed, kicked the plate, and sent the food flying across the veranda.

Sadiyah was the embodiment of humility and faith. She treated everyone with kindness, especially those in need. If a hungry passerby or a wandering fakir knocked on her door, she never sent them away empty-handed—she made sure they had a proper meal. She knew the value of food, understood the pain of the less fortunate, and above all, couldn't stand the sight of it being wasted.

The moment Shahid knocked the plate to the ground, Sadiyah snapped. She had tolerated his tantrums for years, but this was the final straw. Without a second thought, she grabbed him by the hair and landed a sharp slap across his face. Then came a series of smacks on his back and buttocks, each one fuelled by years of suppressed frustration. Shahid wailed, but she didn't stop until his sobs turned into exhausted hiccups.

Still fuming, she dragged him to the dark, musty storeroom—the kind of place where rats and cockroaches thrived. She shut the door behind him as he screamed, begging to be let out, swearing never to misbehave again. But Sadiyah wasn't done. She let him cry there, terrified, for two full hours. No one in the family dared to interfere.

An Indian mother is a blacksmith of character, forging her children's values with the fire of discipline and the hammer of love. Sadiyah was no different. That one incident became a turning point in Shahid's life, leaving a lesson so deep that it changed him forever, guiding him toward the right path.

Shahid begged in the name of Allah, swearing never to repeat his mistakes. He promised to stop bossing people around, stop demanding chocolates and toys, and never misbehave again. His words carried the weight of true regret. Seeing his sincerity, Sadiyah took him to the bathroom, bathed him, and then served him a simple yet wholesome meal—rice, lentils, a green vegetable, and a boiled egg. This time, Shahid ate in silence, finishing every last bite, leaving his plate so clean it barely needed washing.

Later, Sadiyah tucked him into bed, and exhaustion took over. He slept straight through the evening and night, waking only the next morning. The experience had shaken him. He had never imagined his actions could lead to such a consequence, but it changed him in a way nothing else ever had.

Shahid adored his uncle and cherished their time together, but he never walked the same path. He respected his elders, played fair, and always paid for whatever he bought at the local shops. Yet, fate had other plans. His life was standing at the edge of a storm—one that was about to change everything forever.

As the year 2000 neared, Bihar braced for its Assembly elections in March. Lallan Prasad Yadav faced a tough battle, his grip on power slipping—not just because of the Fodder Scam, but also due to the unchecked crimes of his associates. While Lallan's name was tied to financial corruption, his men were knee-deep in far worse—kidnappings for ransom, land grabbing, molestation, rape, and murder. Defeat wasn't an option. Losing power meant disaster for these criminals. So, Lallan turned to his *bahubalis*, the musclemen who ruled Bihar's streets, determined to win by any means necessary.

As Shahid stepped into adolescence and continued Class 6 at an English medium school in Bihar, he took his grandfather's advice seriously—at least on the surface. He stopped visiting Salahuddin openly, keeping his distance. But old habits die hard. Every now and then, when he needed money for a movie, he'd quietly slip away to his uncle, sometimes even skipping school for it. Of course, he made sure his grandfather never found out.

As the Y2K era ushered in the year 2000, change was in the air. The IT sector was booming, media was growing stronger, television reached more households, and mobile phones were slowly replacing landlines. With technology advancing and electronic media keeping a closer watch, the old-school practice of booth capturing started fading.

But politics in Bihar had its own way of adapting. With kidnapping, ransom, and extortion businesses thriving, there was no shortage of money. Instead of snatching ballot boxes, there was always the backup plan - bribe voters, and if that failed, resort to threats.

Salahuddin knew that securing votes in Siwan depended heavily on one man—Mohammed Farukh Eqbal, Shahid's grandfather. Farukh's influence could sway the entire village in his favour. But there was a problem. Farukh despised everything Salahuddin stood for—his crimes, his power-hungry ways. He had always kept his distance, never letting their worlds collide — UNTIL NOW.

Salahuddin arrived at Mohammed Farukh's home, carrying a woven sack—one that usually held rice or vegetables in Bihar. But this wasn't about groceries. This sack had a different purpose today—one filled with cash. The agenda was clear. The election was around the corner, and Salahuddin needed votes. But not through speeches, promises, or rallies. He had a simpler approach—money. ₹50 lakh, in exchange for Farukh's influence. He didn't need Farukh to campaign, just to *direct* the villagers. Because in

Siwan, everyone knew—whoever had Farukh's support was as good as elected.

Mohammed Farukh made Salahuddin wait—maybe intentionally—for a whole hour. Salahuddin saw it as an insult, but he swallowed his pride. He needed Farukh on his side. Just then, Shahid returned from school and lit up at the sight of his favourite uncle in the drawing room. He ran up to greet him, eager to chat. But before they could exchange more than a few words, Farukh walked in. His tone was firm.

"Shahid, go freshen up."

Shahid knew better than to argue and left the room. As soon as he was gone, Farukh turned to Salahuddin, his expression unreadable.

"So, what brings you here?"

'As-salaam Alaikum, Farukh Saab. Please accept this humble gift—a small token of appreciation from a nephew to his beloved uncle' Salahuddin said, pushing the sack forward.

"What's this?" asked Farukh.

'Fifty lakh Rupees'

'For What?'

"Farukh Saab, I'll get straight to the point," Salahuddin said, leaning forward. "All I need is for you to guide the villagers—tell them to vote for me. This sack is just a token, an advance. Once I win, another one will be delivered to your doorstep."

Farukh didn't hesitate and said, "Salahuddin, let me be just as direct. Take your money and leave. Don't ever try to bribe me again. I am not like you. Your ways bring nothing but disgrace to our people, our community."

Salahuddin's expression hardened. The air in the room turned heavy. His voice, now ice-cold, carried an unmistakable threat. "Farukh, just do as I say. Otherwise, this sack—meant for money—might end up carrying your lifeless body."

Farukh's voice grew firm, his tone unshaken. 'Threats work on those who fear you, Salahuddin. I am not one of them. If haven't heard my words, let me make it clearer—take your bag and get out of my house."

As Salahuddin turned to leave, he paused at the door, his voice low but menacing. "I'm going now, Farukh, but you'll pay for your arrogance. Sooner or later, you have to campaign for us, whether you like it or not."

The Eqbal family's future hung in the balance, about to be reshaped by forces beyond their control. Fuming from the confrontation, Salahuddin stormed back to his office, his mind set on revenge. He wasted no time—his most trusted men were summoned. With a cold, calculated tone, he laid out his plan. Mohammed Farukh had dared to defy him. Now, it was time to make him pay.

When Shahid was born, Mohammed Farukh's family was a bustling household of 22 members. But as the years passed, the numbers shrank—daughters got married, sons moved out in search of better careers beyond Bihar. Now only 14 members remained, including five grandchildren—three boys and two girls. Shahid, the youngest of them all was the family's pampered one. Among the grandchildren, Rukhsar (18) and Fatima (20) were pursuing Commerce at the same government college in Siwan. Fatima, incidentally, was Shahid's elder sister.

The very next day, after Farukh's tense confrontation with Salahuddin, disaster struck. Rukhsar and Fatima were on their way home from college when Salahuddin's men intercepted them. Without a trace, they were whisked away to a secluded house on the outskirts of the village—an area so desolate that even the boldest avoided it, fearing the dacoits who lurked there. Back home, as hours passed and the girls didn't return, worry turned into panic. By evening, it was clear—something was terribly wrong.

Farukh and his men searched every corner of the village, desperate for any clue. After hours of frantic inquiries, a local finally spoke—a van, a group of thugs, and two terrified girls. No one mentioned Salahuddin by name, but Farukh didn't need confirmation. Only one man in the entire district had the audacity to target his family. Undeterred, Farukh decided to confront Salahuddin, heading straight to his residence ALONE.

Farukh reached Salahuddin's mansion, only to be met with a thorough frisking by his men. Once cleared, he was led to the drawing room—where he was made to wait. An hour passed, each minute stretching his patience, but Salahuddin made sure to keep him waiting. When he finally walked in, Farukh's fingers twitched with the urge to slap him across the face. But he held back. Barely.

Farukh wasted no time. "Where are the girls?" he demanded.

Salahuddin leaned back, feigning ignorance. "What girls?"

Farukh's voice rose, sharp and unyielding, "Don't play games with me, Salahuddin!"

That was it. In a flash, Salahuddin was on his feet, both hands gripping Farukh's collar. His eyes burned with fury. "Lower your voice," he growled. "This isn't your house where you call the terms. I can have you buried right here in my backyard, and trust me—no one in this entire state will even dare to ask where you disappeared. Got it?"

Salahuddin smirked, his voice dripping with mockery. "Relax, Farukh. Your girls are safe—they're my nieces too, after all."

He leaned in, eyes gleaming with menace. "As long as I'm unharmed, they will be too. But if you want them to stay untouched, unscathed... you know what to do. Convince the villagers to vote for me in the elections. It's a simple deal."

Salahuddin leaned back, his smirk widening. "Of course, Farukh, you're free to refuse. Do whatever you think is right." Then, his tone darkened. "But just so you know, my men possess considerable expertise and proficiency in raping women. Moreover, they derive a perverse pleasure particularly from assaulting young college girls."

Tears welled up in Farukh's eyes as he grappled with the depths of Salahuddin's ruthlessness. The pursuit of power had stripped away any trace of humanity. To ensure the safe return of the girls, he agreed to mediate with the villagers on Salahuddin's behalf. Bound by desperation and a solemn oath to Allah, he conceded to the demands placed before him.

Salahuddin leaned back, his voice calm but laced with menace. "You can go home, Farukh. I'll personally ensure the girls return safely." His tone darkened. "But don't mistake this for generosity. If you dare betray me, there will be consequences. My men won't just abduct—they'll slaughter every male in your family. And the women? They will rape all the women in your family, right in front of you."

As Farukh stepped out of the mansion, he muttered under his breath, "Alhamdulillah, you will die a death so cursed that even your own family won't be able to offer you a proper Janazah. And in your death-bed, the faces you long to see will remain forever out of reach."

When Farukh reached home, both girls were already there, their eyes red with tears. He placed a comforting hand on their heads, his touch soft yet reassuring. "Let's eat something and get some rest," he said gently, trying to restore a sense of normalcy. But while he consoled them, his own mind refused to settle. The thought of campaigning for Salahuddin gnawed at him, leaving him restless—food untouched, sleep impossible.

Farukh had no choice but to give in to Salahuddin's demands. With a heavy heart, he stepped into the village, campaigning for him. In the end, fate played its part—Salahuddin won with ease.

Victory only made Salahuddin more arrogant. Power fuelled his ego, making him feel untouchable. His rule turned ruthless—decisions became arbitrary, his actions cruel. The village's frustration grew, not just against him but also against Farukh, the man who had vouched for him.

After the kidnapping incident, Farukh cut himself off from everyone. He spent days locked in his room, lost in deep thought, his only company—'The Noble Quran'.

Months passed. One morning, two men showed up at his house. Without a word, they walked straight to his room. He sat there, rocking gently, eyes fixed on the holy book. They didn't disturb him. Instead, they placed two sacks in front of him—no explanations needed.

The moment Farukh saw them, he knew—they were Salahuddin's men. His curiosity kicked in. "What's this?" he asked, eyeing the sacks.

One of them smirked. "A gift from our boss," he said.

Farukh opened the bags. Bundles of cash stared back at him. Salahuddin's way of showing 'support' for his election campaign.

Farukh rejected the cash without hesitation, unmoved by the offer, insisting that it would not absolve Salahuddin of his sins. His rejection, however, did not deter the men. They cautioned him against angering their boss, subtly hinting at the risks involved. Accepting the money, they suggested, would be the wiser choice—for his own safety and that of his family.

Their job was done. Without another word, they turned and left, leaving Farukh alone with the weight of their message.

Burdened by guilt, Farukh sought refuge in the Quran, hoping to silence the echoes of his past. But the sight of the two bags shattered his illusion of escape, dragging him back to the days he had campaigned for Salahuddin. Memories flooded in, each one a painful reminder of his choices.

The guilt gnawed at him, pushing him to consider returning the money. His eyes remained fixed on the sacks, his breath turning heavy. Sweat beaded on his forehead as his conscience weighed heavily upon him and immense pain gripped his heart.

Shahid stepped into the room, he called out to his grandfather, inviting him for lunch. There was no response. His eyes fell on the old man, seated motionless near two sacks by his chair. Concerned, Shahid moved closer and placed a hand on his grandfather's shoulder. The moment he touched him, Farukh's body slumped forward, collapsing onto the floor. Panic surged through Shahid as he let out a terrified cry, his heart pounding with the fear that he had caused his grandfather's fall.

Hearing his screams, Arif and Saif, Farukh's sons, rushed in. Their eyes widened at the sight—Farukh lying lifeless on the ground, while Shahid knelt beside him, sobbing uncontrollably.

Arif, Shahid's father, gently lifted Farukh's head, his heart sinking as he felt the lifelessness of his body and the absence of breath. They rushed him to the nearest hospital, clinging to the last thread of hope. But it was too late. The doctors took one look and confirmed—he had been brought in dead. As was common in Bihar, no post-mortem was conducted, and instead, the doctors issued a medical certificate, attributing his death to a severe heart attack supposedly suffered within the hospital premises.

Days passed, and with Farukh's funeral rites completed, his room was finally unlocked for the first time since his death. As the family stepped inside, their eyes fell on two sacks, untouched and forgotten in a corner. Curiosity took over, and when they opened them, they were stunned—bundles of cash lay neatly stacked inside.

No one knew where the money had come from, but its sudden appearance felt almost surreal. With the recent kidnapping still fresh in their minds, the family had been considering leaving Siwan, and this unexpected fortune felt like a sign from Allah—an opportunity for a new beginning, a chance to start over somewhere far away.

Farukh's family lived in constant fear, haunted by the violence in Siwan. But their greatest worry was Salahuddin—if he ever learned about the money, there was no doubt he would come for it, and their lives would be at stake.

Realizing the danger, the four sons made a decision. They would split the cash equally, quietly move their families to different locations, and cut all ties with their past. To ensure a complete break, they agreed to sell the family property in Siwan, divide the proceeds, and leave Bihar for good.

In the end, they executed their plan as intended, walking away from the shadows of their past to rebuild their lives elsewhere, far from the dangers they once feared.

With the money he received, Arif made careful choices to secure his family's future. He deposited half in a Fixed Deposit at the bank, ensuring financial stability, while the rest went into buying a small house in Lucknow, where his wife and daughters lived.

Wanting the best for his sons, he sent them to Dubai for their education, where they stayed with his sister, who was married and settled there. Meanwhile, Arif himself moved to Saudi Arabia, relying on his relatives and connections to find work. Fortunately, securing a job wasn't difficult, and soon he was earning a steady income.

Despite the physical distance, Arif never let his family feel his absence. He regularly sent money to his wife in Lucknow and his sons in Dubai, making sure they had everything they needed. A devoted father, he took extra shifts whenever possible, pushing himself to earn more—not for himself, but for the people he loved.

The weight of Farukh's curse seemed to catch up with Salahuddin as major shifts unfolded in the region. Bihar was no longer the same. A new state, Jharkhand, was carved out, taking with it some of the most resource-rich areas—coal mines, iron ore reserves, and key industrial hubs.

For Bihar, it was a major blow. While Jharkhand held onto wealth-generating zones like the Tata Steel Plant and Bokaro Steel Plant, Bihar was left with vast stretches of farmland and little industry to fall back on. For Salahuddin, this change wasn't just political—it was personal. The regions he had exploited for years, the businesses that fuelled his extortion network, were no longer under Bihar's jurisdiction. His empire, once built on fear and control, suddenly seemed shaky, slipping through his fingers like sand.

Salahuddin's arrogance had reached new heights, incidents like slapping a DSP escalated into full-blown clashes between his men and the police, culminating in the death of a constable. But this time, the cops weren't willing to back down. Unlike before, they ignored political pressure and refused to look the other way.

For the first time, the walls were closing in, and his usual escape routes were disappearing. An FIR was lodged against him, setting off a long and messy legal battle. After years of evading the system, his luck finally ran out—he was arrested in 2003.

In 2004, despite being in prison, Salahuddin once again contested the Siwan Lok Sabha elections. But prison walls were never really a barrier for him. Citing medical reasons, he got himself transferred to the Siwan hospital, where an entire floor was conveniently set aside for his "treatment."

From there, he ran his campaign. Meetings were held, strategies discussed, and visitors streamed in throughout the day—after, of course, getting past his personal bodyguards. Every afternoon at four, he would hold court, listening to grievances, solving problems, and ensuring his grip over Siwan remained as firm as ever, even from behind hospital doors.

Although the elections saw little activity by the opposition – every shop carried a photograph of Salahuddin, and according to a BBC report:

There is almost no sign of the opposition campaigning in the constituency. One villager, pleading that his identity should not be disclosed, said: "Do you want to get us hanged by telling you what we feel about elections here and who we would like to vote for?"

Several phone booth owners and businessmen met brutal ends simply for displaying banners or posters of Salahuddin's opponents. Fear was the law in Siwan, and defiance came at a deadly price.

But as the election drew closer, the tide began to turn. Just days before the polls, the Patna High Court intervened, ordering the state government to shift Salahuddin back to jail, putting an end to his hospital-turned-headquarters setup.

During the elections, large scale rigging and booth capturing were reported from as many as 500 polling stations and re-polling was ordered by the autonomous election conducting body, Election Commission of India.

By late 2005, the Lallan Prasad era ended as Janata Dal (United) won the majority in the Oct-Nov elections, making Nitish Kumar the new chief minister.

In 2005, when he was finally arrested, a police raid at his house uncovered a shocking stash—AK-47s, night-vision goggles, laser-guided guns, and other military-grade weapons meant only for the army. Some of the arms even had markings from Pakistan ordnance factories. The Chief of Police, in his report, claimed that Salahuddin had links with Pakistan's intelligence agency.

Subsequently, eight non-bailable warrants were issued for arresting Salahuddin.

For over three months, the Delhi Police and a special team from Bihar struggled to arrest him. Despite living in his government-assigned quarter and attending parliament regularly, his political influence kept him untouchable. It was only in November 2005 that the police finally managed to arrest him from his official residence.

In May 2006, Nitish Kumar's government set up special courts to crack down on criminal dons.

Salahuddin, however, played his cards well. He claimed he had a slipped disc and couldn't appear in court. But medical reports told a different story—he was perfectly fit to walk. With no other option, two special courts were set up inside Siwan Jail just for him.

The numbers were staggering—over thirty cases pending. Eight for murder, twenty for attempted murder, kidnapping, extortion, and more. And that was just what was on record. Many crimes never even made it to the police files. Siwan had its own dark secrets—mysterious disappearances, whispered rumours of over a hundred bodies buried somewhere in Salahuddin's bungalow. The media had their theories. But the truth? Only he knew.

He tried everything—threatening judges, intimidating opposition lawyers—but nothing worked. He was locked up in Siwan Jail, Bihar, until the Supreme Court intervened and ordered his transfer to Tihar Jail, Delhi. After that, he was just another prisoner, serving his life sentence with no special treatment, no VIP privileges—just cold, hard jail time.

Shahid's life flipped overnight as he moved from the small-town lanes of Siwan to the glitzy skyline of Dubai. It felt like he'd crash-landed straight into a world of luxury and endless possibilities. Thankfully, his family's deep-rooted fluency in Arabic and Urdu—passed down from his grandfather—became his biggest asset. It not only helped him adjust to this new life but also made his studies in Dubai a whole lot easier.

Shahid and his brother got into a public school in Dubai, where education was free. But free school didn't mean free living, so their father still sent money to their aunt to cover expenses. Shahid cleared Grade 10 in 2005 (same as Class 10 in India) and finished Grade 12 in 2007. His elder brother, a year ahead, completed Grade 12 in 2006 and landed a job as a sales manager in a Dubai mall.

Shahid had the looks and the charm, but books? Not his thing. Higher studies in Dubai were expensive anyway, so he took a different route—joined a gym, dreaming of a career in modeling. With his brother working and his father backing him financially, there was no rush to find a job. Life in Dubai felt like a luxury he could afford to enjoy.

In 2008, while most Indians were clicking away on their Nokia 1100 or 6600, Shahid casually flashed an iPhone. It made him stand out, but his real dream—becoming an actor—felt distant. Dubai had top-notch studios, but unlike Bollywood or Hollywood, its film industry barely existed. Making it big in acting here? Not a chance.

Shahid stuck to his gym routine, flexing his biceps and clicking mirror selfies with his iPhone every day. Dubai felt like home, and he had no plans to leave—until fate had other ideas. One day, at a mall, he was on a call with his mother in

Lucknow, speaking fluent Hindi, when Mohit Shetty walked by. Shahid had no clue who he was, but Shetty took notice. Shetty was impressed by his proficiency in Hindi, a language not commonly spoken in Dubai where Arabic prevails.

Mohit Shetty was immediately drawn to Shahid's striking personality, well-built physique, and effortless charm. Without hesitation, he introduced himself and his cameraman, Sid. Intrigued by Shahid's fluent Hindi, a rarity in Dubai, Shetty curiously asked about his background. Shahid, in his usual confident manner, shared his journey of being an Indian settled in Dubai.

Impressed by both his looks and his ease in conversation, Shetty made an offer that seemed too good to be true—an opportunity to train at his acting institute in Mumbai with a stipend of Rs. 50,000 per month, along with free accommodation and meals. The course would last a year, and upon completion, Shahid would have the chance to work in Shetty's films. What made the offer even more tempting was Shetty's subtle hint at the possibility of a lead role in one of his future projects.

For a moment, Shahid was stunned—it felt like he had found water in the middle of a desert. The offer was too good to resist, and without a second thought, he said yes, eager to know when he could start. What he didn't realize was that behind the promise of fame and fortune, something far more sinister was waiting for him.

Before Mohit could respond, his cameraman, Sid, jumped in. "Think of it as on-the-job training," he explained. "For the first six months, you'll learn the basics, then you'll work alongside the crew, picking up skills from experienced actors under Mohit's guidance. But there's one rule—

absolute obedience. Whatever the senior crew asks, you do it. No questions, no complaints. Even if it's something as small as washing cars. One refusal, and you're out. No second chances."

"If I'm getting Rs. 50,000 a month just to wash cars, I'll happily wash the same one ten times a day!" Shahid said with a grin, making all three of them burst into laughter.

Shahid was told to get ready for Mumbai within a week, and he didn't think twice before saying yes. But what truly caught him off guard was the send-off. On the day of his departure, he was surprised to find that Mohit's cameraman had booked him a business-class ticket. Not bad for a newcomer.

Landing in Mumbai felt like stepping into a movie scene. A chauffeur in a crisp white uniform stood at the airport, holding a placard with his name. He was then driven straight to an upscale neighbourhood, where a fully furnished one-room set awaited him. The fridge was stocked with snacks, cold drinks, beer, and whisky, and meals arrived daily from a nearby restaurant. While Shahid, being a devout Muslim, stayed away from alcohol, the rest of the goodies didn't go to waste. If anything ran out, a single call was enough to get it refilled instantly.

Shahid wasn't used to this kind of royal treatment, but he wasn't complaining. At just 19, in 2008, he already felt like a star in the making. His mind raced with dreams—fans screaming his name, girls lining up for selfies and autographs. He could already see it: a life of glitz, cameras flashing, headlines calling him the next big thing.

His biggest fantasy? Buying a mansion right next to Shahrukh Khan's iconic Mannat. Or better yet, making SRK an offer so insane that even the King of Bollywood wouldn't refuse. And why stop there? He saw himself owning an entire floor in Dubai's Burj Khalifa, a home in the clouds where his parents would live like royalty.

The next day, Shahid walked into his acting class, joining a batch of 12 students—5 boys and 7 girls. While the others had already been attending for a week or two, this was his first day. But being Shahid, he didn't take long to make an impression. His charm worked like a magnet, drawing the attention of every girl in the room.

But it was Nikita who made the first move. She struck up a conversation, asking about his background. A casual chat turned into a fast-growing friendship, and within a week, they were inseparable. Two weeks in, and Nikita was in Shahid's room, making memories that neither of them would forget anytime soon.

Nikita's parents lived in Mumbai, and her father, a wealthy businessman, had strong connections. Thanks to his influence, getting into the academy was effortless for her. In fact, most students there had some Bollywood link—either through family or friends. Shahid, however, was the odd one out. He was the only one with zero ties to the film industry.

At 23, Nikita told her parents she'd be staying with a classmate, and they agreed instantly. Her father was always traveling for business, her mother busy with kitty parties, leaving her to be raised by nannies and servants. She had everything—money, luxury, gifts—but not the warmth of family.

So, when she asked for space, they saw it as a step toward independence and didn't even ask for details, assuming it would help her grow. They didn't bother to check who this "classmate" was. If they had, they'd have known it wasn't a girl but a boy—Shahid. The only condition? She had to visit home whenever both parents were in town.

In just 20 days, Shahid and Nikita were in a live-in relationship—something entirely new for him. Coming from Dubai, where even casual interactions between unmarried men and women were rare, let alone living together, this kind of freedom felt unreal. Mumbai was a different world, open and exciting. The more he thought about Dubai's strict rules and conservative lifestyle, the more he realized—maybe buying that floor in Burj Khalifa wasn't such a great idea after all.

Shahid's overflowing testosterone consumed Nikita, drawing her into the fire of their relentless encounters—five times a day, each more fevered than the last. She had known pleasure before, but nothing had ever unmade her quite like this. Shahid's touch sent shivers through her, his firm grip making her body arch in surrender. Every kiss, every caress pushed her further into ecstasy, leaving her gasping, torn between resisting and wanting more. As he moved with a relentless rhythm, she clung to him, her nails digging into his back. She gasped, yet when release neared, waves of pleasure took over, leaving her lightheaded and trembling. Only when Shahid reached his own climax did their storm subside, their bodies collapsed, slick with sweat and tangled in the intoxicating stillness of spent desire.

Their routine revolved around intimacy, five times a day, like clockwork. Mornings began with an intense session before breakfast, followed by another in the shower as they got ready for class. At the academy, they stole moments in the girls' restroom, unable to resist each other. Evenings brought another round as soon as they got home, and after dinner, they gave in once more. No matter where they were or what they did, their minds stayed circled back on one thing—lovemaking.

When it came to pleasure, Nikita defied the common belief that women rarely reach orgasm. She seemed to get there faster than Shahid—whether her pleasure was genuine or merely performed was a secret only she held. Meanwhile, Shahid's neck, decorated with deep love bites, became a hot topic among classmates. At first, he tried to hide them, but the more he covered up, the more attention he got. Teasing followed, and soon, he stopped caring, wearing them like a badge of honour. But not everyone shared his confidence. His teacher, clearly embarrassed, finally asked him to cover them up.

In the race to make it big in the film industry, most students knew that ambition often came with compromises, including the unspoken role of intimacy. The instructors, aware of this reality, turned a blind eye to consensual relationships, as long as they remained behind closed doors. As long as no one complained about public indecency or crossed any obvious lines, no one really cared.

For two months, Shahid attended classes without any issues—until the day he suddenly fainted. Concerned, his classmates rushed him to the hospital. After a quick check-up, the doctor recommended some tests and advised him to rest at home until the results arrived.

The next day, Shahid and Nikita returned for the report. As soon as they sat down, the doctor looked at them and asked, "What's the nature of your relationship?"

Shahid quickly clarified that they were just friends, but the doctor wasn't convinced. He pressed further, asking if they were in a live-in relationship. That was enough to set Nikita off. Annoyed, she shot back, demanding to know why their personal life was any of his concern.

The doctor, clearly irritated but trying to stay professional, took a deep breath before responding. "I have no interest in your private matters," he said firmly. "But his medical report tells a different story. His body is exhausted from excessive sexual activity. There's no illness—just overexertion beyond what his body can handle."

Hearing the doctor's words, both Shahid and Nikita fell silent, their embarrassment confirming his suspicion. He turned to Nikita and said, "If you two are in a live-in relationship, I'd suggest cutting down on the intensity. Twice or thrice a week is fine, but this marathon? Not a good idea. It might not affect you immediately, but at this rate, he'll be back here soon—only in a hospital bed."

After a brief pause, he sighed and said, "That's all from me. If there's anything you want to discuss, I'm here. If not, my next patient is waiting."

For a moment, neither of them spoke. In silence, they gathered the medical reports, neatly tucking them into a folder. Without a word, they left the chamber and walked a few steps before their eyes met. Another glance, and that was it—they broke into laughter, burying their faces in each other's shoulders, both amused and slightly embarrassed.

Onlookers stared, confused. After all, laughter wasn't something you are expected to hear in a hospital corridor.

Back home, they promised to keep it to three times a week. But self-control? Easier said than done. They kept slipping back into old habits, giving in to each other every day. Eventually, though, they found a middle ground—scaling down from five times a day to just once. A small victory, at least.

Shahid was living the dream, and three months passed in a flash. Every month, Rs.50,000 landed in his account, courtesy of Mohit's accountant. With almost no expenses, his savings grew. Nikita took care of his wardrobe, insisting he shouldn't waste money on clothes. So, Shahid spent mostly on mobile recharges and extravagant gifts—for her, of course.

One evening, Mohit Shetty's cameraman, Siddharth—better known as Sid—invited Shahid to his place. He asked him to come at 9 PM, as his day was packed with film shoots. The invitation piqued Shahid's curiosity. Was Sid about to offer him a role? Maybe even discuss payment? The thought was exciting.

Shahid reached Sid's house by 8:30 PM. Sid welcomed him in, and the place was quiet—the servants had the night off. He offered whisky or scotch, but Shahid politely refused, settling for a Coke instead. Sid handed it over with a smile, and as they sipped their drinks, he leaned forward and asked, "Do you have any idea why you're really in the academy?"

Shahid looked puzzled. "I'm not sure what you mean," he said. "Mohit sir personally selected me for the academy."

Sid leaned back, sipping his drink. "What I mean is, look around. Everyone at the academy has some industry connection—family, friends, someone to back them. But you? You're an outsider, no ties to Bollywood. Yet, you're here. Ever wondered why?"

Sid raised an eyebrow, letting the question sink in. After a moment, Shahid shrugged and said, "Because... I have talent and a good physique."

Sid let out a chuckle, almost mocking Shahid's response. "Talent... physique... hmm," he said, shaking his head. "Listen, my friend, Mumbai is full of guys who are more talented and better built than you. They spend years running after directors and producers, hoping for a break. Yet, here you are, already in the academy. Why?"

Shahid frowned, clearly confused, "Then tell me", he said, leaning forward. "Why am I here?"

Sid said, "I was the one who got you into the academy. I saw you at Dubai Mall and convinced Mohit to give you a chance. He wasn't keen on admitting a stranger, but I pushed for it. The deal was simple—if you didn't show promise, you'd be out in three months. I promised to mentor you, to shape you into a real actor. So, if you want to stay, prove you've acquired skills more than just entertaining Nikita in the girls' toilet." His words carried the weight of authority, leaving no room for argument.

Though embarrassed, Shahid acknowledged Sid's help with gratitude. He apologized for his actions in the girls' restroom, admitting his mistake, and assured Sid that it wouldn't happen again.

Sid waved off the apology, telling Shahid it wasn't necessary. In the entertainment industry, one's personal choices are irrelevant to others. What did matter was the rare opportunity he had—to train under Mohit. Sid stressed that such chances usually came at a steep price, making it clear just how exclusive and valuable this break was. If Shahid wanted to stay, he had to be ready to pay the price.

"But I don't have money to pay," Shahid said hesitantly.

Sid smirked. "Who said anything about money? I have plenty of that. What I want from you is something else."

Curious, Shahid inquired, "What is it?"

Sid leaned back, his words slightly slurred from the three glasses of whiskey. "Remember our first meeting in Dubai?" he said, his eyes locking onto Shahid's. "I told you then—follow every order from your seniors, no questions asked. Disobedience has only one outcome—you're out of the academy."

Shahid responded with a suspicious "Yes."

Sid's voice turned firm; his gaze unwavering, "This is your moment—not just to follow orders, but to return the favour I did for you," he said, pausing before giving a chilling command, "Take off your clothes. Now."

Shahid froze, his throat tightened, but somehow, he found his voice—shaky, almost breaking. "Why?" he asked, barely above a whisper.

Sid asserted, "We had a deal, remember? Follow orders, no questions." He let the words sink in before adding with a smirk, "But since you asked, I'll tell you why."

Drunk and unfiltered, Sid disclosed, "Because I'm gay," he admitted, his voice slow and deliberate, "And I want to do to you what you've been doing with Nikita. I've wanted you since the day I first saw you—call it love at first sight if you will."

Sid, drunk and reckless, shed his clothes, standing unabashedly naked before Shahid. A cold wave of shock froze Shahid in place, his breath shallow, his mind scrambling for sense. Before he could react, Sid closed the gap, fingers curling into Shahid's T-shirt, yanking off the T-shirt despite his resistance. Heat surged to Shahid's face—not from desire, but from something rawer, more unsettling. He had stripped before Nikita countless times, but now, an unfamiliar shame coiled inside him. His fingers clenched, his head dipped, chin pressing to his chest—anything to avoid the sight of Sid's bare body.

Shahid refused to move, staying seated on the couch despite Sid's insistence. Growing impatient, Sid grabbed his arm and pulled him to his feet. Without hesitation, he unbuckled Shahid's belt and pulled down his trousers, bringing his underwear down with them. Now, both men stood unclothed, facing each other, but Shahid kept his head down, avoiding eye contact with Sid.

Sid's eyes moved slowly over Shahid's bare body, taking in every detail. His hand followed, gliding over his skin, feeling its warmth. Shahid stayed still, head lowered, chin resting against his chest. A heavy silence hung between them. Sid reached out, gently lifting Shahid's face, forcing him to look up with one hand, while the other hand caressed Shahid's masculinity. After a few moments of tender caresses, Sid leaned in and pressed his lips firmly against Shahid's lips.

The kiss was the breaking point. Shahid shoved Sid away, his patience snapping. "I don't want to be an actor anymore," he said firmly, grabbing his pants from the floor and hurriedly getting dressed.

But Sid, too drunk to care, wasn't ready to back off. He staggered forward, pulling Shahid into a tight embrace, attempting another kiss. This time, Shahid pushed him away even harder, his decision unwavering.

Sid's face twisted in rage as he yelled, "Disobey me, and you're out of the academy by tomorrow!"

"I don't give a fuck about your academy, you bastard."

Sid's anger flared, but Shahid kept pushing him away. Refusing to back down, Sid tried again, forcing himself on him. That was it. Shahid swung his fist, landing a solid punch on Sid's face. Within seconds, he knocked him out. Catching his breath, Shahid didn't wait. He grabbed his clothes, dressed quickly, and walked out, leaving Sid unconscious on the floor.

Shahid sat on Juhu Beach, staring at the endless dark waves for almost an hour. The silence felt heavy, and for a moment, the thought of committing suicide crept in. But he shook it off, refusing to give in. By 1:00 A.M., he finally headed back to his room, where Nikita was waiting, eager to know what had happened.

Shahid walked in, sat beside Nikita, and let the weight of the night sink in. Words failed him. Instead, he buried his face in her lap, tears flowing freely. Nikita kept asking what had happened, but he couldn't speak. Not yet. It took time, but finally, he found the courage to tell her everything. As he spoke, she listened, her own eyes welling up. Without a word, she pulled him into a tight embrace, holding him as they cried together.

The next day, Shahid was expelled from the academy and given just an hour to pack up and leave. His dismissal was swift, though they still handed him his full month's salary before showing him the door. Lost and unsure of what to do next, he turned to the only person he could—Nikita.

Nikita called her father, Mr. Balraj, who was in America, spinning a story about a classmate needing a place to stay. She asked if Shahid could temporarily stay in one of the vacant servant room at their home until he found another place.

Balraj, a London-educated man with a progressive mindset, agreed without a second thought. He was modern in outlook but had zero tolerance for anything indecent. Friendships between boys and girls were fine, as long as boundaries were respected. Without hesitation, he offered Shahid the servant's quarters, saying he could stay as long as he was comfortable.

Nikita was thrilled with her father's response, and Shahid quickly moved into her house. To his surprise, the servant's room was even bigger than his academy accommodation. The plan was simple—he'd stay with Nikita until he found a job and an alternative accommodation.

Staying at Nikita's house felt easier than Shahid had expected. In fact, he got so comfortable that job hunting took a backseat as he began picturing himself as her husband. With her as the sole heir to her family's fortune, she didn't need to work, and if he became her husband, neither would he. Soon, his mind wandered further— expanding Balraj's business, and securing big endorsements.

A 19-year-old's mind is a strange place—full of dreams, yet blind to reality. Often, they are oblivious to the harsh realities of life, instead immersed in their own fantasies and daydreams. They imagine changing the world while failing to see their own life falling apart.

Shahid let go of his acting dreams, knowing Mohit Shetty's influence would shut every door in Bollywood. Someone as powerful as Mohit would never forgive him after what happened with Mohit Shetty's cameraman. Staying at Nikita's house, he started applying for telemarketing jobs. Meanwhile, Nikita continued her classes, barely bringing up his name or his situation at the academy.

With Mr. Balraj away on business most of the month and Mrs. Suneeta busy with kitty parties, the house was practically theirs. Shahid and Nikita wasted no time, slipping back into their old routine— engaging in coitus nearly every day, uninterrupted.

Shahid and Nikita shared her bed every night, careful not to let her parents find out. As months passed, their confidence grew, their boundaries faded, and soon, what started as stolen moments turned into a routine—sleeping naked in each other's arms.

Shahid quickly grew close to Suneeta, who treated him like a son. Whenever Nikita's parents were home, they dined together as a family. Mr. Balraj, generous as ever, let him stay without a second thought. Completely unaware of what was really going on between him and Nikita, they welcomed him with open arms.

As they sat down for dinner, Mr. Balraj suddenly asked, "What do you think about your relationship with Nikita?"

The question caught Shahid and Nikita off guard. Shahid, trying to stay composed, hesitated before saying, "Could you clarify what you mean?"

Mr. Balraj leaned back. "I mean, how do you see Nikita? What is she to you?"

Shahid took a moment, carefully choosing his words. Then, with a polite smile, he replied, "She's like a sister to me."

Mr. Balraj nodded, satisfied with Shahid's response. But across the table, Nikita felt a sting of disappointment. She wanted to say something, but for now, she chose to stay silent.

Later that night, knowing her parents were home, Nikita still couldn't hold back her frustration. Furious at Shahid for calling her his sister, she sent him a message: "Open the door."

As soon as she slipped inside, she unleashed her anger—hitting him on the back with both hands, her voice low but sharp. "How dare you call me your sister, *behenchod*?" she hissed, her frustration pouring out in every slap.

Shahid wrapped his arms around Nikita, holding her close until her anger began to subside. He placed a soft kiss on her forehead, trying to soothe her. Gently, he urged her to listen. Then, with a sigh, he asked, "Tell me, what else was I supposed to say to your father in that moment?"

Nikita crossed her arms and shot back, "You could've just said we're friends. Was that so hard?"

Shahid sighed. "I could've said that, but calling you my sister felt safer. Honestly, I was afraid if I said we were just friends, your dad might have asked me to leave." He smirked, pulling her closer. "But don't worry, darling, I'm Muslim—cousin sisters are totally acceptable in our culture." Nikita burst into laughter, and soon, so did he. Their muffled giggles echoed in the room, though it remained unheard by anyone else.

Shahid suggested she go back to her room, but Nikita had other plans. She pulled him in for a deep kiss, and soon, one thing led to another. An hour later, they lay tangled in each other, bare under the sheets. Before dawn, she slipped out quietly, making sure her parents never suspected a thing. She knew the household staff wouldn't dare say a word—even if they had their doubts.

Six months passed, and Shahid had seamlessly become Suneeta's favorite. Life was easy—no stress, no pressure to earn. The family's warmth made him feel at home, and Nikita quietly covered his small expenses with her pocket money. However, as the saying goes, you can hide love behind words, but lust always reveals itself in actions.

One afternoon, with Suneeta away at a kitty party, Shahid slipped into Nikita's room, his hands traced the curves of her body as he pulled away her top, his touch igniting a familiar fire between them. Lost in their urgent passion, completely unaware of what was coming.

Suneeta, having forgotten her phone, returned earlier than expected. As she passed by Nikita's room, the sound of heavy breathing made her pause. Frowning, she pushed open the half-closed door—only to freeze in shock at the sight before her.

The room fell into a stunned silence. Suneeta stood at the doorway, her breath caught, eyes locked onto the tangled bodies before her. Shahid and Nikita, exposed and motionless, stared back, waiting for her reaction.

But she said nothing. Without a word, she turned around and walked to her own room, sinking onto the bed—lost in a whirlwind of shock, disbelief, and despair.

A few minutes later, Shahid and Nikita walked into Suneeta's room, their heads lowered in guilt. The silence was suffocating—twenty long minutes passed, and no one spoke. Finally, Nikita broke the tension. "Mom, I wanted to talk to you about us for a while, but I never got the chance... you're always busy with kitty parties."

Suneeta sat motionless, her expression unreadable. Nikita inched closer, gently shaking her leg. "Mom, please... say something. Your silence is killing me."

Suneeta finally broke her silence, her voice laced with regret. She admitted her shortcomings, acknowledging how she had left Nikita to be raised by maids instead of being there herself. "Maybe I failed as a mother," she sighed. "But Nikita, your choices... they've only brought pain. And now, you've given yourself to a servant like Shahid?"

Anger flared in Nikita's eyes as she snapped back, "Shahid is not a servant!"

Suneeta raised an eyebrow and asked coldly, "Then what do you call someone who lives in the servant quarters?"

"He's a guest in our home!" Nikita shot back.

Suneeta let out a dry laugh. "Oh, so a guest servant, then?", her tone dripping with sarcasm.

Nikita opened her mouth to respond, but Suneeta raised a hand, cutting her off. "Enough," she said firmly. Shahid tried to speak, but she shook her head and with a dismissive wave, she gestured for both of them to leave.

Without another word, they turned and walked to their rooms, the air between them heavy with unspoken tension.

For the first time in months, Shahid felt the weight of his reality—living in the servant quarters, unemployed, dependent. Shame crept in, and for a fleeting moment, he wanted to leave. But with no money, no job, and no friends in Mumbai except Nikita, where would he even go?

Meanwhile, Suneeta wasted no time. She called Balraj, who was in Delhi, and told him everything. Balraj, sensing the urgency, booked the evening flight.

Nikita, however, was unfazed. This wasn't her first time getting caught. Back in Class 12, her mother had caught her in a compromising position with her ex-boyfriend. So, instead of stressing, she simply locked her door and fell asleep peacefully, exhausted from her erotic workout.

Balraj arrived home late at night, seething with anger. He confronted Shahid, accusing him of betraying their trust and taking advantage of their generosity. Shahid stood in silence, but before he could respond, Nikita stepped forward, fiercely defending him.

Balraj's fury only intensified. "I won't let someone like him ruin our family's name. We gave him shelter, treated him like one of us, and this is how he repays us?"

"I love him, Dad. And I'm going to marry him."

"You're being foolish, Nikita. He doesn't love you; he's only interested in your father's money. He's like a parasite, feeding off the wealth of others through their loved ones, just as he's doing with me through you," Balraj asserted.

Shahid didn't say a word, but Balraj's accusations hit harder than any insult. Deep down, he knew the truth—his feelings for Nikita were tangled with his desire for the life she offered, her wealth more tempting than the love itself.

Balraj ordered Shahid to leave immediately. Turning to Nikita, he informed her that a marriage proposal had come from a business associate. The suitor was an MBA graduate, working as an investment banker at Goldman Sachs in the USA, earning nearly Rs. 3 lakhs a month.

Nikita refused to comply with Balraj's demand for marriage. In a fit of anger, he raised his hand to slap her, but Suneeta caught his arm just in time. His voice thundered through the room. "Had I put you in your place earlier, you wouldn't have dared to defy me like this! The wedding date will be finalized and you will obey. If not, you're free to leave this house and live with that servant!"

Balraj's eyes burned with fury as he spotted Shahid standing nearby, listening in. He shouted, "And what the hell are you doing here, eavesdropping on our family matters, you scoundrel?"

Nikita clung to her father's hands, pleading for Shahid to stay just a few more days. Tears streamed down her face, but Balraj didn't budge. His decision was final—Shahid had to leave. Desperate, she turned to her mother, hoping for support, but Suneeta, too, refused to let him stay.

When her pleas failed, Nikita made one last, desperate move. "If Shahid leaves, I will commit suicide," she declared. Her words sent a shockwave through the room. Balraj stood frozen, while Suneeta broke down, sobbing uncontrollably.

Before things spiralled further, Shahid stepped in. He gently urged Nikita to go back to her room, promising he wouldn't leave without speaking to her first. Though reluctant, she finally agreed, trusting him to handle the situation.

As soon as Nikita left the room, Suneeta unleashed her fury. Her words were sharp, cutting through Shahid like a blade. She called him a thief, a fraud, a man with no morals—someone whose character was a reflection of his upbringing. And then, she crossed the line, dragging his mother into it.

Shahid's fists clenched Anger surged through him, his body itching to retaliate. But he held back. No matter how cruel her words, he couldn't retaliate. After all, this was the same woman who once treated him like a son.

Trying to stay calm, he attempted to explain that Nikita loved him. But before he could finish, Suneeta cut him off, and then, in the heat of the moment, the truth slipped out. "Don't fool yourself, Shahid. You think you're special? You're not the first man she's slept with."

The words hit harder than any slap.

With a heavy heart, Shahid told Suneeta he had no intention of marrying Nikita. He was ready to leave but asked for a few days to convince Nikita to accept the match her family had chosen. He feared that leaving suddenly might push her to do something drastic. Swearing by Allah, he promised that once she agreed to the wedding, he would walk away from her life forever.

Shahid locked himself in his room and collapsed onto the bed, his heart heavy with defeat. Silent tears ran down his face as he buried his head in his hands, muffling his sobs. For the first time, shame hit him—living off Nikita's generosity, without earning a penny of his own.

He skipped dinner, tossing and turning all night, sleep refusing to come. At sunrise, without a second thought, he went straight to Nikita.

"I can't marry you," Shahid whispered, his voice barely audible.

Nikita's eyes widened. "Are you serious?"

"Yes, I am. And you need to see the truth, Nikita. Your father was right. I have nothing—no money, no future. Right now, I'm no better than a beggar."

She opened her mouth to protest, but he cut her off. "Listen to me. Say yes to the guy your father has chosen. If, by the time your wedding day comes, I've built something for myself, then run away with me. If not... then marry him."

Tears welled up in Nikita's eyes as she asked, "Why this sudden change?"

"Because your father was right. Without financial stability, there's no future for us. I can't even provide for myself, let alone sustain a marriage."

"But I love you."

"Love flies out the window, my darling, when hunger walks in through the door," Shahid said softly, his voice laced with resignation.

Nikita clutched his hand, desperation in her eyes "I can't imagine my life without you."

Shahid remained calm; his tone steady. "You'll manage. Time erases everything—like how you moved on from your last relationship after indulging in sex with him."

Nikita froze, stunned by Shahid's words. She had never spoken about her past relationships, yet he knew. The realization unsettled her. Before she could ask, Shahid revealed the source—her mother. Suneeta had told him everything, about her previous boyfriend and their sensual intimacies. A wave of discomfort washed over, as she struggled to process this unexpected betrayal.

"Oh, so this is about my past?" Nikita's voice was laced with anger. "You're leaving me because I had a relationship before you? That's disgusting!"

Shahid sighed, trying to calm her down. "You're getting it all wrong. This isn't about your past—it's about our future. I have nothing. No job, no money. I can't even support myself, let alone both of us. How will we survive?"

Nikita's anger exploded, "Liar! I know exactly why you're backing out, you bastard. Suddenly, you're worried about money? Funny how that didn't matter when you were enjoying my body!"

Shahid's replied with a heavy heart, "Think whatever you want. Call me a bastard, a rascal, a beggar, a servant—anything. Perhaps I deserve it. But please, forgive me. I can't marry you."

Nikita begged him to reconsider, but Shahid stood firm. He urged her to marry the man her father had chosen, knowing he couldn't provide for her. Deep down, he believed she wouldn't survive the struggles of a middle-class life and would eventually regret choosing him.

As Shahid turned to leave, Nikita made one last desperate attempt. She took his hand, leading him to the bed, her eyes pleading for one final moment of passion. She pressed her lips to his, a silent invitation, but Shahid gently resisted.

Instead, he cupped her face, placed a soft kiss on her forehead, and stepped away—ready to walk out of her life.

No words passed between them, yet the farewell was etched in the silence. A blessing unspoken, a wish left hanging in the air—for her to find love, for joy to embrace her, for longing to never haunt her again. And with that, he stepped away, carrying with him the weight of what had been and the finality of what would never be.

As Shahid stepped out, a strange, unspoken emotion gripped him—love, raw and untainted, stripped of greed or lust. He wanted to stay, to marry her, but made a solemn choice— to let her go and never return, ensuring her path was paved with serenity and joy.

Shahid picked up his bag, carrying just two sets of clothes he had bought himself. Everything else—expensive outfits, money, wallet, watches, perfumes, gifts, shoes, and even the phone Nikita had given him—he left behind.

The only thing he took was his old mobile, its memory card filled with moments of their time together. Before stepping out, he pulled out the SIM card, cutting off any chance of Nikita reaching him. And with that, he walked away.

Shahid reached Bandra Terminus Railway Station and asked about the next train to Lucknow. It wouldn't leave for another 11 hours. A new problem hit him—he hadn't eaten in 14 hours and had no money for a ticket or even a meal.

But begging, borrowing, or calling Nikita was out of the question. Instead, he drank water from the station's cooler to suppress his hunger and made up his mind—he would board the train without a ticket. If caught, so be it. A fine, a few slaps, or even a night in jail—none of it scared him anymore.

At 8:00 P.M., Shahid climbed into the overcrowded general coach as the train rolled in. It was unlike any travel experience he had ever known. Though he had seen packed local trains in Mumbai, he had never mustered the courage to step aboard. As he entered the coach, he found no vacant seats. Eleven people crammed into seats meant for four, some barely fitting with their buttocks hanging in the air. Others perched on the upper deck, meant for luggage.

Shahid hesitated to join the chaotic search for a seat, fearing he might suffocate amidst the throng of bodies.

Mumbai's local trains are crowded, yes, but at least the struggle lasts only a few stops. A long-distance journey in the same conditions? That's a whole new level of torture.

They say even chickens in a coop get more space than passengers crammed into the general coach of an Indian train. Ticket inspectors don't even bother stepping in—it's not just about the chaos, but the fear of being pickpocketed amidst the sea of bodies. Surviving 28 hours in that coach isn't just a test of endurance; it's proof that a person can adapt to anything, no matter how brutal.

After hours of standing by the gate, exhaustion finally caught up with Shahid. He squeezed into the tiny space beside the toilet, no longer caring about comfort or dignity. With 28 hours of travel ahead, he let go of self-consciousness, becoming just another faceless passenger in the crowd.

The suffocating heat, the sweat-drenched bodies, the sharp stench in the air—none of it registered. His mind was elsewhere, replaying everything that had happened like a film on loop. Despite the unbearable conditions, he kept his emotions locked away, especially the ones that surfaced for Nikita.

During brief halts, he stepped off to gulp down water, but hunger never came. It had been 48 hours since his last meal, yet his body felt nothing—perhaps because his heart was already too heavy to feel anything else.

As the train approached Lucknow, Shahid felt the crushing weight of his shattered dreams—everything had fallen apart in just 48 hours. His mind was a blur of memories, all revolving around Nikita, leaving no space for anything else.

A sudden halt before the station caught his attention. Passengers began jumping off, crossing the railway tracks toward the nearby road. Curious, Shahid asked why. Someone casually explained—they were avoiding the TTE, slipping away before Lucknow to dodge ticket checks.

Upon hearing this, Shahid swiftly grabbed his bag, leaped from the train, and crossed the tracks to join them. A wave of relief swept over him—he had made it to Lucknow without getting caught, despite not having a single rupee in his pocket. Although he wasn't afraid of being caught, the thought of being humiliated in front of strangers still stung. For the first time in two days, a small burden lifted from his chest, grateful to have avoided the humiliation of being caught without a ticket.

As Shahid stepped into his home, his mother, Sadiyah, rushed to embrace him. It had been nearly three years since she had last seen him. Though surprise flickered in her eyes at his sudden return, it was quickly overshadowed by joy.

Without asking questions, she got to work in the kitchen, preparing a hearty meal. Shahid ate in silence, savouring every bite—it was the first real food he had in two days. That night, as he lay down, exhaustion finally gave way to sleep. No judgment, no shame—just the comfort of home.

For a month, Shahid remained lost in silence, drowning in his own thoughts. He barely spoke, not even to his mother, Sadiyah, who tried again and again to reach him. Most days, he locked himself in his room, avoiding people, avoiding life.

Though thoughts of suicide crossed his mind, but somewhere deep inside, a flicker of resolve remained. He couldn't let his life go to waste. He had to rise, to prove himself.

At Sadiyah's request, Shahid's elder brother, Ahmed, flew in from Dubai. She couldn't watch her son drown in silence any longer. She knew something had broken inside him, but he wouldn't open up to her.

Desperate, she turned to Ahmed—the one person who had been his confidant, his partner in childhood mischief, and the only one who might break through the walls Shahid had built around himself.

The moment Shahid saw Ahmed, he broke down. He clung to his brother, sobbing uncontrollably, letting out weeks of pent-up pain. Ahmed asked again and again what was wrong, but Shahid could only share fragments of the story. Shahid could manage only one confession—he loved a girl. A Hindu girl. Her father had chosen someone else for her, someone with financial stability, something Shahid didn't have.

Ahmed chuckled, ruffling Shahid's hair like he used to when he was a kid. Then, in his usual wise-older-brother tone, he said, "Love at this age feels like the end of the world, but trust me, it's just infatuation."

He told Shahid to focus on his future, not on a girl who might never be his. "Build yourself first, and the right person will come along when you least expect it." Shahid listened, but deep down, he wasn't sure if he could ever feel this way about anyone else.

Ahmed chuckled, nudging Shahid playfully. "Get a good job, make some money, and trust me, girls will line up for you."

Shahid managed a weak smile, but deep down, he knew his brother didn't get it. Love wasn't a transaction for him. He wasn't looking for options—he had already found her. But explaining that to anyone felt impossible.

A few months later, Ahmed got Shahid enrolled in a college in Lucknow for a Bachelor's in Commerce. Thanks to his "contacts," Shahid's two years weren't wasted, arranging for him to join the program with a backdated enrollment. A classic *UP miracle*.

By the time Shahid officially joined, he was already in his final year. It wasn't the path he had imagined, but it was a fresh start. Grateful for the chance, he decided to move forward—one step at a time, leaving the past where it belonged.

In 2009, with a degree finally in hand—thanks to Allah and a few "UP shortcuts"—Shahid stepped into the job hunt. The booming BPO sector seemed like the perfect place to start, and through a recruitment agency, he landed an offer at IBM's call centre in Delhi. A monthly salary of ₹12,500 wasn't much, but it was a foot in the door.

Back home, his mother and cousins supported the decision. A corporate job, even in a call centre, meant stability and exposure—two things Shahid desperately needed.

Before leaving, he hesitated for a moment and unlocked his old phone. Nikita's pictures stared back at him—smiling, laughing, frozen in time. A wave of emotions hit him—love, regret, heartbreak. His fingers hovered over the delete button, but instead, he found himself walking toward an internet café. One last time, he needed to see her, even if just virtually.

Logging into Orkut, he searched for her profile. And there she was, adorned with picturesque snapshots of her honeymoon in Switzerland. Her life had moved on, draped in luxury and happiness. But what struck him the most was the caption beneath one of the images. He stared at the words, letting them sink in. A strange mix of relief and pain settled inside him.

The caption read: "Best Hubby in the world."

He pulled out his phone, scrolled through Nikita's pictures one last time, and pressed delete, bidding them all farewell forever. Two days later, he packed his bags and boarded a train to Delhi, ready for his new beginning.

****

When dreams fall apart

"The pain of shattered dreams lingers, haunting the soul with what could have been."

-Anonymous

(10th December, 2008 - New Delhi)

Aakanksha stepped off the bus at Delhi's Kashmere Gate Bus Stand, her heart pounding. Despite the clock showing noon, the winter clouds shrouded the sun, the city felt trapped in morning haze. As she disembarked from the bus, a wave of fear and uncertainty gripped her as she clutched her bag, stepping into the unknown.

She called Priyanka and took the metro to Laxmi Nagar. Unfamiliar with the system, she embraced the challenge, asking locals, constables, and tea vendors for directions, adapting quickly to Delhi's rhythm.

Laxmi Nagar, a student hub in Delhi, is packed with cramped rooms where strangers become roommates. Beds are rented for ₹3,000 to ₹7,000 per month, with food adding another ₹1,500 to ₹2,500. Priyanka had already arranged with their landlord to reserve a bed for Aakanksha in a small room with two beds, each costing 4,000 rupees, which they would share.

As Aakanksha stepped into Laxmi Nagar, she felt disoriented in its maze of dusty, narrow lanes, where overhead wires hung like chaotic spiderwebs. The buildings were so tightly packed that she found herself envying even the watchman back in Shimla, who probably had more space than most residents here. Priyanka greeted her with a glass of water, already aware of everything from their phone call, making words unnecessary.

Priyanka briefed the PG rules, informing Aakanksha that rent for the bed was ₹4,000, with an additional ₹2,000 for food—optional if she chose to eat elsewhere. The landlord also required a security deposit of two months' rent along with the first month's payment. Despite the formalities, Aakanksha saw this as a short-term arrangement. She was certain that once selected for the national academy, her accommodation and meals would be covered, making this setup temporary at best.

Aakanksha immediately called Vishal to assure him she was safe. She mentioned that her friend had arranged a place for her but skipped the detail that it was just a rented bed for ₹4,000. She outlined her next steps—meeting the instructor recommended by her basketball coach from Shimla and preparing for the upcoming selection trials. Confident in her abilities, she believed that once selected, she would secure a spot in the national academy.

Aakanksha called the basketball instructor in Delhi, who scheduled her trials at Jawaharlal Nehru Stadium in two days at 11:00 A.M. Confident in her skills, she arrived on time and was introduced to the senior coach, who was already aware of her through Mr. Karwal. She requested to play as a center, knowing it was the ideal position for tall and strong players. But the coach denied her request, pointing out that the girls from Haryana and Punjab, being taller and more built, were a better fit. Aakanksha, feeling dwarfed among the towering players, experienced a sharp blow to her confidence. Despite considering herself one of the best players in Himachal, here she was just another player, struggling to match up.

Aakanksha, who had played as a Center for 12 years, was unexpectedly placed as a Point Guard (PG) during the trials. This position, usually assigned to the shortest player, required sharp ball-handling, quick passes, and fast footwork. Unlike her usual scoring role, a PG focused more on creating opportunities for others. The shift threw her off. Used to dominating under the basket, she now had to orchestrate plays, a skill she had barely practiced. Her passes lacked precision, and the opposition intercepted them with ease. As the trials progressed, it became clear—she was the weakest player on the court that day.

The coach's frustration erupted, and he didn't hold back. In front of everyone, he berated her, expressing his disappointment. He had trusted Mr. Karwal's recommendation, but what he saw on the court was a disaster. Comparing her performance to that of a clueless beginner, he made it clear—she had wasted his time.

Aakanksha felt like the ground beneath her had disappeared. For a fleeting moment, she wished she had died. But then, summoning every ounce of courage, she spoke up. She explained that she had spent 12 years perfecting the Centre position, not the PG role. If given a chance where she truly belonged, she was confident she could have delivered a game-changing performance.

The coach, clearly skeptical, agreed to let Aakanksha try the Centre position—more out of respect for Mr. Karwal than faith in her abilities. Stepping onto the court, she felt a surge of confidence. But reality hit hard. Her opponents, towering Haryanvi girls, blocked every move, making scoring nearly impossible. Despite giving her best, she managed just one successful throw out of seventeen attempts.

As the match wrapped up, the coach smirked and said, "Twenty-one years in coaching, and I can tell exactly where a player belongs."

Though he acknowledged her effort, he emphasized that scoring was what truly mattered. "So, tell me, do you still think Centre is your position?"

Aakanksha, her confidence shaken, lowered her gaze and admitted, "No."

Despite her twelve years of basketball training, the coach pointed out that her game still needed work. However, he saw promise in her and advised her to refine her skills by practicing as a point guard (PG) at the Sports Academy for a year. If she improved and impressed the selectors, she could earn a spot in the National Academy next year. The practicing fee was Rs. 1000 per month, a small price for a big opportunity. Aware of the challenges ahead, he assured her of his support during practice, which he did.

Aakanksha quickly did the math—Rs. 4000 for rent, Rs. 2000 for food, and another Rs. 2000 for basketball training and travel. With her savings, she could sustain herself for at least 15 months, more than enough time to secure a spot in the national academy. Once selected, accommodation and meals would be covered, easing her financial stress. Confident in her plan, she wasted no time, signed the paperwork, and officially enrolled in the training classes.

Lost in a whirlwind of emotions, she boarded the packed metro, her mood heavy with disappointment but laced with a flicker of hope. She kept her head down, eyes brimming with unshed tears—defeated yet not entirely broken. She had a year to prove herself, to reclaim her place in the national academy. Deep in thought, she barely noticed when she stepped off at Rajiv Chowk, Delhi's busiest station, to switch trains for Laxmi Nagar. In that moment of distraction, someone seized the opportunity and pickpocketed her cell phone.

When she reached her room and discovered her phone was gone, a wave of helplessness hit her. She knew the chances of getting it back were slim, yet she still dragged herself to the police station to file a report, returning late in the evening. It wasn't just about losing the device—it was the phone numbers, the little connections it held. But amidst the loss, one relief remained—her ATM card, safely tucked away in another pocket, untouched.

Aakanksha didn't bother getting a new phone—there was no one she truly wanted to call. Vishal's number escaped her memory, and reaching out to anyone else meant risking word getting back to her father. After dinner, she replayed the day's events in her head. Was her father right about her basketball skills? Doubt crept in. A fleeting thought of returning home crossed her mind, but the thought of marrying that rascal strengthened her resolve to never go back, regardless of whether she got selected or not. If needed, she'd be working as a waitress at McDonald's or pizza hut, but the idea of returning home was out of the question.

The next morning, Aakanksha started her day with a plate of *poori-chole*, its oil pooling on her plate—probably enough to fry two more *pooris*. She barely noticed, her mind elsewhere. Pushing aside yesterday's doubts, she made her way to practice, blending in with the other girls at the stadium. This time, she didn't argue. Point guard it was. The blow to her confidence still lingered, but she wasn't ready to give up. Dreams didn't come easy, and if hard work was the price, she was willing to pay.

After a few weeks of training, Aakanksha felt her energy dipping. Her focus wavered, her stamina wasn't the same. Worried, she approached her coach. He listened, then asked about her daily routine and diet. It didn't take him long to figure out the problem—she wasn't eating like an athlete. Without proper nutrition, no amount of practice would help. Taking charge, he drafted a meal plan, designed to fuel her body and sharpen her mind, ensuring she had the strength to keep up with the game.

Aakanksha glanced at the food chart as she walked back, scanning the list of fruits, vegetables, milk, dry fruits, and sprouts her coach had recommended. It all sounded great—except for one problem. Following this diet would cost her an extra Rs. 5,000-6,000 a month. She did some quick math. With her savings, she could manage for about 8-9 months. But the trials were still a year away.

Aakanksha made up her mind—she would stick to the diet plan, no matter what. She believed in her ability to handle things. Once her game reached the right level, she figured she could take up a call center job to cover expenses for the remaining months. For now, the goal was clear: train hard, eat right, and make it to the national academy.

At the age of 19, managing finances for the first time can be challenging, especially in a city like Delhi, where temptation lurks at every corner. Aakanksha found herself drawn to branded clothes, expensive shoes, dining out, and unnecessary shopping, typical temptations for a girl from a wealthy background. Before she knew it, she had burned through a lakh in just four months, leaving her with a mere twenty thousand.

With her savings vanishing fast, Aakanksha knew she needed a backup plan. She turned to Priyanka, who suggested a call center job—good pay, flexible hours, and only one requirement: fluent English. It seemed like the perfect solution. Aakanksha decided to give it a shot, balancing work with basketball practice, hoping it would buy her more time to chase her dream.

In the late 2000s, India's BPO sector boomed, particularly in Delhi and Gurgaon. Favorable government policies, a skilled English-speaking workforce, and strong telecom infrastructure fueled its rapid expansion, making call centers a lucrative job option for many youngsters.

Around this time, multinational companies from the US and Europe began outsourcing their back-office operations to India, drawn by its cost-effective workforce and specialized skills. This led to a surge in BPO jobs, fueling economic growth and providing countless opportunities for young professionals.

After multiple interviews, Aakanksha landed offers from four companies, including IBM. But when a call center linked to Amazon offered her ₹18,000 a month—far more than IBM's ₹12,000—her decision was easy. She didn't know much about Amazon back in 2009, but the higher salary was all that mattered. The company assured training for fresh hires, with a permanent position upon successful completion.

Aakanksha, a top student from an Army school in Shimla, spoke English so fluently that even the British would admire it. She secured a job with a ₹18,000 salary, a solid start in Delhi. But somewhere along the way, the dream that had brought her here—the one she had sacrificed everything for—seemed to be slipping away.

Aakanksha put her heart into her first month at work, determined to impress her managers and seniors. When her salary of ₹18,000 finally hit her account at the month's end, the joy was unmatched. To celebrate, she took Priyanka out for dinner at an upscale restaurant, happily spending ₹1,900.

Yet, amidst the thrill of earning, something felt off—she hadn't touched a basketball in weeks. Occasionally, she played at the company's recreational court, effortlessly beating the boys in office, feeling pleased. Yet it was a fleeting satisfaction to quiet her inner doubts. Deep down, she knew she still couldn't match the tall and strong girls from Punjab and Haryana.

Ever since losing her phone, Aakanksha had given Priyanka's number to the coach for any urgent communication. When she missed an entire month of practice, he finally called to check in. She assured him she was fine, making up an excuse about practicing elsewhere due to her new job, which made it difficult to attend sessions at JLN Stadium.

Relieved, the coach suggested she at least come on weekends. She agreed but didn't fully commit. Some weekends, she showed up. Other times, she found reasons to skip—sometimes genuine, sometimes just plain laziness.

The saying holds true: "A salary is the drug they give you to forget your dreams."

She often strayed from her diet, lured by the irresistible aroma of *chole-bhature* and *samosa chaat* from a roadside stall near her PG. And in the midst of these guilty pleasures, she began noticing someone—a young man with a light beard, the kind that hinted at youth yet to fully embrace adulthood.

Their paths crossed almost every Sunday morning at the same food joint in Laxmi Nagar, a place buzzing with students, office-goers, and locals, all drawn by the legendary *chole-bhature*. While others dined in groups, these two stood apart, eating alone but exchanging fleeting glances

The stall had no seating, just round, chest-high tables where 4-5 strangers would huddle together. Some lucky ones found space, while others balanced plates in one hand and ate with the other, perfecting the art of standing meals in Delhi's chaotic street food culture. Amidst the crowd, their silent curiosity for each other grew, woven into the ritual of Sunday indulgence.

One Sunday, fate finally placed Aakanksha and the boy at the same table. Side by side, they tore into their *bhature*, the air thick with unspoken curiosity. They had seen each other here for weeks, yet this moment felt different—charged with an odd mix of familiarity and awkwardness. Halfway through their meal, the silence lingered. Then, just as she was about to take another bite, he spoke, "Hello, I'm Riaz. Riaz Nabi."

Aakanksha felt an unexpected sense of relief. She had been waiting for this moment, though she would never admit it. Without hesitation, she smiled and replied, "Hi, I'm Aakanksha."

As their conversation flowed, he mentioned he was pursuing a Master's in Urdu at Jamia Millia, aiming to become a professor someday. Aakanksha listened intently but couldn't hold back a soft chuckle. "I'm sorry," she said, her eyes twinkling with mischief. "But your accent... it's kind of funny."

Riaz smiled, unfazed. "I know," he said casually. "Even my college friends pull my leg about it. I'm actually from Afghanistan and came to India a few years back to pursue my Master's."

Aakanksha raised an eyebrow. "Why India? You could've chosen any Muslim-majority country where Urdu is widely spoken—Pakistan, Turkey or even an Arab nation."

Riaz smiled and explained, "Urdu is only an official language in Pakistan. In Afghanistan, we speak Pashto, In Turkey, people speak Turkish and Arab countries use Arabic. As for Pakistan, I'd rather stay illiterate than study there. Plus, India's education system offers quality learning at a price that's hard to find anywhere else."

As Aakanksha compared her struggles to someone from a war-torn country striving for education in India, a wave of self-doubt hit her. "Here I am," she thought, "born and raised in this country, yet struggling to make it in basketball."

"So, you're fluent in four languages—Pashto, Urdu, Hindi, and English?" Aakanksha asked, intrigued.

Riaz smiled, "Actually, I know seven—Arabic, Punjabi, Farsi, and the four you mentioned. Learning languages is just something I enjoy."

Aakanksha was drawn to Riaz in a way she hadn't felt before. From that day on, they met whenever they could, sneaking moments between her shifts and his classes. She even bought a new phone—one with a camera—just to capture their time together. Since she didn't want her father to know, she got a SIM card using Priyanka's ID.

Mornings were for work, but her evenings belonged to Riaz. She spent her days lost in thoughts of him, scrolling through their pictures, smiling at the stolen moments. In just a few months, their bond had deepened beyond logic, beyond explanation—something that felt almost unreal, yet undeniable.

Aakanksha slowly drifted away from basketball, skipping even the casual office games. Her priorities had changed—her evenings now belonged to Riaz. They watched movies together, sharing popcorn and stolen kisses in the dark PVR. Ice cream dates turned into long walks, and they'd sip from the same bottle of cold drink, laughing at silly things lost in their own little world.

With Priyanka's varying office shifts, which sometimes included night shifts, Aakanksha found the perfect opportunity to sneak Riaz into her room once the landlord had dozed off. The bed was barely big enough for one, but that hardly mattered. They spent the night tangled in each other's warmth, too lost in stolen moments to care about space. Sleep was an afterthought. Before dawn, before Priyanka's return or the landlord stirred, Riaz would slip out unnoticed, leaving behind whispers of a night that never officially existed.

The August rain felt like soft kisses from the sky, washing away the heat and bringing a quiet calm to the city. It drizzled gently, tapping rooftops, soaking the streets, turning the ordinary into something poetic. In a small cafeteria, Aakanksha and Riaz shared a single ice cream cone, licking from opposite sides, their tongues briefly meeting, sending a shiver of excitement through her. Just then, her phone rang.

It was her basketball coach. The trials, due to unforeseen circumstances, had been rescheduled—much earlier than expected. She hadn't shown up for practice in the last four to five months, and yet, he had called. Maybe because he knew how desperately she once wanted this. Maybe because this was her last shot.

She asked quickly, "When are the trials?"

"Next Sunday, 9 A.M. Same place as last year."

As soon as she heard it, a wave of memories flooded over her— confrontation with Mr. Karwal on that chilly winter night, the night she left home, the dreams she once chased. Overwhelmed, she felt her head spinning and the world around her blurred, her vision darkened, and a strange loud noise filled her ears. Voices echoed, but she couldn't make sense of them. The next thing she knew, her fingers loosened, and the ice cream slipped from her hand.

Five minutes later, a sudden splash of water on her face jolted her back to reality.

Riaz, his face a mix of worry and hesitation, blurted out in one quick breath, "Are you okay? What happened? Wait... are you pregnant?"

Aakanksha shot him a sharp look, "Don't be stupid. I already told you—I'm on my periods."

Riaz had no clue how periods and pregnancy were related—biology had never been his strong suit and neither anyone had ever explained it to him. But from the way Aakanksha glared at him, he got the message loud and clear—she wasn't pregnant.

After a brief silence, Riaz finally mustered the courage to ask, his voice softer than usual, "What's wrong, love? You can talk to me."

Aakanksha broke down, letting out everything she had been holding inside. Riaz listened patiently, then gently suggested she take a break from work and focus on her trials. "You still have a week. You can do this," he assured her. His words provided some relief, but guilt weighed heavy on her chest. She hadn't just skipped practice—she had drowned herself in junk food, soft drinks, and a lifestyle that could undo years of effort. The realization hit hard, sinking her deeper into regret.

Determined to make the most of her time, Aakanksha took leave from work and spent the week training with Riaz at a nearby park. She stuck to a strict diet, conditioning both her mind and body for the big day. When the trial day finally arrived, she reached the venue on time. But before leaving, she asked Riaz to stay back—she didn't want the coach to know about their relationship.

The moment the coach saw her, he raised an eyebrow, "Looks like you've put on some weight. Are you sure you've been practicing?" Aakanksha didn't say a word.

During the trials, Aakanksha was nowhere near her past self. The other girls had sharpened their game, their movements swifter, their passes sharper. Meanwhile, she fumbled, barely holding onto the ball for more than a few seconds. The ten-minute match felt like an eternity, each mistake chipping away at whatever little confidence she had left. One glance at the coach's face was enough—his disappointment spoke louder than words.

There were two rounds before the final selection, with a ten-minute break in between. But before the second round could begin, the coach pulled Aakanksha aside. His tone was firm but not unkind—he asked her to step out, replacing her with another player.

She didn't argue. She didn't plead. Without a word, she lowered her head and walked away, her dreams crumbling with every step.

Realizing she hadn't performed well enough to secure a spot in the national academy, Aakanksha returned home and broke down. She felt like she had let everyone down—her parents, Mr. Karwal, Vishal. But most of all, she had failed herself. Negative thoughts crashed in her mind. Had she really given up on her dream of becoming a basketball player just to turn into the mistress of an Afghan man?

Her father's words echoed in her head, his doubts about her skills, his insistence on marrying Anshuman. In retrospect, she wished she had followed her father's advice. At least then, she wouldn't be drowning in guilt, realizing how much of her parents' hard-earned money she had wasted on mindless luxuries.

When dreams fall apart, a wave of emotions engulfs us. We may feel a profound sadness, mourning the loss of what could have been. The future we envisioned, with its bright possibilities and endless potential, now feels shattered and out of reach. It can be difficult to let go of the dreams we held dear, as they were intertwined with our identity and provided a sense of purpose and motivation.

And then comes the self-doubt. Maybe you aimed too high. Maybe you weren't good enough to begin with. The failure feels personal, like a punch to the gut, making you question everything—your choices, your abilities, even your own worth. The worst part? The emptiness that follows, like being lost in a world that suddenly doesn't know what to do with you.

After her dreams fell apart, Aakanksha found an unlikely anchor—Riaz. He wasn't just a familiar face anymore; he was the one constant in her life when everything else had slipped away. Amidst the disappointment and self-doubt, his quiet presence felt like a refuge, his unwavering support the only thing keeping her from falling apart.

As time passed, their bond deepened. What started as companionship turned into something more—something she hadn't planned for but couldn't ignore. In her most vulnerable moment, she found clarity. She looked at Riaz, the one person who had stood by her through it all, and without hesitation, she asked him to marry her.

At the age of 20, Aakanksha's proposal to Riaz wasn't just about love—it was about clinging to something certain in a life that suddenly felt directionless. Unaware of the intricacies and challenges that come with marriage, she saw marriage as a way to secure her future with him. Her youthful innocence, may create an imbalanced dynamic within the relationship, setting the stage for unmet expectations and future complications.

Riaz had always admired Aakanksha's energy and grown fond of her. As an Afghanistani, life in his homeland had its challenges, and an Indian citizenship could open new doors for him. While Aakanksha's proposal wasn't entirely driven by love, Riaz saw the practical side of it. Their bond had grown over time, and the idea of building a future together—one where they could support and uplift each other—felt like the right move.

Aakanksha's immaturity showed in how easily she made life-altering decisions just to be with Riaz, who insisted he could only marry a Muslim girl. Without fully understanding the religion or its long-term impact, she agreed to convert—driven more by her emotions than by awareness of what it truly meant.

A few weeks later, Aakanksha stood inside a mosque, her heart pounding with a mix of excitement and nervousness. The calm, sacred atmosphere, the intricate designs, and the soft echoes of prayer surrounded her. This was it—the moment that would change everything. As she embraced Islam, she took on a new name, Aafreen, a symbol of her transformation and commitment to Riaz. The Imam led the ceremony, his words of blessing sealing their union as the mosque silently bore witness to a love that had reshaped her identity.

They moved into a new apartment, settling into their life as husband and wife. Everything seemed smooth—until one morning. Aakanksha, getting ready for work, slipped into denim shorts and a t-shirt, unaware that it would spark a problem.

Riaz's face tensed. "Maybe you could wear a salwar suit instead? Or even consider a burqa?" he suggested, his tone careful but firm.

Aakanksha froze mid-motion, then turned to him, her expression sharp. "This is not Afghanistan," she said, her voice unwavering. "If you plan to impose orthodox rules on me, forget it. I was free before, and I won't hesitate to divorce you to reclaim that freedom. I hope that's clear."

Riaz was stunned for a moment, then quickly smiled. "Relax, I was just joking," he said, placing a quick kiss on her forehead as she grabbed her bag and left for work. He hoped that would smooth things over.

From that day, he never brought up her clothes again. Shorts, capris, even mini-skirts—he let her be. It wasn't easy for him at first, but he realized he had two choices: accept Aakanksha as she was or risk losing her. And losing her wasn't an option. She didn't want to be changed, controlled, or moulded into someone else's idea of a wife. She just wanted to be loved for who she was.

This new dynamic lasted for months, and though Riaz didn't say much, he often felt a little uneasy. But over time, something changed. Living in Delhi, he slowly got used to its vibrant culture, its openness. More importantly, he began to see things differently—especially Aakanksha's joy in expressing herself through fashion. Slowly, he realized that giving her the freedom to be herself didn't weaken their marriage; it made it stronger. The more he let go, the more they understood each other.

Over time, Riaz found peace in the blend of their cultures. Instead of resisting, he embraced what made their relationship special—Aakanksha's individuality, her spirit. With mutual respect and a bit of give-and-take, they figured out a balance. They weren't just two people from different worlds anymore; they were a team, building something uniquely theirs.

Riaz chose to become a teacher at a coaching institute, refusing to settle for a BPO job that didn't interest him. His salary was less than half of Aakanksha's, but she never complained. They found happiness in their simple life. Over two years, Aakanksha learned to put their shared life above personal indulgences. She skipped shopping sprees to buy a better mattress, held off on new lipsticks to get kitchen essentials. It wasn't that Riaz didn't contribute—he did—but after rent and food, his earnings just weren't enough to cover everything. So, she adjusted, not out of obligation, but out of love.

Some nights, Aakanksha woke up gasping, her father's and Mr. Kanwar's voices echoing in her head. The nightmares felt too real, dragging her back into a past she couldn't escape. In her dreams, her father's disappointment was unmistakable. His voice, cold and accusing, cut through the silence, "You threw away your basketball dreams. You didn't even marry Anshuman. You betrayed my trust."

Then came Mr. Kanwar, his tone sharp with resentment. He reminded her of the day she had lost her temper at his house, throwing accusations back at him. His words stung as he spoke of missed chances and wasted potential, "Your father was right to doubt you. Maybe you deserved it." And in the background, her mother's broken voice. Pleading. Crying. Begging her to marry Anshuman, to listen to her father.

Aakanksha would jolt awake, drenched in sweat, her chest tight. The weight of unfulfilled dreams, of choices made and paths abandoned, pressed down on her. Some nights, it felt unbearable.

Beside Aakanksha, Riaz slept peacefully, unaware of the turmoil raging inside her. She wiped the sweat from her forehead, her breath still uneven from the nightmare. It had been over a year since she last stepped onto a basketball court. Her once agile body now felt sluggish, weighed down by long hours at the office, leaving her body heavier, slower. The reality was harsh—getting back into the game seemed impossible. Their survival depended on her salary, and even if she tried, it would take at least two years of relentless effort just to reach her old skill level. And even then, how could she compete with the girls from Punjab and Haryana, who had never stopped training?

Her dreams, once so vivid, had slowly crumbled. This was her life now—a life where basketball was just a memory. The thought stung, but she had no choice but to accept it. Aakanksha wiped her tears, muffling her sobs so Riaz wouldn't wake up. Eventually, exhaustion took over, and she drifted back into uneasy sleep.

****

4

Lust is to men – as – Flesh is to Lion

> *"A man is lucky, if he is the first love of a woman,
> a woman is the luckiest, if she is the last love of a man."*
> - Charles Dickens

(5th July, 2010 - Gurgaon, Delhi NCR)

Shahid landed in Delhi and joined IBM, taking up a job at their Gurgaon call center. The company, known for its tech solutions and consulting expertise, had a strong reputation. But for Shahid, it was just a job—like hundreds of others, he was hired as an agent to handle customer complaints and offer solutions.

The first few weeks were tough. Heartbroken and lost, Shahid struggled to focus. But time did its job. A few months in, he pushed past the pain and threw himself into work. Within a year, he was among the top customer service agents. In just eleven months, he bagged the "Best Employee of the Month" title five times. His hard work paid off—his salary jumped to ₹18,000 a month. Not bad for a guy who had started with nothing but heartbreak.

As Shahid's first year at the company came to an end, he began to see life beyond lost love. Nikita wasn't meant for him, and he finally made peace with that. Instead of sulking, he chose to move on—new friends, new experiences.

Parties became a regular thing, and so did alcohol. His confidence, charm, and wit made him stand out. Girls noticed. Some, even those already in relationships, showed interest. He never encouraged them, but he didn't mind the attention either. It felt good to be wanted again.

Shahid's faith in women had eroded, crumbling under the weight of betrayal. Every thought of Nikita felt like a treachery, making him believe that most girls were opportunistic. He convinced himself never to get emotionally attached again. Despite his cynicism, his testosterone-driven impulses urged him towards physical intimacy with girls. But he held back, refusing to let impulse dictate his actions.

Shahid and his colleague, Rijith, decided to share a PG in East Delhi—41 kilometers from their office in Gurgaon. The distance was a hassle, but rent was cheap, making it the best option they could afford. Luckily, their office provided a cab service, which made the long commute bearable. Over time, they got used to it, prioritizing money over convenience.

Rijith Pillai was a paradox—both a miser and an extrovert. A Tamilian by birth, he had moved to Jamshedpur, Jharkhand during his high school years. He was the kind of guy who thought twice before spending a rupee but never held back in any conversation, always speaking in English, no matter the setting. Coincidentally, he had been my classmate back in school.

Both Rijith and Shahid joined the company at the same time, though through different recruitment agencies, landing jobs in Gurgaon. Their bond grew quickly, and soon enough, they decided to share a PG—an already cramped space meant for three people but now home to just the two of them.

Two months later, Arshit Choudhury moved in, becoming the third roommate. A computer engineer from Cuttack, Odisha, he had just joined a telecom company and, with a salary of ₹50,000 a month, was the richest among them. Naturally, Shahid and Rijith wondered—why was a high earner like him staying in their budget-friendly PG in East Delhi instead of a posh area? But Arshit never gave a straight answer. He simply smirked and said he was avoiding someone. Even his job switch, he hinted, was part of the escape.

Unlike Shahid and Rijith, who shared bits of their lives freely, Arshit was different. He kept his past locked away, never revealing much. But one night, after a few too many drinks, he let something slip—he had been arrested. Twice. Out on bail.

There was a brief silence after that confession. No one pressed for details. Arshit didn't offer any. And just like that, the conversation moved on, as if those words had never been spoken.

With no family responsibilities holding them back, the three roommates spent their earnings freely—parties, gadgets, and the latest smartphones. Shahid, especially, found himself slipping into the carefree bachelor life, slowly leaving Nikita's memories behind. Their routine was predictable but perfect. Weekdays were for work; weekends were for excess. The motto? Simple—work hard, party harder.

It was a wild Friday night. Shahid, Rijith, and their colleagues were at a rooftop pub, exclusively booked for the company's employees. The vibe was electric—music loud, alcohol unlimited, inhibitions fading fast. People drank past their limits, some too drunk to remember their actions.

In the middle of the chaos, three girls approached Shahid, one of them kissing him out of nowhere. The moment took over, and without a second thought, he led one of them to a secluded spot in the parking lot. What followed was purely physical—no emotions, no regrets. When they were done, they simply walked back to the party, slipping into the crowd as if nothing had happened.

Rijith, meanwhile, had his own story unfolding. He got caught up with a drunk colleague, one thing led to another, and that night, he lost his virginity. The irony? By the next morning, neither of them even remembered the names of the girls they had been with.

By Monday, Shahid felt a strange discomfort. Facing the girl from the party wasn't going to be easy. He wasn't looking for a relationship, but after what had happened, asking her to forget it and move on felt risky. The last thing he wanted was unnecessary drama at work. His reputation mattered.

Lunchtime at the cafeteria was awkward. Both avoided eye contact, the air between them thick with unspoken words. Shahid considered apologizing, maybe clearing the air, but before he could say anything, she spoke first—her voice low, almost secretive, as if making sure no one else heard.

She took a deep breath and said, "Listen, I regret what happened on Friday. It was a mistake. I'm engaged and getting married in a few months. I can't afford any complications. Please, let's just forget it ever happened. And don't mention it to anyone. Please."

Shahid kept a straight face, but inside, amused at his luck, he thought, "Allah's on my side."

Love has a way of leaving an indelible mark on a person's heart. It possesses the power to etch memories deep within one's mind, creating an everlasting imprint. There are instances, however, when a man, consumed by his desires, becomes blinded in the pursuit of mere lust, overshadowing the love he once treasured.

He held her hand lightly, "I wish I could marry you," he admitted, "but don't worry. I won't bother you again. Let's just forget this ever happened."

She smiled, said nothing, and walked away. A week later, she resigned, her reason simple—she was getting married.

Even more bizarre! Shahid still didn't know her name.

On the flip side, Rijith found himself a girlfriend—Shweta. They talked endlessly whenever they had time and spent weekends going on dates—movies, fancy dinners, and the occasional stay at an OYO room.

Meanwhile, Arshit, too, was in a relationship with Saesha—a girl so breathtaking that even Shahid and Rijith couldn't help but notice. Tall, confident, and with a figure sculpted like a Victoria's Secret model. She had a perfect balance of curves that made people look twice, even the most committed men. With a degree in mass communication, she worked as a Public Relations Manager, effortlessly blending charm with intelligence.

Shahid and Rijith often wondered how Arshit had managed to attract someone like Saesha. A sexy girl from a different organisation and that too—he in IT, she in media relations—it didn't quite add up. Whenever they asked, Arshit dodged the question with a smile, never giving a straight answer. The secrecy only made them more curious. But no matter how much they tried, they couldn't figure out what really sparked the chemistry between him and Saesha.

Weekends had a routine—Rijith and Arshit disappeared with their girlfriends, leaving Shahid on his own. Not that he minded. Relationships didn't interest him. Instead, he preferred the company of beer, cigarettes, and the occasional stranger at a bar.

Occasionally, he'd meet women who were just as unattached as he was. Some nights, he met drunk girls, shared a drink, and if things aligned, ended up in a night together, without worrying about the emotional or moral consequences. He was always clear—no commitment, no expectations. If someone also wanted commitment, he walked away.

Before long, Shahid earned the reputation of a playboy. Most girls avoided talking to him unless they needed a favor. He didn't mind. Shweta didn't like Shahid and thought he was a bad influence but that didn't stop Rijith from hanging out with him. However, Rijith had to maintain a balance. When he was with Shweta, he completely avoided talking to Shahid—almost as if they weren't friends at all. Shahid understood and never complained.

Over time, they realized that getting drunk wasn't as fun as it used to be. Alcohol had become expensive, and worse, their bodies had built a tolerance to it. The buzz didn't last long, but they had grown addicted to the feeling—those few hours of freedom where nothing else mattered. That's when Arshit came up with an alternative—marijuana. It was cheaper, stronger, and way more satisfying. The only catch? It was illegal. Getting it from street peddlers was called "scoring," and the product itself was referred to as "stuff." They'd mix it with tobacco, roll it into a cigarette, and light up—a "joint." And when the high kicked in, they'd call it—"being stoned."

Most of their non-working hours were spent in a haze, comfortably stoned. Their landlord didn't care as long as the rent was paid on time. In fact, when his wife was away, he sometimes joined them for a smoke.

Smoking had become more than a habit—it was a necessity, sometimes even replacing food. Saesha often hung out with them, and weekends were spent in their tiny room, passing joints and devouring pizza. Meanwhile, Rijith's culinary preferences revolved around momos, which he consumed for breakfast, lunch, and dinner, varying only the stuffing. Ever since landing in Delhi in 2010, he had fallen in love with them so much that colleagues had given him a fitting nickname—"Momojith."

Arshit had figured out the best setup—he pushed two single beds together to make a larger one for himself and Saesha whenever she stayed over. Rijith took the remaining bed, while Shahid, ever the accommodating one, chose the floor without a fuss. Shahid's patience went beyond just sleeping arrangements. He often waited for everyone to eat before having his dinner, never once complaining. Oddly enough, their room had no mosquitoes. Turns out, the constant haze of smoke from their endless joints worked better than any repellent.

One weekend evening, Shahid was alone in the room when there was a knock at the door. It was Saesha. "Arshit's not here," he said as he opened it.

"I know," she replied, stepping inside. "He called while I was on my way. Some system failure at work—he might not be back until morning. And he also told that Rijith's off to his hometown for Pongal. So, looks like it's just you here tonight."

Shahid nodded.

"I could use a smoke," she added casually.

Shahid nodded, shutting the door behind her.

Saesha had brought some stuff with her, intending to smoke it with all of them but decided to try it with Shahid till Arshit arrived. They rolled up, lit a joint, munched on burgers, and washed it all down with beer. The hours melted away in smoke and conversation.

By midnight, they decided to call it a night. Saesha dragged a single bed next to Shahid's, then casually removed her T-shirt. "Too humid," she muttered, now in just a black bra, before lying down beside him. Shahid, though high, felt a little uneasy. But he stayed quiet.

Saesha reached for his hand, pulled it close, and rested her head on his shoulder, with her orbs pressing his chest. "I've heard you're quite the playboy at work," Saesha said, a teasing smile on her lips.

Shahid raised an eyebrow, "Who told you that?"

"Arshit. And he heard it from Rijith."

Shahid smirked, "Gossip. None of it's true."

"Hmm... let's agree to disagree." She leaned in closer, her eyes locking onto his. "But I'd rather see your 'playboy skills' myself before deciding if it's just a rumour."

Before Shahid could react, she pressed her lips against his, catching him completely off guard.

A sudden wave of discomfort hit Shahid, and without thinking, he pushed her away. He got up from the bed and walked out, blurting, "Your breath smells like a dustbin."

He hadn't meant to be harsh—he just needed space. But in the moment, he couldn't find the right words, and that's what came out.

Feeling humiliated, Saesha quickly put on her T-shirt, grabbed her phone, and booked a cab. Without saying a word, she walked out. "Boys would kill each other to have a piece of me, and this idiot just rejected me completely," she thought, fuming. "No doubt, 'the playboy' is just a rumor."

For the next two years, the three roommates continued wasting time and money on their reckless lifestyle. Meanwhile, Arshit and Rijith had their own drama—constant fights with their girlfriends, followed by breakups and patch-ups. It never felt like they were meant to be together, but maybe they stayed simply because they had no better options.

None of them had a clear plan for the future, nor did they seem in a hurry to change anything. But one shift was noticeable—they cut down on their wild weekends. Instead of partying non-stop, they now limited it to once a month. The rest of the weekends were spent either with friends or their partners, a small sign that maybe, just maybe, they were starting to grow up.

One weekend, Rijith and Shweta were at a pub in Gurgaon, sipping beers and enjoying the evening—until a heated argument changed the mood. Annoyed, Shweta broke up and stormed out, leaving Rijith alone with his drink.

He moved to a quiet corner, watching the bubbles rise in his glass, lost in thought. The dim lights, the hum of conversations, the faint bass of the music—everything faded into the background.

And then, out of nowhere, a familiar face walked in.

Saesha.

But she wasn't alone. She was with a man—older, well-dressed, and confident. He held her hand, not casually, but with a certain authority.

Rijith's curiosity got the better of him. From his quiet corner, he watched them—talking, laughing, clinking glasses. There was something between them, something more than just casual friendship. As the night wore on, they got up and walked out together. Their footsteps faded into the distance, leaving Rijith with more questions than answers.

Curiosity got the best of Rijith, and without thinking, he followed them, through the empty streets. They stopped at a nearby high-end hotel, where Saesha and the man walked in without a second glance, disappearing behind the grand entrance. Rijith hesitated outside, his heart pounding as he checked his watch, realizing that only a few minutes had passed, yet it felt like hours.

Time slipped away as a drunk Rijith waited restlessly, his mind racing with possibilities. Finally, the hotel doors swung open, and Saesha stepped out with the man. There was something in their expressions—an unspoken secrecy, a story left untold. Rijith walked toward her, his heart heavy with questions. Saesha met his gaze, her eyes a mix of guilt and exhaustion, the weight of the moment pressing between them.

Saesha simply said to the man, he was a friend and that they would leave together. The man offered to drop them off, but she declined, saying they'd stay a little longer. With a nod, he walked away, leaving behind a storm of emotions and unanswered questions.

"You don't need to explain," Rijith said, his voice unsteady, caught between concern and betrayal. "I saw everything."

Saesha's eyes widened, her face turning pale. "Rijith, I can explain," she stammered, struggling to find the right words. "He's the CEO of our company... and I... I got involved to secure a promotion."

The truth hit Rijith like a sudden storm, washing away whatever trust he had in her. His mind spun, torn between two choices. One part of him screamed to call Arshit, to reveal everything. The other, weighed down by confusion and vulnerability, told him to stay quiet. Without saying much, they walked in silence. Eventually, they found themselves near an ice cream parlour, sitting side by side, licking chocolate cones.

"Why, Saesha?" Rijith asked, his voice a mix of concern and disappointment. "Was a promotion really worth losing your integrity?"

Saesha took a deep breath, staring at her trembling hands. "I know, Rijith. I used to think the same," she said, her voice barely above a whisper. "But in the real world, hard work isn't always enough. The corporate game is brutal. Talent alone doesn't cut it—smartness and ambition do. I saw a chance, a shortcut to success... and I took it."

Rijith frowned, struggling to make sense of her words. "But Saesha, what about principles? Values?"

Saesha looked at him, her eyes a mix of regret and defiance. "I never wanted to compromise, Rijith. But the system, the competition... it forces you to. I watched others move ahead—not because they were better, but because they knew how to play the game. I didn't want to be left behind."

Her voice grew steadier, more resolute. "Hard work gets you recognition, but smart work gets you ahead—money, status, opportunities. It's not just about deserving it; it's about navigating corporate politics. And in that game, ambition often outruns morality."

Rijith stayed quiet, absorbing her words. A part of him understood—the race for success, the fear of being left behind. But another part refused to accept it. Shouldn't integrity and love be enough, "And Arshit? What about the love you two share?" he finally asked, his voice laced with doubt.

She let out a sharp laugh. "You really have no idea about Arshit, do you? And trust me, he's not going to tell you either. You'll never know why he was in jail or how we even met. I don't know if he's shared anything with you, but if you ever find out the truth about him, everything will make sense."

Saesha had a sharp eye for reading people, and Rijith's face told her everything she needed to know. He wouldn't be able to keep this secret. He'd tell Arshit. Panic set in. Fear turned into desperation, and desperation led to an impulsive decision. She needed to control the situation. "I'm not feeling well," she said suddenly, clutching her head. "Can you take me to a hotel? Just for a while?"

Rijith hesitated, but eventually agreed to take her to a nearby hotel. Once inside the dimly lit room, she offered herself physically, the air grew heavy. Saesha stepped closer, her every move calculated.

Rijith's heart pounded, caught between his morals and the intoxicating pull of the forbidden. He knew he should resist, that giving in would only drag them both deeper into a mess they couldn't escape. He knew the consequences, the damage it would do to his principles, his self-respect.

Yet, Saesha's beauty, the way she looked at him with vulnerability, pulled him in. The lines blurred as she moved even closer, testing the strength of his principles, one step at a time. His mind screamed at him to walk away, but his body betrayed him, drawn to the moment, the heat, the danger. His judgment blurred, and for a moment, everything else—morality, loyalty, consequences—faded into the background.

He felt her breath against his skin, her body inching closer, closing the space between them. Their bodies intertwined in a passionate dance of stolen moments, each moment carrying with it a profound sense of shame and regret.

As they lay there, the weight of their choices hung thick in the air. The silence was suffocating until Saesha finally spoke, her voice a mix of triumph and bitterness. "See, Rijith," she whispered, her tone laden with accusation. "You lectured me about principles and integrity, yet you couldn't resist the temptation of a beautiful girl. It's always easier to talk about morals than to actually live by them."

As Saesha got dressed to leave, she turned to him, her eyes sharp, her voice cold. "If you ever speak a word about this," she said, her tone laced with chilling warning, "I can always file an FIR for rape. You know what that would mean for you."

Rijith froze. His mind spun, trying to process what had just happened, what she had just said. He stood there, trapped in the mess they had created, teetering on the edge of a disaster he never saw coming.

Rijith met Saesha's gaze, searching for any sign of bluff, but what he saw instead was something new—an unshakable determination. He had seen her argue with Arshit before, even fight passionately, but this was different. This time, she wasn't just defending herself in a relationship; she was protecting her entire existence—personal and professional—and she was ready to do whatever it took.

Rijith swallowed, his heart hammering in his chest. He knew Saesha too well to mistake this for an empty threat. She wasn't just reacting—she had calculated every move, leaving him cornered in a web of confusion and fear, unsure of how to escape.

In that moment, Rijith's instincts screamed at him to stay quiet, to lock away the truth and carry the weight of their secret alone. The fear of losing his friendship with Arshit, tightened around him like a noose, making it hard to breathe.

For a week, Rijith tossed and turned in bed, sleep eluding him. The incident played on a loop in his mind, a tangled mess of pleasure, guilt, and regret. No matter how much he tried to justify it, the thought of betraying Arshit gnawed at him. When Saesha showed up at their place, he avoided her gaze, pretending she wasn't there. But the weight of what had happened sat heavy on his chest. His roommates noticed something was off, but Rijith kept it to himself, unwilling—maybe unable—to talk about it.

One day, Rijith came up with a story. He told Shahid and Arshit that Shweta had given him an ultimatum—either move in with her or risk losing the relationship. He acted torn, pretending he didn't want to leave his roommates but had no choice. Shahid and Arshit believed it instantly. They laughed at his so-called "trouble" and happily gave him their blessing to move in with Shweta. "Lucky guy," Shahid smirked. "But if she ever kicks you out, don't worry. Our door's always open."

A few weeks later, Arshit moved out too, shifting to Okhla with Saesha. With Rijith already gone, that left Shahid alone in the PG. Nights felt longer now. He spent them smoking weed, lost in thoughts—his past, his family, and the memories of Nikita that still lingered.

Months passed, and Rijith eventually settled back to normalcy. The three of them still met once in a while, maybe every few months, but something had changed. The wild parties, the carefree laughter—none of it felt the same. Life had pulled them in different directions, and the bond they once shared had quietly faded into the past. Meanwhile,

Shweta had an arranged marriage within her caste, and Rijith, surprisingly, felt genuinely happy for her.

Shahid no longer felt the need for superficial relationships. His priorities had shifted, and ambition took center stage. His company, known for its progressive policies, never cared about employees' personal lives as long as they performed. Shahid, despite his reputation, was no exception. His choices outside the office never interfered with his professional growth, and he continued moving up, unaffected by whispers or judgment.

Despite his success, and the attention he got, Shahid felt an emptiness he couldn't ignore. The casual flings, the temporary romances—they no longer meant anything. He wanted something real, something beyond just physical attraction. Hoping to find that missing piece, he began dating outside his workplace, searching for someone who could fill the void and bring meaning to his life.

Shahid met several women, each with her own charm. Some were drawn to his confidence, others to the thrill of being with him. But as he navigated these relationships, a realization hit him—none of them offered the love and connection he craved. They were exciting, but empty. Meaningless. And with every passing day, the void inside him only grew deeper.

Determined not to give up, Shahid put himself out there. He attended social events, joined clubs, and explored places where he might meet like-minded people. Along the way, he met others who, like him, were searching for something real—companionship beyond momentary attraction. Through these interactions, he realized he wasn't alone in his quest.

Late at night, when sleep evaded him, memories of Nikita surfaced like uninvited guests, settling deep into his soul. No matter how much time passed, she remained a part of him, a love that refused to fade. As time passed, he started valuing real connections, choosing emotional intimacy over physical desires.

Yet, there are moments when Shahid, driven by primal urges, lost himself in the pursuit of physical pleasure, losing sight of the love he once held dear. Lust, with its seductive allure, blinds him to the beauty of true love, clouding his judgment and distorting his priorities.

Shahid no longer insisted on keeping things casual. He stayed with the same woman for months before eventually parting ways. He genuinely wanted love but refused to compromise his self-respect and values for it.

Even when deeply drawn to someone, his principles remained intact. If a relationship felt forced or unfulfilling, he and his partner chose to step back, giving each other the space to grow and reflect rather than clinging to something that wasn't meant to be.

Caught in this pursuit of lust, Shahid momentarily forgets the woman he once loved. The deep connection, the quiet moments of tenderness, the vulnerability they shared—all of it faded into the background. The memories that once felt sacred were drowned by the thrill of the present, blurring the lines between love and desire.

****

5
The Curse

*"When God gives you a new beginning,
don't repeat the same mistake..."*
-Anonymous

(07ᵗʰ September, 2012 – High Court, Delhi)

A bombing took place in India's capital on Wednesday, 7 September 2012, outside Gate No. 5 of the Delhi High Court. A suspected briefcase bomb detonated at the court's reception, a spot crowded with people attending hearings. The blast claimed 15 lives and left 79 injured, turning an ordinary morning into chaos and tragedy.

According to reports following the blast, the terrorist group Harkat-ul-Jihad al-Islami (HuJI) claimed responsibility. They allegedly demanded that Mohammed Afzal Guru, convicted for the 2001 Indian Parliament attack, not be hanged as ordered by the Supreme Court.

On the night of their third wedding anniversary, Aakanksha poured her heart into the celebrations. She cooked Chicken Biryani, Mutton Korma, and Vegetable

Raita, filling their home with rich aromas. She decorated the space with flowers, balloons, and soft candlelight, creating the perfect setting for a romantic dinner with Riaz.

Completely unaware of the day's events, she was excited to surprise her husband. Riaz, too, walked in with a gift for her, but his mood was slightly off—his mind still lingering on the tragic incident at the High Court earlier that day.

Not wanting to dampen Aakanksha's excitement, Riaz masked his emotions and reached into his office bag. "Close your eyes," he whispered. She obeyed, smiling with anticipation. Turning her gently, he clasped a gold necklace around her neck, its heart-shaped diamond pendant catching the candlelight.

When she opened her eyes and saw it, her lips parted in awe, her fingers trembling as they traced the delicate piece. "Riaz... this is beautiful," she murmured, still mesmerized.

"This looks expensive." She remarked.

" "It is," he admitted with a smile. "But nothing compared to you. I know I haven't given you many gifts over the years, and I wanted to make this one special, something you'll always remember."

Aakanksha kept insisting on knowing the price of the necklace, but Riaz just smiled and refused to answer. After their romantic dinner, they went to bed, wrapped in the warmth of the evening. She rested her head on his chest as he leaned against the headboard, his fingers gently tracing her back. Riaz kissed her forehead, then moved closer, about to kiss her lips when she stopped him. "Tell me first," she whispered. "How much did it cost?"

He sighed, realizing she wouldn't let it go. Finally, he reached for his phone and showed her the bill—₹1,25,000. Her eyes widened. "Riaz, where did you get that kind of money?"

He hesitated for a moment before answering. "I borrowed it from a friend, Ushman."

"Ushman? But none of your friends are well-off enough to lend that much."

"Well, you've never met him. Back in 2006, when I first came to Delhi, Ushman and I shared a room in North-East Delhi. I didn't know a soul in the city, and he had already been here for two years. He had come from Pakistan to study software engineering." Riaz continued, "He was quiet, and we barely spoke. Some days, he'd attend college regularly, and then there were weeks when he wouldn't step out of the room at all."

"So weird."

""Yeah, definitely weird," Riaz said. "I moved to Laxmi Nagar for my studies and never thought about him again. Then today, after 4-5 years, I ran into him—outside a jeweller's shop." He paused, recalling the moment. "I was just looking at the gold on display, checking out the price tags, wishing I could buy even a small ring for you. Just as I was leaving, he called my name." Riaz exhaled, still puzzled. "Maybe he had noticed me staring at the jewelry. I told him about us, our anniversary, and how I wanted to buy you something but couldn't afford it. And then... he did something strange."

"What did he do?"

"He took me inside the store and insisted on buying the necklace for you. I told him a simple gold ring in the ₹5000-6000 range was enough, but he refused and went for the necklace instead." Riaz paused, recalling the moment. "I told him I might not be able to repay him anytime soon, but he just smiled and said I could return it whenever I could. He didn't even give me his phone number—just told me to visit him at the same room we once shared in North-East Delhi."

"He must have a really kind heart," Aakanksha said, lost in thought, wondering about the generosity of Ushman.

Riaz's face grew serious as he said, "I don't know. But today has been strange... and dangerous. I thank Allah that I'm here with you, celebrating our anniversary. If I had been just 30 minutes late, I might not have been alive to see this day."

Aakanksha's brows furrowed with concern as she asked, "Why do you say that, Riaz? What happened?"

After buying the gift, Riaz was about to leave for his university when Ushman stopped him with a request. He looked rushed, explaining that his day was packed—an important meeting with an international client and a legal hearing at the Delhi High Court regarding some income tax issues. He pulled out a briefcase, secured with a number lock. "This has important business documents," he said, his tone urgent. "I can't afford to miss either of my appointments. Can you do me a favour? Just drop this off with my lawyer's driver. He'll be waiting for it near Gate No. 5 of the High Court."

Curious, Aakanksha asked, "And then?"

Ushman assured him that finding the driver would be easy - a young man in his twenties, wearing a maroon T-shirt with the phrase "If we must die, we die defending our rights" written in Urdu. Since Riaz could read Urdu, there was no chance of missing him. Riaz hesitated for a moment, aware of his packed schedule and looming lectures. But Ushman had helped him and therefore, Riaz agreed to do him the favor.

Riaz took a deep breath and looked at Aakanksha. "You probably haven't heard the news yet," he said, his voice tense. "There was a bombing at the Delhi High Court today. A terrorist attack—right at Gate No. 5." Aakanksha's eyes widened in shock, but he continued. "That's exactly where I delivered Ushman's briefcase. If I had been just 30 minutes late... I might not be sitting here with you right now."

Aakanksha froze, his words echoing in her mind. A chill ran down her spine and without thinking, she threw her arms around him, holding him as if she might lose him any second. Tears streamed down her face as she whispered, "You're all I have, Riaz. Promise me... you'll never leave me."

Riaz held her close. "We're not alone, Aakanksha. Allah is with us."

He wiped her tears, reminding her of the day's unexpected blessings. "I got you the perfect gift without planning, and we escaped something terrible."

She sighed, holding him tighter, feeling a wave of relief. In that moment, love overshadowed fear. In that tender moment, he reciprocated her embrace, and together they embarked on a romantic journey, celebrating their most extraordinary anniversary ever.

Sketches of the three suspects were distributed across intelligence units and Delhi police stations. Despite an intense manhunt, the second suspect remained untraceable. Just as Delhi was still reeling from the blast another shocking incident shook the city within three months.

On 16 December 2012, in Munirka, a neighbourhood in South West Delhi, a horrific crime shook the nation. A 22-year-old physiotherapy intern was brutally assaulted, tortured, and gang-raped inside a private bus while traveling with her male friend. The six men on board, including the driver, attacked them both. The woman suffered severe injuries and was rushed to Safdarjung Hospital. Eleven days later, she was moved to Singapore for treatment, but two days after her arrival, she succumbed to her injuries. The incident sent shockwaves across the country, igniting a movement for justice.

Since Indian law prohibits revealing a rape victim's name, she came to be known as Nirbhaya, meaning "fearless." Her fight and tragic death became a symbol of women's resistance to sexual violence worldwide. The 2012 Delhi gang rape and murder was forever remembered as the Nirbhaya case.

The incident sparked nationwide outrage and global condemnation. Media coverage was relentless, both in India and abroad. Aakanksha felt a personal connection to the victim, as if the attack had happened to her. Anger burned within her—not just for Nirbhaya, but for every woman who lived in fear. She blamed the authorities, convinced that if the police had been more vigilant, this tragedy could have been prevented.

Women's rights activists and NGOs called for nationwide protests, urging women from across the country to march toward Parliament and Rashtrapati Bhawan on 21st December 2012. The outrage spread like wildfire. In Delhi, thousands took to the streets, demanding justice and clashing with security forces. Similar protests erupted in major cities, a collective outcry against the government's failure to ensure women's safety. Aakanksha, unable to sit back, took leave from work and joined the protests. She stood among the crowd, her voice loud and fearless, demanding answers from the government and police.

The incident dominated news channels, with powerful images and videos of determined women marching toward Rashtrapati Bhawan, their voices echoing across the nation. As the protest escalated, thousands clashed with the police and Rapid Action Force units. Baton charges, water cannons, and tear gas filled the streets, but the crowd refused to back down. The standoff led to multiple arrests, but the fire of resistance only burned stronger.

Colonel Jitendra Singh Rana sat glued to his television screen, closely following the escalating protests. As an army officer, he viewed the situation through a different lens—what had started as a peaceful demonstration now seemed hijacked by unruly elements and politically driven activists. To him, it was no longer just about justice; it was a security threat that needed to be controlled before it spiralled further.

As he watched the footage, his eyes narrowed at a particular scene—a woman locked in a heated scuffle with the police. They grabbed her arms, trying to drag her into a police van, but she fought back fiercely. With one swift side kick, she sent a policeman tumbling to the ground. Another tried to restrain her by yanking her hair, but she twisted his arm and threw him down as if he were a bean-bag. Before anyone could react, she darted into the dense crowd, disappearing into the chaos, before two policemen chasing her, lost sight of her in the crowd. The moment played on a loop across news channels, leaving Colonel Rana in a storm of emotions—pride, anger, disbelief, as he witnessed the awe-inspiring spectacle. The fearless girl on the screen, defying authority, fighting back with all her might, was none other than his daughter, Aakanksha.

The next day, on 22nd December, authorities shut down seven metro stations in Delhi to curb the growing protests at Raisina Hill. By 24th December, the police tightened restrictions further, blocking roads leading to India Gate and Raisina Hill and closing nine metro stations, leaving thousands of commuters stranded.

Media access was restricted, with journalists barred from covering the protests. Section 144 was imposed, banning gatherings of more than five people, and a curfew was enforced near the Presidential residence. Reports emerged of excessive force—375 tear gas shells were fired at India Gate and other parts of Delhi to disperse the protesters.

Colonel Rana wasted no time. He reached out to his contacts in the army, informing them about his daughter's presence at the protest. The regret of his past mistakes weighed heavily on him—he had to find her, to bring her back home.

His associates in Delhi immediately alerted the Commissioner of Police, explaining that Colonel Rana's daughter was missing and had last been seen at the protests near India Gate, captured in a news broadcast. The

Commissioner swiftly acted, gathering details about the news channel and the exact time she appeared on screen.

Video footage was retrieved from the news agency, and soon after, the Commissioner contacted Colonel Rana, seeking more information about his daughter.

Colonel Rana recounted everything to the Commissioner—the events that led to Aakanksha leaving home, the anger and humiliation he had felt when she tarnished his reputation in society. He admitted that while he had tried to locate her, he had never truly put in the effort, convinced she would eventually return on her own, defeated and exhausted.

But after seeing her on TV and after four days of reflection that followed, he realized that it wasn't entirely her fault. He had been wrong too. She was just 18 when he tried to force marriage upon her, when he should have been guiding her toward education and a career.

Watching her fearlessly fight for her rights, made him see her in a new light. She hadn't changed. She was still the same girl—strong, defiant, unwilling to bow down to anyone who tried to take away what was hers. And just like that, his resentment melted away. All the mistakes, all the past conflicts seemed insignificant. She was still his daughter, and she deserved another chance.

The Commissioner reviewed the footage and issued an urgent alert to all Delhi police stations, instructing them to locate Aakanksha but not to harm her. Knowing her strength and resistance, he ordered that at least three to four female constables be assigned to detain her, a single constable may not be able to take her down. Once found, she was to be escorted safely to Shimla, with strict orders that no case be filed against her. Additionally, it should be ensured that she is not given access to any media or lawyer.

After a two-day search, a tip-off led the Laxmi Nagar Police straight to Aakanksha's location. Without wasting time, they moved in. As they approached the house, an unusual sight greeted them—four to five men in plain clothes lingering nearby. It was clear who was in charge—one man stood apart, commanding silent respect from the rest.

To clear the path for his Police Station In-Charge, a constable stepped forward, brimming with authority, barked at the group's leader, demanding he clear the way. His tone carried an air of arrogance, expecting immediate obedience. The leader, unfazed, met his gaze for a brief second before delivering a sharp, resounding slap. The impact was brutal—the world momentarily distorted for the constable, as if day turned to night in the midst of broad daylight, leaving him to see stars.

The entire police team stood frozen, stunned by what had just unfolded. Before they could react, the mysterious leader calmly reached into his pocket and pulled out an ID card. He held it up, just enough for the Police Station In-Charge to catch a glimpse of the bold lettering: "National Investigation Agency".

In that instant, nothing else on the card mattered. The In-Charge snapped into a salute, quickly followed by the other constables. Their arrogance vanished, replaced by silent submission. Without a word, they stepped aside, making way for the NIA officer.

The NIA officers exchanged glances, a flicker of doubt passing through their ranks. Their mission had been discreet, yet somehow, the local police had caught wind of it. Not wanting to compromise the operation, the senior officer signalled his team to hold back, warning against any hasty moves. On the flip side, the local police were equally perplexed. Who was this woman, Aakanksha? What had she done for the NIA to personally intervene in her capture?

The NIA team reached Aakanksha's fourth-floor apartment; their presence discreet but heavily armed. A few officers remained hidden, scanning the surroundings, fingers ready on the trigger in case things went south. A firm knock on the door jolted Aakanksha from her thoughts. She opened it, surprised to see a group of serious-looking men in front of her. Before she could process what was happening, one of them cut straight to the point— "Where is Riaz?"

Before Aakanksha could even respond, Riaz stepped out of the bedroom, his face clouded with confusion. The moment he appeared; the lead NIA officer's hand flew instinctively to his gun. "Hands up! Kneel!" the officer shouted.

The room tensed in an instant. Aakanksha froze, eyes darting between Riaz and the officers, struggling to grasp what was happening. The remaining NIA officers followed suit, separating Aakanksha from Riaz, their guns stayed locked on him as they edged closer and pressed Riaz for a surrender.

The police officers stood on the ground floor, watching as the NIA team escorted a man in handcuffs. His voice rang out in frustration, demanding to know why he was being taken. Behind him, Aakanksha struggled, her face red with panic as she tried to push past the officers. She pleaded, but they blocked her at every step. Without wasting another second, the NIA agents forced Riaz into their vehicle and sped away, leaving behind a cloud of dust and unanswered questions.

Amidst the chaos, it initially appeared that the NIA had come for Aakanksha, but their real target was Riaz. Meanwhile, the Commissioner of Police had ordered her arrest, leading to a bizarre twist—two people from the same house were now wanted by two different law enforcement agencies.

The police officers stood frozen, their minds struggling to keep up with the madness unraveling before them. "What the hell just happened?" one of them muttered, but no one had an answer.

Aakanksha lay on the road, her face streaked with tears of pain. Two lady constables approached, each extending a hand to help her up. Their voices were calm yet firm as they asked her to come with them to the police station. She didn't resist. In her mind, she connected the people who had taken Riaz with the police officials. She believed they were one and the same, and that they were leading her to Riaz's location. Filled with this conviction, she followed them willingly, without putting up any resistance.

The moment Aakanksha stepped into the police station, her eyes darted around, searching for Riaz. But he was nowhere to be seen. Panic set in as she turned to the officers, demanding answers. Their silence only deepened her unease. The Police exchanged confused glances, as if they, too, were trying to piece things together. Finally, one of them informed the commissioner—they had brought in the girl who had been living with the man, arrested by the NIA.

The commissioner, stunned by the revelation, instructed his team to quietly detain Aakanksha for a few days. He needed time to dig deeper into her connection with the man she had been living with. The shocking truth unraveled—Riaz, the second absconding terrorist, linked to the blast, wasn't just any suspect. He was Aakanksha's husband. When the commissioner relayed this to Colonel Rana, the news left him shaken, grappling with the weight of what it meant and what he should do next.

The commissioner was certain that Aakanksha had no involvement in the case. However, given her marital ties to Riaz—now confirmed as a terrorist—he needed clearance from the NIA before sending her to Shimla. Colonel Rana, determined to bring his daughter home, reached out to his senior contacts in the army, who in turn liaised with the NIA. The outcome was reassuring—Aakanksha had been under NIA surveillance and her innocence had been observed by the vigilant NIA. She had no link to the blast, sparing her from arrest.

With no charges against her, Aakanksha was finally released—but not to freedom. A few days of confinement later, she was quietly escorted into a private vehicle under the watchful eyes of lady constables. The journey unfolded under the cover of night, stretching through winding roads and fading city lights.

By dawn, they arrived at a secluded villa, its surroundings blanketed in pristine snow. As she stepped out, her eyes fell on a familiar figure at the entrance—a tall, imposing man in a dignified grey overcoat. 'The Colonel'.

Unaware of the maneuvers happening behind the scenes during her custody, Aakanksha found herself trapped in a maze of uncertainty. The silence, the unanswered questions, the abrupt transfer—it all felt like a conspiracy. In the absence of clarity, her mind filled in the blanks, weaving a web of misunderstandings.

Aakanksha was certain that her father was the mastermind behind all her suffering. In her mind, he had orchestrated Riaz's arrest and torn them apart once again. The struggles she faced in Delhi had, for a brief time, softened her resentment, even allowing traces of forgiveness to creep in. But now, this fresh betrayal reignited the bitterness, stronger than it had been four years ago. It was as if nothing had changed—her father remained the same, rigid and unyielding. Memories of her forced engagement to Anshuman resurfaced, each one a painful reminder of the battles she had fought, only to find herself trapped in yet another.

Overcome with emotion, she burst out, "Why can't you just let me live in peace? I never asked for your help, yet you always find a way to ruin my happiness."

The Colonel struggled to understand the storm inside Aakanksha's mind. He could only assume she was furious about being forced back home. Instead of arguing, he remained silent, knowing she had every right to be upset with him.

Hearing the commotion, Gayatri quickly followed the noise and stepped outside, finding Aakanksha standing there. Without a second thought, she walked toward her. The moment Aakanksha saw her mother, all her anger melted away. She rushed into her arms, holding her tightly as tears streamed down their faces. For four long minutes, neither of them let go. Then, with quiet understanding, Gayatri led her inside, offering the warmth and comfort of home.

After freshening up and having breakfast, Aakanksha's curiosity turned to her brother. Gayatri smiled as she shared the news—he had cleared the Services Selection Board (SSB). He's currently in training, aspiring to follow in the footsteps of Captain Vikram Batra, the courageous Kargil Hero.

Then, after a pause, Gayatri opened up about Anshuman. She revealed how deeply hurt he had been after Aakanksha left. This deeply affected him, leading to a period of sadness where he lost both his job and Aakanksha. He even claimed that you told him that you weren't a virgin. For a while, he was under depression. But with time and medical support he managed to recover. He later pursued an MBA from IIM and secured a job abroad. Now, he had moved on, settled in another country, with no plans of ever returning to India.

"Did he get married?"

"No, not yet. He even mentioned that he intends to marry a girl of his own choosing, someone who he believes has good character, unlike what he thought about you."

Aakanksha felt sorry for him and let out a bitter laugh, saying, "And what about his father?"

"He was the calmest of them all," Gayatri said. "Your father was torn between anger and betrayal. Anshuman crumbled into depression. Your brother was furious, not because of what you did, but because he couldn't stand seeing your father so broken. But amidst all this, it was Anshuman's father who remained unshaken. He carried on as if nothing had happened, managing his responsibilities like any other day. He even advised your dad to take a few weeks off, putting everything aside, and return to work without letting emotions cloud his judgment."

As the day went on, Gayatri lovingly cooked all of Aakanksha's favorite dishes. On any other day, she would have savored every bite, but today, the flavors felt distant. Her mind was elsewhere—restless, heavy with worry for Riaz. No matter what, she had to find a way to help him.

After lunch, Aakanksha gathered her courage and approached her father. "I want to leave," she said firmly. "I'm married, and I need to be with my husband."

Her father's expression hardened. He had expected resistance but not this. He stared at her for a moment, searching for some hesitation in her eyes. Finally, in a steady voice, he asked, "Do you even understand what your husband has been accused of?"

Aakanksha's voice shook with fury as she snapped, "He's innocent! You framed him just to bring me back here. But let me make one thing clear—I won't abandon him, no matter what you say. You already shattered my dreams when you kept me off the basketball team. And now, you expect me to believe these lies about my husband?"

The Colonel tried to reason with her, but Aakanksha refused to back down. Her resolve to be with Riaz only strengthened. Frustrated, he finally lost his temper and thundered, "You're staying in this house, and that's final! Do whatever you want—play basketball, go to college, stay single for life—but you're not going back to Delhi."

Sensing the tension rising, Gayatri quickly stepped between them. She placed a reassuring hand on Aakanksha's shoulder and gently led her away. "Not now," she whispered. "Let him cool down first. Talk to him when he's in a better frame of mind."

Through her tears, Aakanksha sobbed and asserted, "Riaz is not a terrorist."

Gayatri said, "He is. Riaz is the second suspect—the one who handed over the bomb to the person behind the explosion."

"How can you be so sure? Just like father conspired against me four years ago, maybe he's done the same to Riaz. And yet, you believe it."

"No, he's changed. You don't know this, but the day he saw you on TV, protesting and kicking that policeman, he broke down. He regretted every selfish move he made against you. He wanted to make things right. He swore that if you ever came back, he'd let you play basketball, never force you into marriage. But he had no idea you were already married. When he asked the Commissioner of Police to bring you home, he learned the truth—that you were married to an Afghan man, a suspected terrorist."

"How do you know all this?"

"Your father told me."

"I see. But what if he has concocted another story like he did with me? I can't trust him. I know Riaz better than my father or the Commissioner of Police. He's not a terrorist."

A few days of commotion went by, but the grand villa began to haunt Aakanksha. She longed for the warmth of her husband's embrace and the coziness of their small apartment, which the villa failed to provide.

That night, as her parents slept, Aakanksha decided to leave—just like she had four years ago. She was certain no one would notice, just as they hadn't back then. But as she stepped onto the veranda, ready to disappear into the night, her father's voice cut through the silence, "If you walk out of this house for *that* bastard, consider yourself *disowned.*"

Aakanksha halted for a moment, her eyes locking onto her father's. With unwavering resolve, she said, "I don't need you as long as I have Riaz." The words hung heavy in the air. Hearing the commotion, her mother rushed in, only to find her daughter standing at the door, a bag of clothes in hand, ready to walk away.

"I will not leave Riaz. Why should I leave my husband? Is marriage the cheapest relationship ever? Just as a mother doesn't abandon her son or a sister her brother when he is unlawful, then why should I? I won't abandon my husband because of some dirty tricks of yours," she declared firmly as she turned away and continued walking.

Gayatri's voice trembled with desperation as she called out, "Don't go, beta. I've already suffered enough. You're choosing a stranger over your own family, and one day, you'll cry for this decision. Please, my child, come back. Please." Tears rolled down her cheeks as she pleaded, her voice cracking under the weight of heartbreak. Gayatri's desperate pleas fell on deaf ears.

When pleading failed, Gayatri's voice turned sharp with desperation. "If you leave, I curse you—you will never find happiness with him," she warned, her words heavy with pain. But Aakanksha didn't stop. Even as her mother's sobs and threats echoed behind her, she didn't waver. She remained firm and left the house without hesitation. Without a second thought, she turned away, stepping out of the house, determined to find her way back to Riaz.

As soon as she reached Delhi, Aakanksha headed straight to the police station. Desperation filled her voice as she demanded to know about Riaz. The policemen, indifferent at first, dismissed her questions. But she didn't give up. After repeated pleas, a reluctant lady constable finally spoke. "You can't meet him," she admitted. "He's in police remand— first for 15 days, then extended for another 15—under terrorism charges."

Aakanksha inquired, "What is the difference between police remand and Jail?"

The lady constable sighed, as if she had answered this question a hundred times before. "When the police arrest someone, they keep them in custody for questioning— figuring out their involvement, intent, and gathering evidence. That's police remand," she explained. "Once that period is over, the court decides—either the person gets bail or is sent to jail. If they're in jail but haven't been convicted yet, they're called an under-trial prisoner. That phase is called judicial custody."

Aakanksha's heart sank as she listened to the constable's words. Desperate, she pleaded, "He's innocent! You're making a mistake!" But the constable remained unmoved.

"His remand period ends in four days," she informed Aakanksha. "He'll be presented in court then. If you really want to help him, get a good lawyer. You'll need one—it won't be easy to defend someone facing terrorism charges."

Determined to fight for Riaz, Aakanksha wasted no time. She walked into a jewellery store and sold the gold chain he had gifted her. With the money in hand, she approached a well-known lawyer, who agreed to take up Riaz's case and signed the paperwork.

"This will cover the initial process," the lawyer said, scanning the documents. "But you'll need more funds for the legal proceedings."

Aakanksha nodded. "Give me a few days. I'll arrange the rest from my savings and provident fund."

On the day of the trial, Aakanksha sat in the courtroom, her heart pounding. The moment Riaz was brought in, his eyes met hers—surprised, yet relieved. She gave him a reassuring nod, standing beside their lawyer.

The police argued for a 10-day extension, claiming Riaz's responses during interrogation had been evasive. But the judge wasn't convinced. "Where's the concrete evidence of his involvement?" the court demanded.

The police had no solid proof.

Riaz's lawyer fought relentlessly, arguing that there was no concrete evidence linking him to terrorism or the bombings. However, the court remained unconvinced, refusing to grant bail, stating that the allegations were too serious to ignore without a thorough trial. At the same time, the prosecution's request for an extension of police custody was also denied. With no legal grounds to keep him in remand, the judge ordered Riaz's transfer to Tihar Jail as an under-trial prisoner, where he would await the next phase of his legal battle.

As the policemen led Riaz out of the courtroom, Aakanksha couldn't hold back any longer and she ran toward him, wrapping her arms around him in a desperate embrace.

The officers hesitated for a moment but eventually pulled her away.

The lawyer caught up, assuring Riaz, "I'll visit you in jail. We'll discuss the next steps." Riaz nodded, his eyes holding Aakanksha's, heavy with unspoken words.

Two days later, after carefully studying the case files, the lawyer met Riaz in jail, with Aakanksha by his side. He urged Riaz to be completely honest, leaving out nothing. The room was empty except for the three of them. Riaz repeated what he had told both Aakanksha and the police—he had run into Ushman at a jewellery store, who had asked him to deliver a suitcase filled with documents to a man outside the High Court.

The lawyer leaned forward and asked, "Did you check what was inside the bag?"

Riaz shook his head. "No, I didn't."

Before he could say more, Aakanksha added, "And Ushman gave him money for delivering it." Riaz's expression hardened. He shot her a sharp look, silently warning her to keep quiet.

"Money? What money? There's no mention of that in the case papers filed by the police." the lawyer questioned, clearly intrigued by this unexpected information.

Aakanksha remained silent, but the lawyer sensed that something was fishy.

"It's because I haven't mentioned the money I received from Ushman to the police," admitted Riaz timidly.

"How much?" pressed the lawyer.

"One lakh twenty-five thousand," confessed Riaz.

The lawyer leaned in, his voice firm. "Kid, I've been in criminal law for 15 years. I know when someone's hiding something. No one pays ₹1.25 lakh just to move papers. Listen, I'm your lawyer, your only shot at freedom. You're already at a disadvantage being from Afghanistan. Tell me the truth, or forget about getting out of here."

At first, Riaz hesitated, but eventually, the words spilled out. Back when he had first come to India for his studies, he lived in North-East Delhi. That's where he met Ushman, a Pakistani, supposedly here for education. But unlike him, they had little interest in books or degrees. His real motive was something else—money minting through drug dealing.

The lawyer cut in, skeptical. "Pakistani nationals don't get Indian visas that easily. How did he manage?".

Riaz nodded, expecting the question. He explained that they had secured student visas during a brief phase of improved India-Pakistan relations around 2005-06, after India's cricket tour to Pakistan. It was a different time—before the Mumbai attacks, before the visa restrictions tightened. Back then, students could still get in. Now, post-26/11, visas were nearly impossible, granted only for medical or rare exceptions.

"Okay. So, they were involved in drugs, and after that?"

Riaz revealed that Ushman and his friends were involved in smuggling drugs, arms, and ammunition, moving them from one location to another. Their operation thrived on a steady influx of new people, as fresh faces were less likely to attract police suspicion. Struggling financially, he found himself vulnerable. They tried to rope him in, offering quick money for seemingly simple tasks—just delivering parcels, no questions asked.

"Did you participate?"

Riaz hesitated, forcing the lawyer to repeat the question. Finally, he admitted, eyes downcast, that he had been involved in the illegal trade three times.

The lawyer leaned in. "Then why did you leave?"

Riaz exhaled. "It was 2007. The first two times were easy. But the third time, a rival gang tipped off the police. I barely escaped, slipping through the dark, narrow alleys of North-East Delhi. That night, fear got the better of me. Terrified, I left everything behind and moved to Laxmi Nagar."

"That's where you met Aakanksha and got married," the lawyer remarked.

"Yes, we've been married for three years now."

The lawyer exhaled, his gaze sharp, "Fine. I get your past. Now tell me about the present—why did you deliver that bomb?"

Riaz's voice cracked as tears welled up in his eyes. "I didn't do it. I just needed money to buy Aakanksha a gold chain for our anniversary. That's all. I thought they were still dealing drugs and agreed to one last delivery. I had no idea... no clue they had planted a bomb in that suitcase."

Aakanksha's heart sank, her world crashing around her. The trust, the respect—everything she had for Riaz—shattered in an instant. Her father's warnings rang in her ears, hauntingly accurate. Was he right all along? Had she been blind? She had given up everything for Riaz, and now, it felt like the biggest betrayal of her life.

"I just wanted to make you happy," Riaz pleaded.

"By killing innocent people?" Aakanksha retorted bitterly.

"I'm sorry, Aakanksha. I really am. I just wanted to give you something special."

"Did I ever ask for anything? Weren't we enough for each other, Riaz? I didn't need gold or luxury to be happy with you."

"I know. I was blinded by greed and didn't bother to question what was inside the suitcase," Riaz confessed tearfully.

The lawyer, his patience wearing thin, cut through their emotional exchange. "Enough of this. Focus on what matters right now," he said firmly. Aakanksha wiped her tears, while Riaz took a deep breath, regaining his composure.

"Now," the lawyer continued, his voice sharp, "what exactly did you tell the police?"

"I told the police that Usnman, my old roommate met me on the way to college. He said he had an urgent meeting and asked me to deliver a suitcase filled with papers to his associate at the High Court. Since it was on my route, I agreed," Riaz paused, lowering his gaze. "But I didn't mention the money he gave me."

"I know you're telling the truth because the exact same words are in the police case files," the lawyer said, 'And let me tell you, you're the luckiest criminal I've ever met. Perhaps lady luck is on your side."

Riaz frowned, confused. "I don't get it. What do you mean?"

"First, you got away with transporting drugs in 2007—no criminal record, nothing to link you to your past. Second, the only person who could expose you, Ushman, was shot dead while running from the police. So, there's no one left to testify about the money you took for delivering that suitcase. That's a stroke of luck, Riaz." The lawyer paused, studying him. "But tell me, how did you survive police custody? They must have beaten the hell out of you to make you confess."

Riaz was pleased to hear the lawyer's praise and responded, "Sir, you're forgetting—I'm from Afghanistan. What they call torture here is nothing compared to what men back home endure. Either from the Taliban Militants or the American army, beatings are a way of life there. The torture here in India, is nothing more than a warm-up in Afghanistan."

As Aakanksha stepped out of the jail, tears blurred her vision. The lawyer, walking beside her, finally broke the silence. "Are you still willing to stand by him, knowing the truth?" She stopped for a moment, wiped her tears, and looked at him with unshakable resolve. "He's still my husband," she said softly, "And I won't turn my back on him."

For the next 18 months, Aakanksha showed up at every court hearing, carrying the weight of disappointment and heartbreak. She never spoke to Riaz, never even met his eyes. Her silence wasn't just anger—it was the ache of shattered trust, of dreams broken beyond repair.

The Indian court upholds the principle that even if a hundred guilty individuals walk free, no innocent person should be wrongfully punished. With insufficient evidence against Riaz and India being accountable to the Afghan government for imprisoning one of its nationals without proof, the court had no choice but to order his release.

However, at the request of law enforcement agencies, the court directed the revocation of Riaz's visa, paving the way for his deportation to Afghanistan. While the court acknowledged that Riaz may not have known about the bomb, his role in transporting the suitcase made him legally responsible, leading to the decision.

Riaz's lawyer contended that despite his Afghan nationality, he was entitled to Indian citizenship through his marriage to an Indian woman, making deportation unjustified.

The court then demanded proof—a valid marriage certificate or *'nikahnama'*—and requested Riaz's wife to appear in court. The lawyer gestured towards Aakanksha, confirming her as Riaz's wife.

Summoned by the judge, Aakanksha stepped into the witness box.

The judge turned to Riaz. "Is she your wife?"

"Yes, your honour," Riaz affirmed.

The judge then shifted his gaze to Aakanksha. "And is he your husband?"

Aakanksha stood frozen, her mind torn between memories and reality. Moments with Riaz—love, laughter, fights, and dreams—flashed before her, only to be overshadowed by the horrific scenes of the High Court blast. The chaos, the lifeless bodies, the shattered families—it all came rushing back.

The judge's voice cut through her thoughts, "Is he your husband?", he asked again.

Aakanksha's voice rang through the courtroom, firm and unwavering. "No, he is not my husband."

A stunned silence followed, the judge and the lawyer exchanging surprised glances. Even Riaz looked at her, disbelief clouding his eyes.

Perplexed, the judge sought clarification, "Are you sure, he is not your husband?"

"Absolutely," she affirmed. "We were never married. We were in a live-in relationship in Laxmi Nagar, but that's all. There is no nikahnama, no marriage."

Riaz, visibly stunned, remained silent, his gaze shifting between the lawyer and Aakanksha, his eyes in disbelief.

The Judge, realizing the gravity of the situation, pressed further, "Are you absolutely certain of your statement? If he is deported, he may never set foot in India in his lifetime."

Aakanksha met his gaze without hesitation. "I understand, Your Honour. And I stand by it. I don't want him to ever return."

The court ruled in Riaz's favour, granting him freedom, but on the condition that his visa be revoked, leading to his deportation to Afghanistan. There was no chance to plead, no final words. He was taken straight from the courtroom. Aakanksha, eyes brimming with tears yet unwavering in her decision, walked out of the courtroom. She had chosen solitude over a life with a man tainted by innocent blood.

Just as she was about to leave, the lawyer stopped her. "You fought so hard to save him. Why abandon him now?"

Aakanksha's voice was steady. "I saved him because he was my husband. But I left him because his actions took innocent lives. If those families never got their loved ones back, why should he get a second chance?"

"But what about you? You'll suffer too. Why punish yourself for something that wasn't your fault?" the lawyer inquired.

"I didn't choose this. It was inevitable. A mother's curse never goes unanswered."

Back in her Delhi apartment, she rummaged through a plastic folder filled with important documents. Her fingers stopped at one—Nikahnama, their marriage certificate. Without hesitation, she walked to the kitchen, turned on the gas stove, and watched as the flames consumed the marriage certificate, burning it to ashes.

The curse had taken its course.

****

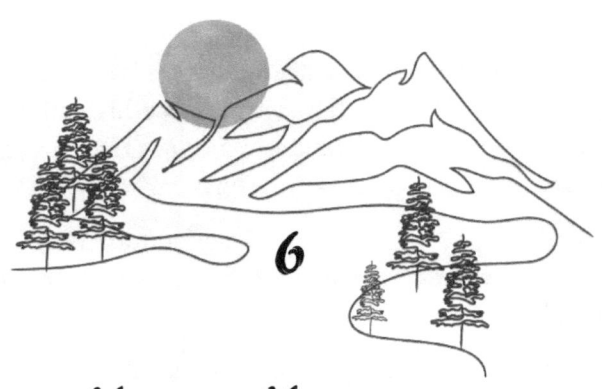

Kismat Konnection

"May you fall in love with someone, who never gets tired of saving you from your own chaos."

- Anonymous

(30th June, 2015 – Gurgaon, Delhi NCR)

Almost a year had passed since Riaz's deportation, and Aakanksha had slowly learned to find solace, carrying the weight of two deep scars—being disowned by her parents, a burden she blamed herself for, and the pain of her husband's departure.

A fast-growing startup, "Metroclap", was on a hiring spree. Backed by heavy funding from global investors, the company had caught the attention of venture capitalists betting big on its future. With fresh capital pouring in, Metroclap was gearing up for rapid expansion, eager to build a strong team to drive its vision forward.

Metroclap was on a hiring spree, scouting for skilled professionals with hands-on experience. To attract top talent, they offered lucrative salary hikes—some as high as

50%. Fortune favored both Aakanksha and Shahid, who secured positions with the company, each earning a hefty 50% raise from their previous pay.

Rijith also landed a job at Metroclap, though with just a 3% salary hike. He didn't mind—it was still better than getting fired from his previous company, which could have happened any day. Brilliant but lazy, he had a work ethic that was anything but conventional. Some days, he'd walk into the office with unkempt hair, skipping a bath altogether. Summers saw him in shorts—not for comfort, but to flaunt the oversized tattoos etched on his bulging, fatty skin. Adding to the challenge, he never spoke respectfully to managers or team leaders. The only reason the company kept him? His work. Despite his laid-back attitude, Rijith never missed deadlines.

After training, Aakanksha secured the top spot, with Shahid trailing right behind. The recruits were split into two groups—freshers and experienced hires. Teams were formed under different leaders, ensuring a balanced mix of both. Since Shahid and Rijith already knew each other, they requested to be on the same team, and HR obliged. Aakanksha was assigned to their team as well, while the rest were inexperienced freshers.

Their office was in Gurgaon, and Aakanksha, living nearby in Sultanpur, was the only one with a convenient commute. To cut down on travel time, Shahid and Rijith decided to move closer. With Aakanksha's help, they found a 1BHK apartment in her building. She lived alone on the fourth floor, while the two of them settled into an apartment on the second.

Aakanksha was usually reserved, but spending time with Shahid and Rijith brought a lightness to her life she hadn't felt in years. Since leaving Shimla, she had only survived, battling challenges alone. Meeting them made her realize she had never truly lived, despite earning more than both. In Delhi, she had been stuck in a troubled marriage, her savings drained by legal fights. But with them, the past felt distant. They became close friends, even though Rijith often playfully flirted with her. She didn't mind—it was harmless fun. Deep down, both knew they were never meant for each other.

Being a Tamilian, Rijith's battle with Hindi was a source of endless amusement for Aakanksha. When he first landed in Delhi, he stuck to Tamil and English, refusing to even attempt Hindi. But that didn't sit well with the girls in his office. They made it clear—if he wanted to be part of their circle, he'd have to speak Hindi, no matter how terrible. Left with no choice, he broke his self-imposed rule and started speaking Hindi, albeit in a broken and amusing manner. Surprisingly, his efforts in speaking Hindi, despite their imperfections, attracted more girls to him, a feat that would have been challenging solely based on his tattooed arms and bulky physique.

The trio was inseparable, almost like modern-day musketeers—always united and always supportive of each other. Weekends meant celebrations, weekdays meant sharing a cab to the office. Aakanksha always took the back seat, and Rijith, as a rule, never let Shahid sit beside her. His hilarious Hindi slip-ups, like saying *"Main peeche se ghusega"* instead of *"Main peeche baithega,"* had the entire cab, including the driver, laughing. The best part? Rijith never even got the joke.

Days turned into months, and while Rijith remained blissfully unaware, something was changing between Aakanksha and Shahid. An unspoken connection was forming—one neither of them acknowledged but both felt. Although they both recognized their love, they hesitated to express their feelings, haunted by their respective pasts. Another bond that drew Aakanksha and Shahid closer was their shared birthday, perhaps deepening their closeness.

During Diwali, Rijith headed home to Jamshedpur, leaving Shahid and Aakanksha alone in their respective apartments. That evening, Aakanksha called Shahid over, asking him to bring some rum and a joint from his usual peddler, while she prepared snacks. Outside, the city was alive with celebrations—fireworks lit up the sky, and children's laughter echoed through the streets, reaching even the top floor of their building.

Aakanksha didn't have a dining table, so they settled comfortably on a thick woolen mat in the living room. Over drinks and snacks, they gossiped about colleagues, cursed their bosses, and laughed at office drama. As the evening unfolded, Shahid felt something shift within him. The warmth in her eyes, the ease in their conversation—he realized she had unknowingly become the most important person in his life. He wanted to be close to her, to protect her, to never let her go. But love, as always, came with its own complications. How was he supposed to tell her? Where would he even start?

Lost in thought, he stood at the crossroads of his past and present. He had to face the wounds he had inflicted, the love he had let slip away, and the quiet ache of emptiness that followed. Only by embracing his mistakes could he begin to understand what truly mattered. Love was never about momentary pleasures—it was about holding on, about cherishing, about becoming worthy of the one he had lost.

As Shahid finally confessed his love, Aakanksha felt a rush of emotions—an unspoken joy mixed with a quiet fear. But before he could say another word, she stopped him, "Wait... let me speak first," she said, "There's something you need to know. Hear me out, and then decide if you still feel the same way."

Despite Shahid wanting to speak first, Aakanksha held her ground. "I have a grey past," she confessed, "And I don't know if, after hearing it, you'll still feel the same about me."

Shahid smiled reassuringly. "If your past is grey, mine is pitch black. Trust me, once you hear my story, you'll realize you have nothing to be ashamed of."

Aakanksha let out a small, nervous laugh before taking a deep breath. Then, with a quiet intensity, she said, "I'm married."

Shahid's heart skipped a beat, his ears grew warm, and his mind went blank. All he could manage was a stunned, "That can't be true."

Aakanksha clarified, " Technically, yes. I'm still married... just not divorced yet."

"Explain."

Aakanksha took a deep breath and started from the beginning—her love for basketball, the betrayal by her coach, and the night she ran away, just two days before her wedding. She spoke of missed opportunities in Delhi, her entanglement with Riaz, and the tragedy that unfolded in the court.

Shahid listened attentively, the way a child listens to his mother's bedtime story—hanging onto every word, afraid to miss even a single detail.

"Why didn't you file for divorce after he was deported?"

"I couldn't," Aakanksha sighed, "In court, I lied—said we were never married, just in a live-in relationship. If I file for divorce now, it would mean admitting to perjury. My lawyer warned me that I could end up in jail. So technically, I'm still married... and I can't even seek a divorce."

"He's been deported and can't return to India. So who's stopping us from getting married?" Shahid asked.

"He might be banned for life, but he can still try to defend himself. If he manages to challenge the deportation order in the High Court, then who knows what might happen."

Shahid took a slow drag of the joint, followed by a sip of rum, his mind racing, "Did you ever register your marriage in an Indian court?"

"No, we didn't think it was necessary. Our Nikahnama was all we had."

"Any wedding photos?"

"None. He used a basic phone, and all our wedding pictures were on my old Nokia 6600, which I deleted."

Without a court registration and the Nikahnama destroyed, there was no digital proof of Aakanksha's marriage. The only remaining record was in the register maintained by the Kazi who had officiated the ceremony.

Shahid proposed a bold idea—if they could somehow destroy that record, Riaz would have no legal standing if he ever tried to return. Aakanksha saw the logic but knew it wouldn't be easy. She looked at Shahid, curiosity flickering in her eyes. "How did you come up with this plan so quickly?" she asked.

Shahid felt pleased at Aakanksha's compliment, a flicker of pride in his eyes. Her words stirred memories of his uncle Salahuddin, who was serving time in Tihar Jail. Though Shahid had cut ties with him long ago, the sharp instincts and street-smart tricks he had picked up from his uncle's life had undeniably left an imprint on his character.

Aakanksha snapped him out of his thoughts, curious about his past. Shahid hesitated, "Let me get properly drunk first," reaching for another drink. A few sips, a few laughs later, he finally began telling his story.

Shahid took a deep breath and began unraveling his past—the story of being the nephew of a gangster-turned-politician, his time in Dubai, and how fate had led him to work with a Bollywood director. He spoke of Nikita, his once-fiery romance, and the unexpected favor a cameraman had asked of him. Aakanksha intervened, expressing a particular interest in the cameraman more than anything else. Her curiosity led to a string of questions, making Shahid squirm a little. But with a half-smile and a reluctant sigh, he answered them all.

Shahid then opened up about the darkest phase of his life—the humiliation he faced at the hands of Nikita's parents, who saw him as servant. The rejection crushed him, pushing him to the brink of despair, even suicidal thoughts. But his family pulled him back. He then shifted to lighter memories, sharing how he landed a job in Delhi, met Rijith and Arshit, entertaining Aakanksha as he recounted their wild parties, Arshit's gorgeous girlfriend, and the chaos that followed their nights out.

As the conversation deepened, Shahid bared his past, admitting to mistakes he once justified in the name of love. Betrayal had left him bitter, making him believe that all women were cheaters and gold-diggers. Disillusioned, he stopped seeking love and instead indulged in physical pleasures, treating relationships as nothing more than one-night stands. If a woman agreed, he stayed; if she didn't, he moved on without a second thought. He even confessed, with a tinge of shame, to having slept with some women whose names and faces he couldn't even remember.

Aakanksha listened, surprised but not entirely shocked—after all, such things were common in Delhi-NCR. Still, she needed answers. She took a deep breath and asked three pointed questions. First, had he ever crossed the line with Arshit's girlfriend? Second, just how many women had been a part of his past? And lastly, the most important one—why should she trust him, knowing his history?

"NO. Not Saesha. I never slept with a whore."

"Whoever she may be, never disrespect a woman in front of me. It's very easy to comment on a woman's character without knowing her background," Aakanksha warned firmly.

"But why are you so angry?" Shahid asked, confused. "Ask Rijith. He slept with her too. He even saw her with her boss, trying to trade a promotion for a night."

"Doesn't matter what she did. Don't use words like that. Similarly, Anshuman once labelled me a whore. It's always the same story—if a woman doesn't fit into a man's expectations, she's branded with terms like 'whore'."

Shahid paused, his expression softening. "I'm sorry for what I said about Saesha. I shouldn't have used those words. And I won't, ever again."

As for Aakanksha's second question, he sighed, "I don't remember the exact number... maybe 20-25, including Nikita."

But when it came to the last and most important question, his voice turned firm. "I know my past is messed up, but I swear, you can trust me. I love you, Aakanksha."

Aakanksha remained silent, listening as Shahid poured his heart out. He didn't beg for her love but made one thing clear—if she ever chose him, he'd be there. No conditions, no doubts. Just unwavering commitment through every storm.

"But what if Riaz returns to India?" she asked, her voice laced with curiosity.

"I will handle that situation. I assure you."

Aakanksha had been alone for too long. Riaz's absence had left a void, and though her mind wrestled with doubts, her heart craved companionship. As Shahid pulled her close, she didn't resist. She let herself lean into him, surrendering, if only for a moment, to the warmth she had been missing.

In the end, Shahid's journey was proof that love is what truly lasts. Lust may tempt and thrill, but it is love that gives meaning, heals, and stays. His mistakes had taught him what mattered—love wasn't about casual moments, but about finding someone worth holding on to and never letting go.

As Shahid leaned in to kiss her, Aakanksha didn't resist. Lost in the haze of alcohol and marijuana, they surrendered to the moment, letting passion take over. Promises were whispered; loyalty pledged. Around them, the night told its own story—an empty bottle, scattered cigarette ashes, half-eaten food, and discarded chicken bones. Wrapped in each other's arms, they drifted into sleep on the mat, the world outside forgotten.

Shahid quickly succumbed to exhaustion, his snores echoing through the room. But sleep refused to claim Aakanksha. Lying beside him, she stared at the ceiling, her mind tangled in doubts. Tears welled up as she questioned her choices. Riaz had deceived her, but Shahid had been honest in his intentions. Yet, fear still gripped her—fear of what the future held, of what would happen if Riaz ever returned? Her thoughts wrestled with uncertainty until exhaustion finally won, pulling her into a restless sleep.

At 2:00 in the afternoon, Aakanksha woke up to the sharp whistle of a pressure cooker. Groggy but curious, she called out to Shahid, asking what was cooking. "Biryani for lunch," he replied casually. She stretched her arms, feeling a sense of peace she hadn't known in years. For the first time since Riaz's departure, she had slept deeply, without nightmares, without restlessness. Smiling, she reached out and whispered, "Give me a hug." Shahid wrapped his arms around her, holding her close.

A few days later, she suggested they move in together. Shahid agreed without hesitation. That evening, he shifted his belongings from the second floor to Aakanksha's apartment on the fourth. Meanwhile, Rijith remained blissfully unaware, still busy enjoying his extended Diwali holidays back home.

When Rijith returned home after a week, he found the apartment unusually empty. Shahid's belongings were gone. Confused, he tried calling him, but his phone was switched off— as per the office security protocol.

His overactive imagination jumped to the worst-case scenario. Robbery! It never occurred to him that a thief would probably ignore clothes and personal belongings. But Rijith, in his self-proclaimed brilliance, decided not to take chances. Without thinking twice, he called the police and insisted they file an FIR for the theft.

Two constables arrived at Rijith's apartment, scanning the place with mild curiosity. One of them asked, "So, whose belongings are missing?"

Rijith, brimming with certainty, replied, "My flatmate Shahid's. He's at work right now."

The constables raised an eyebrow. "And you're sure it was stolen? Not, say, packed and taken away voluntarily?"

Rijith, still convinced of his theory, explained that Shahid's belongings had been there when he left for his hometown but were missing now.

The constable, tapping his baton on the floor, asked, "And what about your stuff? Anything missing?"

Rijith confidently shook his head. "No, sir. My clothes, watches, laptop, everything is right where I left them."

The constable let out an exasperated sigh, "Are you serious? So, you're telling me a thief broke in, ignored all your valuables, and only took your friend's stuff? What kind of thief does that?"

Rijith was left speechless, unsure of what to say. The constables then pressed him for Shahid's workplace details. With the information in hand, they called his office and demanded that Shahid be allowed to leave early on account of an emergency.

Later that day, Shahid and Aakanksha rushed to Rijith's apartment, only to find the constables still waiting. When they explained what had happened, they revealed that Shahid had moved to another apartment. Shocked, Rijith realized that Shahid had left without telling him. The constables, growing impatient, then threatened to file an FIR against Rijith for wasting the police department's time.

Despite Shahid's repeated apologies, the constables weren't ready to let Rijith off the hook. Their patience had worn thin, and they insisted on being compensated for their "wasted time." They started with a demand of ten thousand but, after some back-and-forth negotiations, settled for five. Shahid and Rijith pitched in two thousand each, while Aakanksha handed over the remaining one thousand. Only then did the constables leave.

The moment they were gone, Rijith exploded. "You moved out without telling me? What the hell, man?"

Shahid tried to explain, but before he could, Aakanksha stepped in, "Rijith, calm down," she said, placing a hand on his shoulder. "Shahid proposed... and I said yes."

Feeling saddened, Rijith questioned, "But why did he move out of the apartment?"

Aakanksha blushed and responded, "You didn't get it. We're live-in couple now. He didn't leave; he simply moved from the second floor to the fourth floor."

Rijith's heart sank deeper than the Titanic, yet he forced a smile and congratulated them. Once they left, he shut the door, sat on the floor for hours, lost in thought. He wasn't sure what stung more—Aakanksha choosing Shahid, the two thousand rupees he had to shell out to the constables, or the brutal realization that next month's rent would now be entirely on him.

The next day at the office, Rijith learned that all three of them had been moved to different projects based on their performance reviews, which also meant new shift timings. Aakanksha was placed in the morning shift, Shahid in the evening, and Rijith in the night shift. However, this turned out to be a blessing in disguise for Rijith when he noticed a new addition to his team—a North-Eastern girl from Manipur.

Her name was Angelina Ngangom, inspired by the Hollywood star Angelina Jolie. The only difference? She was half the height and nearly seven times chubbier. But with her round cheeks, twinkling eyes, and radiant smile, she had a charm of her own. In the office, she was nicknamed "Angie."

Rijith quickly fell in love once again, feeling that Angie was the perfect match for him, especially considering their similar physical attributes. Angie, still adjusting to the fast-paced life of Delhi, was a little hesitant but eager to blend in. So, when Rijith casually asked her out for coffee, she smiled and said yes.

A girl's presence can change a man in unexpected ways—turning even the stingiest into a generous spender. Rijith was no exception. His love for chicken momos became a shared obsession with Angie, deepening their bond. They spent most of their time together, both at work and outside, lost in easy conversations and laughter. Encouraged by their closeness, Rijith finally mustered the courage to ask her to stay in a live-in relationship with him. But Angie, with a soft smile, gently refused.

One morning, like always, Rijith strolled into the office late, expecting another routine day. But as he passed by Angie's desk, he noticed something unusual—tears rolling down her cheeks. Concerned, he asked what was wrong. Angie quickly wiped her face, forcing a smile. "Nothing," she muttered, avoiding his gaze.

In a hurry to catch up on work, Rijith let it go—for the moment. But the image of her tear-streaked face lingered in his mind, making it impossible to focus. He waited impatiently for their break, and as soon as they stepped out, he pressed her to tell him what had happened.

At first, Angie hesitated, but then, with a trembling voice, she revealed the truth. Their team manager had called her into his cabin, and he mocked her accent, ridiculed her appearance, and hurled racial slurs at her. If it had been about her work, she could have handled it, but this was different. He had called her 'Chinky,' and even made lewd remarks—saying she resembled a Japanese porn star and should move to China or Japan to make porn films instead of working at this office.

Rijith, feeling furious, exclaimed, "I know the manager is arrogant and rascal. But why did you go to his cabin?"

Angie sighed, wiping her eyes, "A Haryanvi customer had called with a complaint, but I couldn't understand his accent, and he couldn't understand mine. It was a mess. He got frustrated and demanded to speak to the manager, so I called him over to my desk. The customer was loud, aggressive, often using words like 'ben-cho,' which I didn't even understand. After the call, instead of handling the situation professionally, the manager dragged me to his cabin and started saying absurd things."

"It was the customer's fault, not yours. The manager had no right to speak to you like that," Rijith said.

"Should I file a complaint with HR?" Angie asked hesitantly.

"No need. I'll handle it. He will apologize to you—I promise."

As their shift ended in the early morning, Rijith sent Angie home before heading straight to the basement parking lot to confront the manager. The guy was massive—broad shoulders and bulging biceps. Rijith, in comparison, was no match. But courage isn't always about winning; sometimes, it's just about standing up. And sometimes, so is stupidity.

Still, fuelled by a mix of anger and a desperate urge to impress Angie, Rijith squared his shoulders and said, "You owe her an apology."

The manager replied, "Go home, dumbass. Unless you want me to make you cry like your little bitch."

Rijith lost it. He threw a punch at the manager but the guy wasn't expecting it. The punch landed on his face, but it hurt Rijith's hand more than it hurt the manager. Furious now, the manager kicked him in the stomach and punched him in the face. Within seconds, he was on the ground, curled up, gasping for breath. The manager walked off, leaving Rijith writhing in pain. He lay there for about 20 minutes, clutching his stomach. Finally, he struggled to his feet, limping towards his cab outside the campus. Once home, he popped a paracetamol and crashed into bed.

Rijith slept the whole day, missing work and ignoring phone calls. Talking was too painful. After two days of him not showing up at work, Angie called Shahid to check on him. Shahid explained that they barely saw each other during the week due to their different work schedules, only meeting on weekends. But the moment he realized Rijith hadn't shown up for two days, he rushed to his apartment and banged on the door.

When Rijith opened the door, Shahid was shocked to see his black eye and the difficulty he had speaking. "What happened?" Shahid asked, but Rijith hesitated. After some pushing, he finally opened up and told Shahid everything. He explained that he could barely see from the bruised eye for the past two days, and only started seeing a little better today.

When Shahid asked why Rijith hadn't called him during the incident, Rijith shrugged it off. "I didn't want to bother you and Aakanksha. Angie's my girlfriend; I thought I could handle it myself."

It was 11 PM, but Shahid told Rijith to get ready. He booked an Uber, and when Rijith asked where they were going, Shahid stayed silent. After 45 minutes of driving, the cab stopped at an apartment building. Shahid led Rijith to the second floor and knocked on a door.

It was the manager's house, and he was partying with two friends, enjoying his week off. Shahid stormed in, punched the manager, and knocked him out cold. He then took care of the other two, sending them to the ground and keeping them there for the night. Meanwhile, Rijith cranked up the music, trying to block out any screams.

Next, Shahid turned to the manager, grabbed his hands, and slammed his knee into his arm with a sickening crack.

The manager screamed in pain. Shahid didn't stop, punching him repeatedly, bruising both his eyes and knocking out a molar. He only stopped when the manager pissed himself. Finally, Shahid made him type an elaborate sorry message to Angie and beg Rijith for forgiveness.

In pain, tears streaming down his face, the manager clutched Rijith's feet and composed a WhatsApp message to Angie: "India is my country, and all Indians are my brothers and sisters. You are my sister too. I apologize for the insults and name-calling. Please forgive me. I hope someone as kind-hearted as you can forgive your elder brother."

Shahid booked a cab to take them home. On the way back, Rijith's pain eased, and his vision cleared. He messaged Angie on WhatsApp: "I promised I'd handle it, and that bastard will apologize to you."

Angie replied with a kissing smiley: "Love you, darling."

Shahid and Rijith were happy with how things had turned out, unaware of the trouble waiting for them at the office on Monday. When Monday arrived, they were both summoned to the office simultaneously, despite having different shift schedules. The senior officers were waiting for them.

As they walked into the office, they were greeted by the sight of the manager, his hand plastered, eyes swollen, and bruises darkening his face. It became apparent that the manager had filed a complaint against them with the management. Disciplinary officers questioned them about the incident. Shahid admitted to hurting the manager, but Rijith intervened and said, "We both did it."

Rijith then explained the entire incident, describing the manager's racist remarks and inappropriate comments about female colleagues. When asked for proof, he called Angie and showed the WhatsApp messages the manager had sent her. The HR team also questioned other female employees, many of whom shared similar complaints. In the end, the disciplinary team concluded that Shahid and Rijith were telling the truth, and the manager had made false accusations to cover up his own wrongdoings. The management also told the female employees not to tolerate such behavior and encouraged them to report it directly to HR without fear.

The management quickly fired the manager for his inappropriate behavior and comments towards female colleagues. However, they also asked Shahid and Rijith to resign. When questioned, HR admitted the manager's fault but pointed out that resorting to violence wasn't the solution. They should have reported the issue to the company first. Recognizing that Shahid and Rijith weren't fully at fault, the company decided not to fire them immediately, as it could hurt their future job prospects. Instead, they were asked to resign, which, in office terms, was known as being 'Asked to Leave' or 'ATL'.

With no other choice, Shahid and Rijith reluctantly agreed to the ATL and resigned. If they hadn't resigned, they would've been fired. When Aakanksha arrived at the office, she quickly learned about their departure. Outraged, she drafted her resignation and handed it to HR. Inspired by Aakanksha, Angie also found the courage to resign. Within just four hours, all four of them were jobless.

Aakanksha and Angie arrived in a cab at Aakanksha's place, where Shahid and Rijith were discussing their next move. As they walked in, they announced their resignations in protest. Shahid looked at Rijith, noticing his exhausted face, and said, "Why did you both resign? How will we pay rent and buy groceries now? It would've been better to wait a few months until we found something else."

Aakanksha and Angie soon realized the mistake they'd made.

"Can we take our resignation back?" Angie asked.

"No. Don't take it back," Shahid replied. "We'll figure something out."

The four of them requested the withdrawal of their PF and reimbursements to settle their debts. They started using credit cards for groceries and asked their landlord for an extension on the rent, given their sudden unemployment. Luckily, the landlord—rare in Delhi—sympathized and gave them more time. They sent out resumes to recruitment agencies, anxiously waiting for interview calls.

Three and a half months passed, and they had burned through their salaries, PF withdrawals, and struggled to make credit card payments. While three of them got interview calls, Angie, new to Delhi with little experience, had a tough time landing a job. As their finances shrank, Angie found it harder to cover her expenses and decided to return to Manipur. She agreed to do interviews over the phone and planned to come back to Delhi once she had a job offer.

For the last 12 days, Aakanksha, Shahid, and Rijith had been living on a simple diet of bread, jam, rice, butter, and boiled potatoes. They had just enough cash to buy a joint every day and whiskey twice a month. After attending numerous interviews, they were anxiously waiting for the final call. Feeling the pressure of being cooped up, Aakanksha suggested they unwind and celebrate with whiskey at a pub. It had been four long months since she'd had a reason to celebrate.

Despite his own financial struggles, Shahid agreed to go with Aakanksha to the pub and put the bill on his credit card, adding to its pending dues. Once there, Aakanksha downed seven shots of tequila and danced non-stop for two and a half hours. Reluctant to stop, she wanted more tequila, but Shahid stepped in and led her outside. Drunk, Aakanksha's movements became erratic, walking in a zigzag pattern. Without waiting for Shahid to get a cab, she impulsively ran off and Shahid chased after her. By the time the cab arrived, Aakanksha had already wandered 300 meters away from the pub.

On the way home, Aakanksha passed out in the cab. When they reached, Shahid carefully woke her, but she was disoriented and mumbling nonsense. Not giving up, Shahid hoisted her onto his shoulders and carried her like a sack of rice up to the fourth floor. Arijit, hearing the noise, joined them and lit a joint, adding to the relaxed atmosphere.

As they sat together, smoking joints, Aakanksha mentioned wanting to go back to the same pub the next day. Shahid, however, admitted he'd maxed out his credit card and couldn't afford another trip. Aakanksha asked when they could go again, and Shahid promised he'd take her once he landed a job and got his next salary.

Taking a deep drag from the joint, Aakanksha, completely off track from the intoxication, remarked, *"Tum apna gaand de diya hota, toh, aaj tu bhi hero hota. Phir hume paise ki koi tension nahi hoti,*" and burst into uncontrollable laughter, completely unaware of how absurd she sounded.

Rijith didn't understand, so Shahid clarified, "She means, if he'd given his ass to the cameraman in Mumbai, he'd be a hero now, and we wouldn't be broke." Rijith couldn't stop laughing for the next two minutes. Their laughter echoed through the room, the first real sound in four months, tears streaming down their faces. Just then, an email notification popped up. Shahid clicked open the email, and the subject line read:

"Letter of appointment for the role of Quality Assessment Manager against your interview dated 15th March, 2016."

****

7

Love beyond Faith

"Love is a fire. But whether it is going to warm your hearth or burn down your house, you can never tell."
-Joan Crawford

(30th September, 2016 – Jamshedpur, Jharkhand)

I was born into a lower middle-class Bengali family in Jamshedpur, Bihar (now Jharkhand) on 5th February 1989. I'm Samitabh Sarkar, the older of two brothers. My relationship with my father was always strained, leading to rare and brief conversations between us. In March 2014, the last words I spoke to him in Bengali were, *"Tomar morar pore aami tomake mukhe aagun debo na,"* which translates to, "After your death, I won't perform the final rite of lighting your funeral pyre," a traditional Hindu ritual performed by the eldest son for a deceased parent.

In November 2014, when my father passed away, I chose not to perform the cremation ritual. Instead, my younger brother took on that responsibility. Perhaps, I still don't regret my decision, but I do regret our last conversation.

Coming from a middle-class background, my biggest dream was to land a stable, well-paying job. While working at a private firm in Jamshedpur, I kept applying for government roles, including bank exams, but faced disappointment, either in the written tests or interviews. Then, six months after my father's death, a rare opportunity came up: the Airports Authority of India (AAI) advertised for two Junior Executive (Company Secretary) positions with an application fee of Rs. 500. Although the limited vacancies and high fee made me hesitant, my mother insisted, so I applied. Eight months later, in January 2016, the written exam was held. To my surprise, in August 2016, I got the news that I had cleared the written test and was called for an interview in New Delhi scheduled ten days later.

Given my tight finances and the slim chances of success with only two vacancies, I was reluctant to travel to New Delhi on such short notice, especially with train tickets costing around Rs. 4-5 thousand. But while I was contemplating this, I noticed a line in the last paragraph of the interview letter: *"You will be reimbursed AC III Tier fare or actual Bus fare by the shortest route on production of proof of travel, provided the distance travelled by Rail/Bus each way exceeds 80 Kms."*

Since the organization would cover travel expenses, I decided to head to Delhi, though I was doubtful about clearing the interview, assuming the seats were likely reserved for well-connected candidates. To sort out my stay, I contacted Rijith, an old schoolmate, who kindly offered accommodation at his place. With travel, food, and lodging sorted, I ended up spending more time researching tourist spots in Delhi than focusing on the interview.

The interview went well, and the organization had already paid for the rail tickets before my interview began. Receiving the amount made me feel more relaxed than giving the interview. I spent the rest of days of my trip in Delhi visiting Akshardham, Red Fort, India Gate, Lotus Temple, Gurudwara Bangla Sahib, and Qutub Minar. I also met Aakanksha and Shahid and partied with them.

On September 30th, 2016, the final interview results were announced. Sitting in my office in Jamshedpur, I checked the list and saw two roll numbers of the selected candidates. I checked my 10-digit roll number nearly 15 times, barely believing it. I had secured the top spot and was selected as Junior Executive (Company Secretary) at the Airports Authority of India. The posting? New Delhi.

That evening, as I was about to leave the office, it started raining. I rode my Hero Maestro scooter to work every day, covering 16 kilometers each way. Though I had a raincoat in my bag, I decided not to wear it—or the helmet.

For the first time in decades, I cried for continuous 35 minutes in rain; as I drove the 16 kilometers from office to home. For the first time in decades the raindrops soaking my clothes brought a sense of pleasure rather than irritation. For the first time in decades, the cold air, piercing my body like needles, gave me comfort rather than chills. For the first time in decades, two souls wept together for thirty-five minutes, unnoticed and unjudged. And perhaps, for the first time in decades, my father and I, cried together.

Within a month, all the medical and formalities were completed, and I joined AAI in November 2016. At first, I stayed with Rijith in his apartment before moving to a new flat near my office, leaving Sultanpur behind. Living with Rijith introduced me to new friends in Delhi. He told me stories of Aakanksha, Shahid, Arshit, Saesha, and his beloved, Angie. He spoke of how they had all faced unemployment for months, but in the last 4-5 months, they had found new jobs. While Aakanksha and Shahid had secured their jobs on their own, Arshit had played a crucial role in helping Rijith find his. Angie, however, had not returned to Delhi since then, though she planned to come back in a few months. Listening to their stories, I felt a deep connection with them, as if I had known them for years, even though I had not met all of them yet.

In my hometown, winter was bearable, but in Delhi, it could freeze your bones. It was my first taste of such biting cold. Most of my free time was spent with my newfound friends after work. It was the time of demonetization, and as a result, clubs, bars, and public places stood quieter, less crowded. Two months passed in the blink of an eye, and they became the finest months of my life. We danced through the night, explored new cities on weekends, savored midnight snacks, and laughed beneath the stars after our late-night drinks. Fun, after all, is always sweeter, more peaceful, and unforgettable, especially when you have money in your pocket.

It was a freezing winter night, the kind that pierces through your bones, and here we were, five millennials crammed into the cozy, yet chaotic four-storey apartment of Aakanksha and Shahid, the live-in duo whose birthdays we were toasting to. The arsenal for the night included two bottles of Old Monk, a couple of scotch, and a rogue bottle of vodka. By the time the clock struck 2:00 A.M., three bottles were already history, casualties of our midnight revelry.

Aakanksha, the birthday girl, shared her special day with Shahid, who had earned himself the title, 'Chef of the Night', thanks to his killer fried chicken. The squad—Rijith, Arshit, and myself—completed the circle.

Everyone, barring me, was deep into smoking up 'joint' and chugging rum as if tomorrow was a myth. With three bottles down, the consensus was clear: no one leaves until we are out of booze. Totally smashed, I watched as Arshit, high on the night's vibe, rallied for another round, his voice cutting through the haze, "Let's pop another one, saalo!" His call went unanswered at first, but his persistence paid off. At that moment, I stood alone in my unwillingness, while everyone else was more than enthusiastic to obey Arshit.

Unwillingly, I gave in to the peer pressure, the brotherhood of the night winning over my sober senses.

Another bottle was freed from its cork. Joints were rolled, and rum flowed like water. We smoked like a chimney and drank like a fish. As we cracked open the fourth bottle, the cold night air mingled with our laughter and the clink of glasses, celebrating the couple of the hour.

Midway through, Aakanksha's mood flipped like a switch, tears streaming down her cheeks, her sobs a sharp contrast to the evening's cheer. We rallied around her, a chorus of soothing words, yet the more we consoled, the louder she cried.

Each of us prayed for her tears to cease, aware of the doggy ears of other residents of the apartment. The prospect of explaining why a young woman was sobbing at 02:00 AM, in the presence of four drunk guys was something we all wanted to avoid. Finally, her sobs quieted, and she whispered through her tears, "I'm sorry, guys. I just miss my mom a lot. I haven't seen her since that night in January 2013, when I fled from home for the second time. It's been rough with Dad. After that, he cut me off completely and even told my relatives to ignore me or else..." Her voice trailed off, lost in the echoes of her broken family ties.

We tried to comfort Aakanksha when Rijith told her not to be so upset. He reassured her that Shahid and the rest of us were like family to her. We all made sure she never felt the absence of her own family, and we still do. She shouldn't let her father's actions trouble her. In time, they will surely accept her. Time has a way of healing everything.

Aakanksha replied, "You are right, but I really miss them. You may remember, I have a younger brother. In our childhood, we fought endlessly, yet the love we shared was boundless. It has been 11 years since I last saw him, but his voice, his scent, still linger in my mind. I found out on Facebook that he's getting married, and it hurts to know I won't be there to witness it."

Even the coldest of hearts could see the pain in her eyes. She was tired of being single and living in a live-in relationship. She longed to have a family of her own and wanted to make sure Shahid would stay with her. She was tired from fighting alone and just wanted someone to call her own.

Yet, within the depths of her soul, she still held on to pieces of love. The live-in relationship had left her feeling empty, her heart quietly yearning for something more profound. The echoes of past love beckoned, urging her to break free from the fleeting dream and seek a love that nourished her spirit, not just her desires.

Shahid's family remained unaware of his live-in relationship, believing instead that he was still living with Rijith. Months passed, and Aakanksha asked Shahid to marry her. Overjoyed, Shahid agreed and traveled to Lucknow to share the news with his mother and elder brothers. Whenever his father, who worked in Saudi Arabia visited India. Shahid would visit his family. However, his sudden arrival in Lucknow in his father's absence took them by surprise. Shahid shared his intention to marry Aakanksha, a Hindu girl, which shocked them deeply. His brother urged him to reconsider, citing societal norms that would never accept his marriage to a Hindu girl.

Shahid, weary of his brothers' incessant chatter, chose to ignore their advice. Instead, he went to his mother, seeking her blessing. Yet, she, too, stood with his brothers, urging him to part ways with Aakanksha. She warned him against marrying a Hindu girl, fearing it might endanger their family.

Shahid stood firm, asking why he couldn't marry the girl he loved just because she was Hindu. He criticized his brothers and mother for their traditional beliefs and urged them to be more open-minded and realistic.

His eldest brother explained, "You are so consumed by love that you fail to see the broader picture. Society cannot accept the union of a Muslim boy with a Hindu girl. It not only poses a threat to those involved but also threatens our community as a whole. Some have stained our community's reputation by marrying Hindu girls and then abandoning them. The relationship you seek, is now called Love Jihad. It has destroyed many families, and we don't want to be in the news for the wrong reasons. We have families and children, and I hope you wouldn't want to put them in danger."

Shahid implored, "This is not Love Jihad, *bhai*. My love for her is true, and I am ready to sacrifice everything for it. I am aware of the world around me, but I wish our love could rise above religious boundaries. I want to show the world that our love is pure, not confined to labels like 'Jihad.' There are many examples of well-known figures, like Shahrukh Khan, Aamir Khan, Irrfan Khan, Saif Ali Khan, Farhan Akhtar, and others who have married Hindu women."

"First, society may not see your love as you do; their biases will lead them to label it as Love Jihad. Second, you're neither a celebrity nor wealthy like them. In India, societal norms bind us, unless you're exceptionally rich. So, either amass wealth before marriage or forget about marrying Aakanksha. As for your cinema reference, recall Ramadhir Singh's words in Gangs of Wasseypur: "*Jab tak sanima hai, tab tak log chutiya bante rahenge.*" On another note, I have arranged your marriage with our paternal uncle's daughter, Shifa. She is beautiful, talented, and well-respected in our family.

Shahid stood firm in his resolve, declaring his intention to marry Aakanksha or remain unmarried forever. Yet, his family, especially his eldest brother, opposed this decision with great force. They feared the societal consequences and would not let Shahid risk the safety of their family. He insisted that Shahid either agree to marry Shifa, their paternal uncle's daughter, or another Muslim girl, or choose lifelong bachelorhood, but never think of marrying a Hindu girl.

Repulsed by his family's narrow views, Shahid left without hesitation, resolute in his decision to marry Aakanksha and no one else. His brother's warning followed him, harsh and final: if he pursued this path, he should die in Delhi, rather than endangering the lives of their family in Lucknow.

Shahid returned to Delhi, his heart heavy with the events that transpired in Lucknow. Aakanksha, feeling disheartened, grappled with the realization that her dream of a family seemed increasingly distant. She held Shahid's hand in silence, longing for reassurance that he would never abandon her, despite the challenges they faced. True to his promise, Shahid comforted her, saying he would stand by her, despite his family's objections. While Aakanksha's face showed some relief, she still felt unsure about how Shahid could go against her family's wishes to marry her.

Shahid felt anxious after the heated argument with his brother, but he remained committed to Aakanksha. He tried to find a way to convince his mother and brothers, considering every option, but none seemed right. A colleague suggested a court marriage, but Shahid hesitated. He didn't want to reveal their identities in court, fearing the risks of being exposed, both in the court and outside.

His final option was to consider marrying in a mosque, though the bride was required to be Muslim. He proposed to Aakanksha that she might temporarily convert to Islam for the ceremony, and after the wedding, continue practicing her own religion as she wished.

Though Aakanksha had converted to Islam at Riaz's request, she soon regretted it, feeling she had been too naive. She struggled with inner conflict, feeling trapped and longing to break free from the pain of leaving her religion.

She was upset because her initial condition with Shahid was clear—she would not convert to marry him, and Shahid agreed. She was determined to follow her own beliefs and refused to let anyone impose their religion on her Shahid's idea of marrying in a mosque after her conversion left her heartbroken. Aakanksha even argued, she would rather face her fate alone than marry under such terms, but Shahid was firm in his desire to marry her. Together, they decided to wait and try to convince Shahid's parents to accept their marriage. In the meantime, they chose to stay together and explore other options for their wedding.

Shahid struggled to persuade his parents and lacked the courage to pursue a court marriage. Although he knew they could easily get married in Delhi without trouble, he hesitated, fearing the risk of an inter-religious marriage and the potential repercussions in Lucknow. Meanwhile, Aakanksha grew increasingly impatient, and started doubting Shahid's intentions. She had never met his family and only had his words to rely on. Sometimes, she wondered if he was being unfaithful but her heart reassured her that if he truly wanted to leave, he would have done so long ago, instead of constantly arguing with his family over the phone.

After two years of struggling with their situation, Shahid came to my apartment one day asking for help. With some hesitation, I asked what he needed. Shahid explained that he and Aakanksha were planning a court marriage and wanted to keep it private because of the complexities of their inter-religious marriage. They decided to marry in Delhi, to avoid unwanted scrutiny in Lucknow. They needed three witnesses for the court process, and Shahid asked if I could be one of them.

I was afraid to witness their marriage—it confused my senses. Partying with them was completely different from being a witness to their inter-religious marriage in court. Being a government employee, I didn't want to get involved in anything that might cause trouble later. We were good friends, and I didn't want to upset Shahid, but I couldn't find a way to say no to him, and again, I was sure that I didn't want to get involved in this mess.

I said, "I am sorry, Shahid Bhai, but I cannot be a witness to your court marriage. Given your Muslim background and Aakanksha's Hindu identity, I fear that any trouble in the future might drag me into unwanted complications. I have earned this job through great struggle, and I cannot risk it under any circumstances."

"What kind of trouble?" he asked.

I explained, "If, by any chance, Aakanksha's family files a complaint with the police, I wish to avoid any problems. Please understand, Shahid *Bhai*."

Shahid's face fell, and I braced myself for his anger, expecting him to grab my collar and strike me. I prepared for the worst, resolved not to retaliate. But, to my surprise, he simply tapped my shoulder and said, "It's alright. Before coming here, Aakanksha predicted that you wouldn't help us, but I was confident you would. Turns out, she was right."

Had Shahid punched me, leaving bruises and blood, it would have been less painful than the sting of his words. After he left, I sat in the same place for hours, lost in thought, questioning my decision. For the next two days, I lacked the will to eat or drink. A sense of betrayal weighed on me, as though I had betrayed my friends and spent days thinking about my choice, but I never found the courage to be a witness to their marriage.

Before they could register their marriage, March 2020 arrived, and India found itself gripped by an unprecedented crisis. The entire nation came to a standstill as fear of an unknown Chinese virus spread. With uncertainty in the air, people stayed indoors, avoiding the unseen threat outside. Streets that had once thrived with life now stood empty, and the usual sounds of daily life were replaced by an eerie silence.

As days turned into weeks, fear and anxiety hung heavily in the air, affecting everyone. Families stayed indoors, only interacting with those in their homes, each one gripped by the terror of the unseen virus. Every cough or sneeze became a source of worry, stirring waves of anxiety through every household.

After facing the challenges of the lockdown, Shahid and Aakanksha found a silver lining in 2021. As restrictions began to ease and the courts resumed their functions, albeit with limited capacity, Shahid devised a plan to marry quietly. They chose a courthouse wedding in Delhi, believing that the smaller, restricted gathering and social distancing measures would keep their marriage unnoticed. The police presence, due to COVID guidelines, would ensure a smooth ceremony with little attention.

Rijith and Arshit, volunteered as witnesses, lending their support to the couple's secret marriage. To further safeguard the legality and privacy of the ceremony, Shahid enlisted the help of a junior from his office to be a witness.

In the quiet corridors of the courthouse, a small group gathered, their presence solemn as Shahid and Aakanksha signed the marriage certificate, formalizing their union. With the necessary documents signed, including those of the witnesses, the couple was bound in matrimony, their fate sealed in the peaceful atmosphere of the courthouse.

A few days later, Shahid gathered the courage to contact his mother, though he still lacked the courage to tell his brothers. He shared everything with her, including their marriage, and said that they would stay in Delhi if his family refused to accept Aakanksha as their daughter-in-law. Troubled by this, his mother urged his father to visit India. Upon his arrival, Shahid's father asked both him and Aakanksha to come to Lucknow.

Despite their hesitation, Shahid and Aakanksha made their way to Lucknow. Upon reaching home, Shahid's eldest brother and mother erupted in anger. They feared that, despite their love marriage, their marriage would be branded as "Love-Jihad," drawing the attention of 'moral policing' groups. They warned that if their relationship became public, their homes could be targeted by an angry mob. Yet, they spared Aakanksha from any direct hostility. Shahid's father intervened, calling for calm, reminding them that their marriage was legal and there was no reason for opposition. Still, he warned them to stay cautious, as the situation could put their safety at risk.

The father spoke with firm resolve, declaring that since his son had brought his wife, they would treat her with the respect due to a daughter-in-law. He instructed his other sons to arrange a reception for their relatives. Due to Covid restrictions limiting gatherings to fifty people only, they decided to keep it small, inviting only close family. They would tell the guests that Aakanksha was Muslim, orphaned in a car accident as a child, and raised by her maternal uncle in a boarding school in Shimla. Furthermore, they agreed to ensure no extended conversations took place with Aakanksha, to avoid any suspicion about her religion.

A week later, the reception was held in Lucknow, with sweet packets distributed in the neighborhood, explaining that due to Covid restrictions, they could not invite everyone. Aakanksha was kept in a separate room, allowed little interaction with visitors. Rumors were spread that she had a cough and cold, possibly signs of Covid, urging neighbors to keep their distance. Fearing the virus, the neighbours didn't even go near the front doors as long as Aakanksha remained in the house.

The reception unfolded as intended, with only the closest relatives present. Shahid rumored that the bride was unwell, suffering from a cough and cold, prompting many to refrain from attending the reception. Instead, they sent their gifts for the bride through courier.

The reception unfolded quietly, with no suspicions aroused in Lucknow regarding Aakanksha's religious background. Sadiyah insisted that, as Shahid's wife, Aakanksha should embrace Islam. Yet, Shahid's father adopted a more tolerant view, allowing Aakanksha the freedom to follow her own religion, prioritizing her happiness above all. Still, Sadiyah made one final request—that Aakanksha wear a *'besar'*, a traditional nose ring worn by married women in some regions. Reluctantly, Aakanksha agreed to have her nose pierced at her mother-in-law's demand and was presented with a beautiful gold nose pin as a gift.

Upon their return to Delhi after the reception, Aakanksha was furious with Shahid for not standing firm when his parents insisted, she get her nose pierced. For a week, she refused to speak to him, while Shahid remained silent, knowing that Aakanksha had married with the condition that no rituals would be forced upon her. Torn between his love for her and respect for his parents, Shahid couldn't refuse their request, as they had already done so much for them. Yet Aakanksha's anger was justified, for Shahid had broken his promise. And so, he endured her reproach quietly.

In May 2021, Aakanksha saw on Facebook that her brother had become a father to a son, whom he named 'Atharv'. Overjoyed for him, she sent blessings to the newborn. Aakanksha yearned to hold her nephew, show him love, and play with him, but her heart ached with sorrow as she couldn't. She prayed for his bright future with all her heart.

When Shahid returned home from work, Aakanksha was eager to share her news, but she saw that he was troubled, his face clouded with concern. On her asking, he spoke of two sad news. First, his maternal uncle, Salahuddin, had passed away in the hospital from complications due to Covid. Though he had been kept in isolation, it was believed that he had contracted the virus from an asymptomatic jail officer. Despite their strained relationship and Shahid's dislike for him, a wave of sorrow and nostalgia washed over him, as he remembered the good moments they had shared in his childhood.

"What's the second news?"

"In a separate incident, a young woman named Shraddha Walkar was tragically murdered by her 28-year-old boyfriend and live-in partner, Aaftab Amin Poonawala, in Delhi. After an argument, Aaftab strangled Shraddha and then dismembered her body into 35 pieces, reportedly burning her face to conceal her identity. He stored the body parts in a 300-litre fridge, and disposed of them piece by piece in the Chhatarpur forest over the next 18 days, under the cover of night to avoid suspicion. Shraddha, a Hindu, had moved in with Aaftab, a Muslim, in 2019, despite her family's objections to their inter-religion relationship and her living with someone she barely knew. After Aaftab's arrest, the issue of 'Love Jihad' was raised aggressively by 'moral policing' groups, who now call for a ban on interfaith relationships like theirs.

The news of the Shraddha incident spread like wildfire, quickly catching the attention of the entire country, with every news channel covering it. Though they were safe in Delhi, Aakanksha and Shahid were filled with fear, dreading the trouble they might face. Anxiety kept them awake all night; their hearts gripped by the thought of the consequences if they were ever caught. The next day, Shahid's mother called, worried, while the noise of his eldest brother shouting echoed from the background. Shahid's father, calling from Saudi Arabia, advised them to temporarily move to Lucknow while he made arrangements. Without hesitation, they agreed.

When they arrived in Lucknow, they stayed for a week until Shahid got a call from his father. His father asked Shahid to go to Dubai to help his aunt, who was struggling after her husband's death due to Covid complications. She owned a restaurant, but with no one to manage it, the business was in trouble, and her health was declining with age. Shahid fondly called her "Phuphi," meaning father's sister in Urdu. Curious about her children, Shahid learned that her son was settled in the USA, working for an IT company, while her daughter was married to a doctor in

Australia. Though her son had suggested she move to the USA, Phuphi couldn't leave everything behind on such short notice. Emotionally tied to the 27 years spent with her husband in Dubai, she couldn't bring herself to leave the place.

Shahid was flooded with guilt as he realized he hadn't checked on Phuphi or kept in touch with her or her children for years, despite the fond memories from his childhood. He felt a deep need to be there for her now, knowing how much she had shaped him into who he was. Wanting to help, Shahid turned to Aakanksha to discuss the possibility of moving to Dubai.

Tired of constantly worrying about their safety, Aakanksha decided it was time to start fresh in Dubai. When they returned to Delhi, they submitted their resignations and requested their final settlements. After working for 5-6 years since they first met, they had saved up around 22 lakh rupees in their provident fund, personal savings, and gratuity, all of which they received when they left their jobs.

The day before their departure to Dubai, Aakanksha and Shahid hosted a wedding party in Delhi, inviting all their friends and colleagues, including me. Though I felt ashamed attending, I went anyway, bringing a small gift and a bouquet as a gesture of goodwill. They greeted me warmly, treating me with the same respect they gave everyone else. As the party ended and I said my goodbyes, I apologized for not being there as a witness. They both looked at me with understanding and hugged me together. Shahid stayed quiet, but Aakanksha reassured me, saying, "It's okay. If I were in your place, I would've done the same."

Since Shahid had lived in Dubai for many years and his aunt was a permanent resident, getting a visa during the COVID restrictions was not a problem. Once they arrived in Dubai, they went to his aunt's apartment. As Shahid entered, Phuphi hugged him tightly for two minutes, clearly showing how much she had missed him. Then, she turned to Aakanksha and gently kissed her forehead, warmly welcoming her as her new daughter-in-law.

Phuphi asked, "What happened? You went to India to become an actor, but ended up as a lover instead?"

Shahid blushed and stayed silent.

The next day, Phuphi took them to her restaurant, which had seen a decline in customers due to Covid. She shared that she had been suffering losses for the past few months, something unheard of in the last two decades. When she asked about their work in India, they told her about their experience in the BPO sector. Phuphi smiled, noting that running a restaurant requires the same patience—satisfying customers' hunger instead of their problems, just like in the BPO sector. The only difference, she explained, was the personal interaction needed in a restaurant, as opposed to handling things over the phone. She emphasized the importance of a human touch in this business to succeed.

Phuphi had always worked alongside her husband to manage the restaurant, so after his passing, she took charge effortlessly. She spent a month teaching them the ins and outs of running the business, which became a bit easier due to fewer customers because of Covid restrictions. She covered everything—from renewing licenses, sourcing raw materials, and preparing dishes, to managing spices, the signature dish, staff salaries, increments, bonuses, and holidays. Despite their detailed training, the month still ended in losses due to reduced sales and limited number of customers.

One night, Phuphi called them to her room, her worry evident in her voice. She expressed her concerns about the city's situation post-Covid, feeling overwhelmed and unsure if she could carry on her husband's legacy. With losses in 8 of the last 10 months, she questioned if it was worth continuing. A businessman had offered her 2 million Dirham to buy the restaurant and turn it into a sports car showroom. "My son in the USA advised me to take the offer, and I was nearly ready to sell," she said. "But then your father called and spoke about you two. I don't know why, but it felt as if my late husband was whispering to me, telling me that with your help, the business could be revived."

Shahid spoke with confidence, "It will recover, Phuphi. Just give it time until the Covid situation settles."

Phuphi sighed, her worry evident, "I know, but my savings are running low, and I'm reluctant to ask my son for help. He wants to shut down the restaurant. I know he'd support me financially, but I can't bring myself to ask."

Before Shahid could reply, Aakanksha spoke up, "Why depend on your son? We've brought our savings from India, and we're willing to invest in the business. We don't want to burden you—we want to share the challenges together."

Phuphi's voice was firm as she said, "I will never let you think of yourselves as a burden. Shahid is like my son, and you, as his wife, you're my daughter. I've raised Shahid, and I consider you both part of my family."

Feeling intimidated, Aakanksha quickly changed the subject, apologizing for her choice of words. " I'm sorry for any misunderstanding. I didn't mean to imply burden, but rather responsibility. As part of your family, we are equally responsible of supporting the business. We have enough funds for ourselves and are ready to invest whatever is needed. Your guidance is all we need."

Phuphi was delighted by Aakanksha's selflessness and immediately entrusted them with the responsibility of managing the business their way. She shared her own story, telling how she and her husband had built the business from scratch 25 years ago, learning from their mistakes along the way. She encouraged Shahid and Aakanksha to invest their capital, learn from any failures, and use their skills to make the business a success. Aware of her age, Phuphi wanted to leave the business in capable hands. But she had one condition.

"What's the condition?" they asked, eager to know.

Phuphi replied, "You'll run the business, and after covering expenses, calculate the monthly net profit. Donate 2.5% of that profit to charity as *zakat*. The rest will be split— 40% for me, 60% for you."

Curiously, Aakanksha inquired, "What is *zakat*? And what if we face losses?"

Phuphi explained that zakat is an Islamic practice, requiring a person to donate a portion of their wealth to charity, as one of the pillars of the faith. It's usually 2.5%, or 1/40, of one's total profit. However, if there are losses, zakat isn't mandatory. Still, if they wish, they can choose to donate from their savings, even after a loss.

She added that until the business becomes profitable and recovers from losses, Shahid and Aakanksha wouldn't need to pay her the agreed 40 percent share. They would start paying her once the losses are covered, and the business begins making a regular profit again.

Aakanksha, a bit embarrassed, asked, "How will you know if we're actually profitable and not deceiving you?"

Phuphi laughed and said, "I raised your husband, dear. I trust Shahid completely. He may face losses, but he would never betray my trust. That's why I'm not insisting on any paperwork. It's all based on mutual respect and verbal agreement between Shahid and me."

Aakanksha's swelled with pride as she heard Phuphi's praise for her husband.

Phuphi expressed her hope that Shahid and Aakanksha would carry on her husband's legacy by successfully running the restaurant. Aware of her growing age, she shared her wish to move to the USA to live with her son. She entrusted them with the responsibility of preserving the restaurant and its legacy. Phuphi asked them to take charge of the restaurant and make it successful. She encouraged them to save from the profits, and once they had saved two million Dirham, they were to transfer the amount to her. In return, she would transfer ownership of the restaurant to them. After acquiring it, they would no longer have to share 40 percent of the profits anymore and could keep all the earnings, and even renaming the restaurant as they wished.

The deal with Phuphi became a major motivator for Shahid and Aakanksha to make the restaurant a success. They threw themselves into the project, adding new dishes like South Indian and Bengali cuisines, and drawing ideas from YouTube and Instagram for fresh business strategies. Using social media, they created engaging content to promote the restaurant and attract customers. They also invested around 8 lakhs of their savings into renovations and operations. Their hard work paid off as Covid restrictions eased and vaccinations rolled out. Dining out became popular again, and the restaurant quickly regained profitability. Weekends saw large crowds, with customers often waiting hours for a table. Phuphi visited occasionally and took pride in watching the restaurant thrive.

By December 2023, Shahid and Aakanksha had saved 4 lakh Dirham. In the 28 months since they took over, they had been profitable for 22 months, with an impressive 18-month streak of increasing profits. Shahid decided to apply for a loan to buy the restaurant, using his strong financial record and the restaurant's steady earnings as leverage. The bank, impressed by both, approved a loan of 16 lakh Dirham. After completing the paperwork, Shahid bought the restaurant from Phuphi, paying her 2 million Dirham with a mix of the loan and their savings. Phuphi was happy to transfer ownership, knowing the business was in capable hands and would remain within the family.

On 14th January 2024, both Aakanksha and Shahid's birthdays, Shahid surprised Aakanksha with the gift of the restaurant. In return, she kissed him on lips and made a special request: to rename the restaurant. Shahid with a smile and without any hesitation, agreed. A few days later, Aakanksha chose a new name for the restaurant and renaming it after her nephew —"Atharv Indian Restaurant."

****

Karma's a dog

"Learn how to see. Realize that everything connects to everything else."
— **Leonardo Da Vinci**

(11th February, 2024 - Dubai)

It was a typical Tuesday in Dubai, with a gentle sea breeze creating a refreshing vibe. Shahid was focused on the restaurant's finances, while Aakanksha prepared a list of raw materials to order. The restaurant hummed with activity as lunchtime drew a crowd, and the waiters stayed busy taking orders.

As the afternoon sun bathed the busy streets of Dubai, a Mercedes pulled up to the restaurant. The driver quickly got out, rushing to open the rear door. A woman stepped out, a vision of elegance and energy, walking into the restaurant with confidence. Dressed in a colorful salwar suit, intricately embroidered, she seemed to carry the vibrant cityscape outside with her.

With stylish blue sunglasses perched on her head, she radiated sophistication. But it was her hair, dyed with henna, that truly stood out—its earthy tones blended perfectly with her natural beauty. Each strand seemed to weave a story of tradition and modernity coming together effortlessly.

As she walked towards the cashier, her graceful movements caught the eye of everyone around. With confidence and charm, she asked about meeting the manager or owner. Her demeanor carried a sense of purpose, as if she had a mission or message waiting to be shared.

Shahid approached her and immediately recognized her. The girl, too, was surprised—it was Saesha. He greeted her warmly, just like any other customer, without dwelling much on their past. He called Aakanksha over, much to Saesha's surprise, and the two friends shared a warm hug. When she learned they owned the restaurant, Saesha genuinely congratulated them and wished them the best for the future.

Saesha had heard positive reviews about the restaurant's authentic Indian cuisine, prompting her visit. With her husband's birthday just two days away, she planned to surprise him with a special candlelit dinner. She requested that everything be perfect and the dishes delicious for the occasion.

When Shahid asked about her husband, Saesha beamed with pride and shared that he was an IIT and IIM graduate with gold medals in both and was currently the Vice President for the Dubai region at a multinational bank. She mentioned that while she could've chosen a five-star venue for his birthday, her husband often dined at such places for work, so she wanted something different. Although she had heard great things about the restaurant's Indian menu, she remarked that it seemed small compared to five-star options. Shahid, feeling slightly insulted, quietly muttered that his restaurant's food was far better than any five-star's, though his words went unheard. Recognizing her husband's wealth, he offered a private terrace with a sea view for 7,000 dirhams. Aakanksha was surprised, as they usually charge 2,000 to 2,500 dirhams for such reservations. Nonetheless, Saesha agreed and paid upfront.

Shahid's cunning smile didn't go unnoticed by Aakanksha, who wasn't impressed. She shot him a stern glance from the corner of her eye, feeling displeased at the exorbitant charge but choosing to remain silent, not wanting to risk losing a wealthy customer. Aakanksha then led Saesha to the terrace to show her the dinner spot. As they reached the top, Saesha was captivated by the breathtaking sea view and stood mesmerized by it.

Aakanksha was curious about why Saesha had broken up with Arshit and if her marriage had been arranged. Saesha explained it was a love-cum-arranged marriage but didn't want to talk about Arshit. Noticing Saesha's discomfort, Aakanksha decided not to push further, respecting her boundaries. Instead, she ordered a cool, non-alcoholic blue lagoon for Saesha, which she enjoyed in the hot afternoon.

After finishing her drink, Saesha asked if the restaurant served alcohol. Aakanksha shook her head politely. Saesha's face showed a trace of disappointment—she longed to sip a few glasses of vodka to beat the heat.

Saesha politely requested Aakanksha if she could arrange some beers or, even better, vodka for her to enjoy at the restaurant.

Aakanksha, with a gentle tone, explained the risks involved, mentioning that if caught serving alcohol, it could lead to the cancellation of their license. She suggested that Saesha go to a licensed bar where she could enjoy drinks freely, especially since there were no restrictions on women drinking in Dubai.

"I know women can drink freely in Dubai, but my conservative husband is a big problem," Saesha said, worried.

"I don't get it,"

"My husband provides everything I need, but there's a catch. He gives me 15,000 dirhams a month for shopping, but he's very traditional and suspicious. While he's happy to buy me new dresses, he insists I wear traditional Indian attire like a Salwar suit or saree wherever I leave the house. No jeans, no t-shirts, just traditional wear. Sarees are too difficult for me to handle, so I stick to salwar suits. Before we got married, he made it clear he wanted a traditional housewife, so I left my job. He also forbids me from drinking alcohol, and I promised I wouldn't. While I'm okay with not working and wearing traditional clothes, my craving for vodka is testing that promise. I miss it, but I can't go to a bar alone—the driver is always with me, and I'm not allowed to go anywhere alone. If I were to disobey, he'd find out from the driver, and I'd be in serious trouble."

When asked about her love marriage and whether she knew about his traits beforehand, Saesha explained, "I was tired from barely getting by on my meager income. He makes 2.2 million Dirhams a year, and I realized the pocket money he'd give me was five times what I earn. So, I agreed to marry him. It was indeed my love marriage. My love for money." she chuckled.

Aakanksha laughed along with Saesha, though a hint of jealousy lingered in her mind. She couldn't help but compare their struggle to pay off the 2-million-dirham loan for their restaurant, while this guy was making 2.2 million dirhams a year. Despite these thoughts, Aakanksha kept her emotions in check and instead supported Saesha's decision, saying, "I completely agree that money is very important. Love may be temporary, but luxury is permanent. So, crying in a Mercedes with a pizza in your lap is far better than crying under the sun with an empty stomach."

Impressed by Saesha's honesty, Aakanksha offered to get vodka for her if she really wanted it. Saesha quickly agreed and even offered to cover any extra costs. Aakanksha went downstairs, asking Shahid to keep an eye on the car and the driver while she and Saesha snuck out the back door of the restaurant to hit the nearest pub for drinks. When Shahid asked why they were using the back door of the restaurant, Aakanksha promised to explain later.

Aakanksha and Saesha headed to the nearest pub, which Aakanksha knew well from their connections in the restaurant owners' community. She spoke directly to the manager, requesting a private cabin for their drinks. The manager agreed and provided them with temporary seating arrangements in a secluded cabin, usually used as a storage room. It was comfortable enough, and a waiter soon arrived to take their orders. Saesha went for a bottle of vodka, while Aakanksha ordered beer, along with some snacks to enjoy with their drinks.

Saesha relished three pegs in just five minutes, her reaction as if she had tasted nectar. She savored each sip, reflecting on how much she had missed this, having gone almost two years without it. During the Covid period, she married and moved to Dubai two months later. Her honeymoon in Singapore had been great, but eventually, neither wealth nor luxury could quench her deepest desires.

Saesha kept chattering while Aakanksha listened closely. She ordered three more pegs and drank them down. Then, she asked for a cigarette, which was handed to her, and she lit up. Once the pegs were finished, she started sharing details about her personal life, even answering questions that Aakanksha hadn't even asked. Meanwhile, Aakanksha quietly sipped her beer and nibbled on the snacks.

Saesha went on, "In Delhi, I was in love with Arshit, but I also wanted a life of luxury. The problem was, Arshit had his own issues with the police. He'd been arrested twice, but never told me why. He was out on bail, with most of his money going to lawyers and bribes to avoid being arrested again. He always said he was innocent, that someone had framed him. But honestly, to this day, I still don't know if he was telling the truth."

"Why did you break up with him then?" Aakanksha asked.

Saesha ordered more snacks, took a sip of vodka, and lit another cigarette. It felt like a rare opportunity, maybe even a once-in-a-lifetime chance, and she was determined to drink as much as she could, so she wouldn't feel the craving to drink it again in future.

Saesha sighed and continued, "Like I said, he couldn't give me the luxurious lifestyle I wanted, and I wasn't making enough to fulfil my desires. I tried everything—compromising with CEO and Managers, even trying to manipulate them for promotions and pay hikes, but there were limits to what they could do. One night, drunk, I ended up in a compromising situation with one of my colleagues. Arshit video-called, and without thinking, I answered, not realizing he'd find out about it."

While smoking, she continued, "When I got home, he was waiting. Asked me where I'd been. I tried to lie, but he already knew. The moment I spoke, he slapped me sending me to the ground. I got up, furious, shouting at him. Told him he had no right to question me, not after being arrested twice and hiding the reasons from me. I warned him—touch me again, and I'd call the police."

She exhaled, the smoke curling into the night. "But he was drunk, raging. He didn't stop. He punched me again. I hit the floor, barely conscious. Then he left, came back with a rope from the kitchen. Tied my hands behind my back. I fought, but he was stronger. He ripped my clothes off, piece by piece, no hesitation, no mercy. When I tried to scream, he shoved my torn panty into my mouth."

Her fingers trembled as she flicked the cigarette ash, "He beat me. Kicked me. Raped me. All night. And you know what's worse?" She let out a bitter laugh, "I'd slept with him willingly before. But that night... that was different. Perhaps, it's difficult to put into words, but the pain of rape was unbearable. It's different when you're intimate by choice and when you're being raped by the same person. I wanted to scream, but all I could do was choke on silence."

Aakanksha, with a gentle yet concerned voice, asked, "Why didn't you go to the police?"

"I couldn't. We were already in a live-in relationship and I was scared the police wouldn't believe me. The neighbours would have testified we were just another couple, lovers who had been together for years. Plus, my family is in Moradabad, and I feared that if I made a complaint, the police would've dragged them into this, and ruined my name in their eyes. I wasn't ready for that."

She took a slow breath before continuing. "The next morning, when he sobered up, he untied me. My body was covered in bruises. He apologized, but I had nowhere to go, no backup plan, no safe escape on such short notice. So, I stayed. A couple of days later, once the pain dulled enough for me to function, I went back to work. But I knew I had to get out. I started applying for jobs outside Delhi, sending my CV everywhere I could. I was lucky enough to get an offer from a renowned magazine in Mumbai. Within a month, I ended things with him and moved to Mumbai to begin a new chapter as a reporter."

When Aakanksha asked about his whereabouts, Saesha's response was far from hopeful. "I have no idea where he is," she said. "I blocked him on Facebook and Instagram and changed my number without telling him. The last I heard from Rijith was that he'd gone to Russia. It could be to avoid the police or maybe to chase Russian women. I only found out about his interest in them after we broke up."

Aakanksha asked if Saesha was still in touch with Rijith. Saesha replied that they kept in contact through Instagram. Rijith had updated her about Arshit and mentioned he was now in Manipur with his wife, Angie. However, when Saesha asked about his job, Rijith dodged the question. Jokingly,

Saesha added, "I hope he's not involved in the cultivation of marijuana in Manipur."

Aakanksha, noticing Saesha was tipsy and more likely to open up, decided to press on. She asked, "I've heard you slept with both Shahid and Rijith. Is that true?"

"No, not Shahid. I tried to lure him to make love with me once, but he completely ignored my advances. Stupid Shahid. But yes, I did sleep with Rijith once, just to keep his mouth shut."

Aakanksha felt a strange satisfaction hearing praise for Shahid. But as Saesha's behavior grew more erratic, she couldn't help but think of her undergoing a "Narco test"—where she'd reveal anything asked of her. Though taken aback by Saesha's unfiltered talk, Aakanksha found herself intrigued. Caught up in the openness of it all, she posed a more intimate question, her curiosity mixing with a touch of apology: "What is your body count?"

Saesha, without hesitation, revealed that she had been with seven men before her marriage, sipping vodka casually, having consumed pegs equivalent to three-fourth of a bottle and the effects already showing. Aakanksha, shocked by the confession, expressed her surprise. Saesha, unbothered, grinned and added, "Make that eight, if you include my husband." Intrigued, Aakanksha continued to probe, asking for names of her partners, thoroughly enjoying their cajoling conversation.

Saesha casually shared her romantic past, starting with her five-year live-in with Arshit, which Aakanksha already knew. She went on to admit to having slept with two managers and a CEO from different companies, hoping to get career boosts and salary hikes. There was also that one time with Rijith, and a drunken action with a colleague. She ended by recalling a week in Manali with a doctor's assistant, calling it an "FWB" relationship.

"How did you become FWB with a doctor's assistant?" Aakanksha asked, genuinely curious. Saesha chuckled, admitting it was a long story. Aakanksha, however, assured her she had all the time in the world, having already ordered lunch for both of them and eager for the full tale With a smile, Saesha decided to share.

Saesha picked up where she left off, "When I first arrived in Mumbai for my assignment, I was asked to cover a press conference held by a doctor for my magazine. The topic was hymenoplasty, a term I had never heard before. But the doctor explained the procedure eloquently, that I started to understand it. After the event, I approached one of the assistants to gather more details for my article. The assistant was happy to share information on hymenoplasty, its benefits, and why some women choose it."

Aakanksha interrupted, "What exactly is hymenoplasty?"

Saesha explained, "The hymen is a thin membrane that partially covers the vaginal opening. In India, it's often tied to the idea of virginity. Many believe that if a woman's hymen is intact, she's a virgin, which is why the hymen is so significant in traditional views. However, some women may still be virgins but could rupture their hymen through physical activity or an accident—like gymnastics, cycling, or using tampons. In cultures where the bride's virginity is highly valued, women may undergo hymenoplasty to restore their hymen. This surgery either stitches the torn hymen or reconstructs it using vaginal tissue. Hymenoplasty, also known as hymen repair or hymenorrhaphy, is done to 'repair' or 'rebuild' the hymen."

Aakanksha understood the concept but was confused about why it mattered to Saesha. Taking a sip of her vodka, Saesha asked for patience, promising to explain. She initially found the idea absurd, wondering why anyone in the 21st Century would need to prove their virginity to their spouse. She felt that any such demand should be a dealbreaker, and the woman should walk away from the relationship immediately. Aakanksha couldn't agree more.

Saesha shared that she had asked the same question to the doctor. The doctor explained that some women, especially those who had suffered from rape or sexual abuse, wanted to keep their past hidden. They sought a fresh start, free from the stigma and painful memories, and hymen reconstruction could offer them that opportunity.

Saesha said, "I remember this one time at a brand event for my magazine. That's where I met my future husband. He had just been promoted to Vice-President at an MNC Bank, and he was immediately taken by my looks. He came up to me, and what started as just a simple conversation turned into a full-blown romance. So, as we started dating, he asked me if I was a virgin. I didn't want to lose him, so without thinking, I said yes. Then he said something that stuck with me: 'If you've had other boyfriends, I wouldn't even consider marrying you.' I couldn't let him go, so I lied and said I'd never been with anyone before because I'd never found someone worth dating."

Although her husband had a modern education, Saesha found his views on virginity outdated, reminiscent of caveman mentality. She claimed that many men are born bastards and the presence of a hymen held significant importance to them, granting them a sense of conquest upon its removal, being the one to 'break the barrier', like it's some trophy.

She criticized men, noting their hypocrisy in expecting their wives to be virgins while they themselves engaged in debauchery. She criticized such double standards, highlighting the hypocrisy of expecting purity from their wives while engaging in multiple relationships.

Aakanksha asked, "So what did you do next?"

Saesha smiled, remembering. "Well, I had become friends with the doctor's assistant. So, I approached him for help, and he was willing. He agreed to assist, arranged for me to get the surgery done earlier than expected. The cost? 1.5 lakh rupees. I mean, the cost varied from doctor to doctor, but it was still way too high for just a tissue repair that was bound to be destroyed again. So, I asked him if there was a way to get the procedure done for much less—around 10 to 15 thousand rupees."

The assistant hesitated at first, refusing to budge. But I kept pushing, and after a moment, he leaned in closer. His gaze sharpened, and in a voice barely above a whisper, he said, "I can't make it cheaper. But if you want it for free, there's a favour I need from you."

Saesha's expression flickered and a mix of disbelief and resignation crossed her face. She understood the gravity of his words, the darkness lurking beneath them, and the price she had to pay. The lines between right and wrong blurred, with ambition clouding their judgment. A pact was silently made, sealing their destinies together in secrecy.

The assistant planned a week-long trip to Manali and Saesha accompanied him. For the first three days, he didn't let her leave the hotel room. It wasn't until the fourth day that they finally went out for sightseeing. When they returned to Mumbai, he arranged the surgery with the doctor. Saesha never asked how he managed to pay for it, but she didn't spend a penny on the procedure.

"So, this is how you proved your virginity."

"Darling, virginity can't really be proven to these stupid people; it can only be shown. A few drops of blood on the wedding night bedsheet—that's all it takes."

"Did you ever feel guilty about what you did, or even worse, about cheating on your husband?"

Saesha, tipsy and rambling, responded, "Guilty? There's no guilt when karma takes its revenge. It's all karma— mine and my husband's. They say karma is a bitch, but trust me, karma is a dog, not a bitch."

Aakanksha laughed bitterly and asked, "How can you say karma is a dog?"

"Karma is not a bitch because bitches bite, and dogs fuck. Bitches bite when they're wronged, or when their pups are in danger, but a dog sees no time, day, or place. Therefore, karma is like a dog— It can fuck you anytime, any day or anyplace like a dog does. Karma has no menu; one receives what they deserve. It fucked me because I tossed my morals aside for desires. Now, despite having wealth, I must dress in traditional attire like salwar suits or sarees. I can't drink like I did in Delhi or Mumbai. I have all the money but no pleasure."

By now, Saesha was barely conscious from the alcohol. She asked for a floor mattress and collapsed onto it, drifting off to sleep. Aakanksha, still awake, sipped her beer and snacked on the food in front of her. As she sat there, she wondered if perhaps it was a sign for Saesha to become faithful, to finally commit to her partner and stay loyal for life. There was a hint of regret in Saesha's words as she wished she could erase her past and start anew. Saesha accepted her fate, understanding that she was facing consequences for her past deeds.

Aakanksha couldn't shake off Saesha's words about karma. It hit her hard because, deep down, she knew karma had already shaped their lives. Despite receiving a second chance, she had made the regrettable decision to leave her family, and working like a donkey in a foreign land. Even though she had a loving husband, the emptiness of family love still stayed with her, the very reason she had married Shahid. Even in marriage, they remained isolated, devoid of the warmth of family. The pain she had inflicted upon her parents and brother continued to haunt her in the form of karma. Despite her efforts, karma was depriving her of the embrace of a loving family. She remained without the presence of a brother, sister, father, or mother. While her in-laws visited them in Dubai, their stays were temporary. Aakanksha had severed ties with her family, and karma seemed to ensure that she remained permanently estranged from any family.

Aakanksha remembered her father's lecture from 2012 as though it had happened yesterday. He had warned her about the millennials of today, stuck in a web of endless choices, unaware of the consequences. According to him, most of them were chasing money, fame, or love, ignoring their responsibilities to their families and opting for a nomadic life. He also pointed out that many got married and had children due to societal pressure, not because they truly wanted it. In his eyes, they were the "misfit millennials," rejecting the norms of society. Back then, Aakanksha had dismissed his words as nonsense. But twelve years later, she couldn't help but see how right he was. Karma, it seemed, was settling scores.

Aakanksha's next thought was, "What did Shahid do to deserve this? Why is he suffering?" Then it hit her—he had betrayed Nikita's parents, getting involved with their daughter despite being treated like a son by them. He had also gone against his own parents' wishes, marrying a Hindu girl, which led to their curse and pain. However, despite his wrongdoings, he had somehow built up some good karma. Whenever they were in trouble, someone always came to their rescue. Karma, she realized, was like an elephant—it never forgets—and like a dog, it really fucks hard.

After finishing lunch, Aakanksha lay beside Saesha, her mind heavy with the consequences of their actions. She thought about how everyone's suffering seemed tied to their own karma. But then, the thought of innocent children losing their parents in accidents troubled her. How could karma be responsible for the suffering of a 3-year-old orphan? She wondered why some are born into wealth while others face poverty, or why some are born with disabilities. The questions lingered in her mind, filling her with more doubt than clarity. It shook her, making her get up to order another beer. She downed the whole bottle in one go.

After finishing the bottle, she thought, "Forget about others' suffering—what did her husband do to deserve a wife like Saesha?"

Saesha woke up in the evening, feeling content, and settled the bill with a smile. She thanked Aakanksha for the drinks before heading to the restaurant through the back door. The driver was waiting patiently in the parking lot. Aakanksha handed her a mint to freshen her breath and suggested keeping the windows open on the ride back to get rid of the vodka smell. Saesha left, promising to return in two days for her husband's birthday.

Saesha told her husband that the restaurant was owned by a couple from Delhi, who happened to be her friends. On February 13th, 2024, around 9 PM, the couple arrived to celebrate the husband's birthday. Saesha wore a salwar suit while her husband wore a men's suit. They were warmly welcomed by Shahid at the entrance, and led them upstairs to a private space reserved just for them.

The terrace was beautifully set up for the couple, with soft candlelight casting a warm glow. Saesha and her husband stood at the terrace entrance, captivated by the decor, the ambiance, and the warm hospitality of the restaurant. Shahid called Aakanksha to meet Saesha's husband, but she was busy on the other side, adding the final touches and arranging candles on the terrace alongside the staff. The dim lighting made it hard to see faces from a distance.

As she walked towards him, extending her hand to wish him a "Happy Birthday," she caught the full view of his face under the soft glow of the candlelight. Her eyes lit up, and a smile spread across her face as she looked at Saesha's husband. Unable to hold back, she laughed loudly, a triumphant sound that seemed to echo in the terrace. Proudly, she raised her hand above her head, her face turned to the sky, clapping as if in admiration of the karma from the heavens, applauding the cosmic justice at play. Once her laughter died down, she shook his hand, skipped the birthday wish, and said instead, "You deserve her."

Saesha's husband took it as a compliment, thinking Aakanksha was praising him for marrying her. He proudly smiled and said, "Thank you." It was Anshuman from Shimla, the IITian.

****

Epilogue

"One day you will tell your story of how you overcame what you went through and it will be someone else's survival guide."

- Brene Brown

(10th April 2024 - Dubai)

Shahid celebrated Eid in Dubai with his family, who had come to visit him for the holidays. With the restaurant closed for the week, Aakanksha prepared delicious meals for her in-laws and cousins. The family was thrilled for the couple, proud of the name and success they had built in Dubai. It was a joyful day, and Aakanksha had the best Eid celebration in years. The next day, Shahid called his friends and cousins in India to wish them a 'Happy Eid,' since Eid was celebrated a day later in India due to the moon sighting differences.

As night settled in, Shahid lay half asleep, while Aakanksha tossed and turned, her mind drifting to friends and family back in India. Memories of her loved ones and the friends who had supported her during tough times flooded her thoughts. It had been three years since she'd last seen her friends from Delhi, and she longed to visit them. She especially missed Rijith, Arshit, Angie, and me.

Aakanksha woke Shahid, telling him she wanted to go to India to meet her friends. At first, Shahid thought she was out of her mind, but when she kept insisting, he gave up on sleep to hear her out. She asked him to manage the restaurant for 4-5 months while she reconnected with her friends in India. Shahid was concerned—she seemed uncertain about her own plan, and he couldn't understand why she was so determined on meeting them.

Aakanksha explained to Shahid that her decision to go to India wasn't sudden; it had been brewing for a while, sparked by her conversations with Saesha. She was curious about her friends—Rijith, Arshit, and others—wondering how their lives had turned out, based on their karma. She had questions: why Arshit had been to jail twice, how Rijith, a Tamilian, ended up in Manipur, and why Samitabh had such a strained relationship with his father. These mysteries had been lingering in her mind.

"Why go all the way to India when you can just ask everyone on the phone or WhatsApp? You have their numbers, don't you?"

Aakanksha smiled and said, "But secrets aren't spilled over the phone. You have to get them drunk to spill the truth. I need answers, especially after meeting Saesha and Anshuman. It's just for me, no one else. I might not find all the answers, but I want to try. Who knows, maybe one day I'll write a book about their stories."

Shahid chuckled when Aakanksha mentioned writing a book, but he eventually agreed and told her to book the tickets whenever she wanted. She was thrilled and immediately called me. It was 12:30 a.m. in Dubai, 2:00 a.m. in India. As I lay next to my wife and kid, the phone rang, sending a wave of anxiety through me—calls at 2 a.m. never bring good news. I answered, half-dreading the worst, but it turned out Aakanksha just wanted to chat.

The phone rang in the dead of night, and both my wife and I froze. I answered the call and told her it was just Aakanksha checking in, nothing serious. But instead of feeling relieved, my wife got upset, muttering curses at both me and Aakanksha before going back to sleep.

During our two-hour chat, Aakanksha mentioned her plan to visit India soon. She was curious about the lives of her friends, including mine, as she was thinking about writing a book. I didn't want to share much, but I knew, with her determination, she'd eventually get it out of me.

A few weeks later, Aakanksha booked her tickets from Dubai and found herself at the airport, waiting for her flight to India. While browsing through the shops for gifts for her friends and their kids, she noticed a 3- or 4-year-old boy crying for a Hamley's toy. His tantrum caused a scene, and his father, clearly embarrassed, seemed hesitant to buy the pricey toy.

When Indian bystanders asked, the father explained that he was on vacation in Dubai and was heading back to India. He mentioned that the toy his son wanted cost 1400 dirhams, about 33,000 rupees, and he had already spent a lot during the trip. He felt it was unnecessary and couldn't afford such an expensive gift, even if he wanted to. The onlookers sympathized and pointed out that the same toy could be found in Delhi's Chandni Chowk for just 500 rupees.

Aakanksha, standing behind, overheard their conversation and silently walked up to the counter, asking for the toy to be packed. It cost her 1400 dirhams. She then handed it to the boy as a gift. At first, the father hesitated, ready to return it, until he recognized Aakanksha. Their eyes lit up as they hugged, surprised and happy to see each other. It had been 16 years since Vishal had helped Aakanksha escape from Shimla in 2008, and the reunion felt special. Vishal was happy to hear that she had settled in Dubai, but he still expressed concern over the costly gift.

"You don't have to do this," he said, urging her to return it.

Aakanksha smiled and said, "I'm not doing you a favor. I'm just paying you back for the 1400 rupees you gave me in 2008. You gave me 1400 rupees in India, and I'm returning 1400 dirhams now, since I live in Dubai. Same to same." Vishal laughed and agreed to disagree, ultimately took the toy for his son.

There, in that moment, the debt was repaid—not just in money, but in a bond of friendship and gratitude that had endured all these years.

Aakanksha felt that her journey was beginning on a positive note, believing that God was offering her a fresh start. The loose ends in her life seemed to be coming together, and just when she thought she had reached the end of her quest for growth, a new chapter emerged. She was filled with excitement and happiness at the prospect of embarking on a new opportunity that life had bestowed upon her. In the stillness of her heart, she joyfully echoed the famous line of T.S. Eliot's poem, as if they had been written just for her: "In my end is my beginning."

****

www.ingramcontent.com/pod-product-compliance
Lightning Source LLC
LaVergne TN
LVHW041910070526
838199LV00051BA/2561